At the Lighthouse

edited by

Sophie Essex

At the Lighthouse
edited by Sophie Essex

ISBN: 978-1-913766-23-8

Publication Date: September 2023

The stories in this collection copyright © 2023 by their original authors.

Cover art and interior design by David Rix, copyright 2023

EibonVale

www.eibonvalepress.co.uk

Contents:

7	Sourmouth-on-Sea Heritage Trail (A Walk In Seventeen Stages) – Jason Gould
21	Keepers – Andrew Hook
35	The Zond Tower – Terry Grimwood
53	The Sirens Are Calling In – Rory Moores
61	The Lighthouse at Addenbay – Pete Sillett
83	The Keeper – Ariel Dodson
109	Sea Glass – Julie Ann Rees
117	Three Days In The Grave of Sam Poe – Matt Leyshon
125	Night Lamp Lotus (An Attempt at a Strategic Guide) – Damian Murphy
147	Rising Tall and Slender – Tim Lees
161	The Lighthouse Sisters – Rhys Hughes
173	Safe Passage – Brittni Brinn
183	Not Sideways, But Upwards – Charles Wilkinson
199	House of the She-Devil – Tom Johnstone
213	Cygnus – Douglas Thompson
227	The Volkhova Perplex – Ashley Stokes
251	Turn Again, O My Sweetness – C.A. Yates

Sourmouth-on-Sea Heritage Trail

(A Walk in Seventeen Stages)

by Jason Gould

This heritage trail is free to visitors and residents. It begins at the car park on Merhill Rd, from where it winds its way down into the quaint seaside town of Sourmouth-on-Sea, taking in multiple points of historical interest and local colour, before arriving at the harbour and lighthouse. At the lighthouse, it is possible to climb the spiral staircase and view the inner workings of the sadly now defunct lamp-room, before choosing from a range of light refreshments in the competitively priced café.

Visitors should note that Sourmouth-on-Sea is renowned for its soul-stirring ability. Walkers are liable to lose themselves in strange thoughts and peculiar fancies, especially those considered questionable in character.

Many find it impossible to turn back before the trail is complete.

1. Merhill Car Park and Public Convenience

Constructed in 1987, this moderately sized car park is located on the site of a former pond and beauty spot, filled in and concreted over to make way for increased numbers of tourists. Secluded by overhanging trees, Merhill pond was popular for many years with courting couples and bored spouses wishing to engage in casual infidelities under cover of darkness. Its hillside location half-a-mile above town ensured freedom from prying eyes and ruinous gossip, and was used as far back as the 19th century by those for whom love had to remain in the shadows.

Local legend suggests that an avid visitor to Merhill pond in the late 19th century would have been Mr Reginald Braithwaite. Official records show Mr Braithwaite to be the Sourmouth-on-Sea lighthouse keeper between 1870 and 1875, suggesting he would have been substantially out of his way up here on Merhill, far from his station. What brought him to these dark waters in the depths of night? Was it connected to stories of a prehistoric underground stream, said to feed the pond from the sea, along which a shoal of "sylph-like wenches" was thought to swim from time to time, to bare their scaly breasts while basking beside the pond on hazy summer evenings?

Nowadays, the car park is protected by multiple CCTV cameras for the safety and security of the public, and the area remains generally free from the undesirable activity by which it was once plagued.

2. Village Road

The only road into and out of Sourmouth-on-Sea predates the Roman occupation of the United Kingdom by several centuries. Eminent archaeologists believe it was originally scraped from the mud by Ancient Britons. It would have been an unpaved track used to transport fishing boats to and from the bountiful sea. In recent years it has been resurfaced by National Highways (formerly the Highways Agency) as part of their infrastructure investment programme which seeks to provide easy access to areas of outstanding natural beauty for the motorist who prefers to wander off the beaten track on a Sunday afternoon and investigate the more scenic route.

Before you follow the road down to sea level, taking care to stick to the grass verge and not stray into the path of oncoming traffic, you might like to pause and drink in the picture postcard view – white three-storey houses, smooth blue sea, idyllic bay carved from the coastline like the downturned mouth from which the village is proud to take its name.

As you descend into Sourmouth-on-Sea, your eye will be drawn to the lighthouse, at the furthest point on the peninsula, patiently waiting.

3. Bartlett's Field

This square of arable land forms the eastern edge of the Bartlett family estate. Originally the hunting lodge of Lord Bartlett until his death in 1842, the estate has been farmed by successive generations and, in recent years, diversified to include a number of log cabins, yurts, and even a shepherd's hut for the modern-minded tourist. Unremarkable in many respects, Bartlett's Field – to your left as you follow Village Road down to the sea – has twice found itself the subject of local interest. It first drew attention in 1805, when Lord Bartlett, hunting stag in the woods to the west, spied through his field glasses "a thing human in shape and guise, yet not" pulling itself across the ground in the direction of Merhill Pond. In 1874, following an "unexplained collapse of earth" ("sinkhole" would be the scientific explanation today), Bartlett's Field found itself invaded by hordes of excited geologists keen to examine the "entrance to hell".

Later that year, Merhill Pond began to stagnate, suggesting the underground stream thought to join this landlocked pool to the sea might have been blocked by the sudden structural fault. Reports of the Sourmouth Sirens (long thought to be the stuff of legend) swimming in Merhill Pond ceased after the incident in Bartlett's Field, as did reports of the lighthouse keeper, Mr Reginald Braithwaite, haunting the banks beneath the overhanging trees – "haggard in countenance, lascivious in eye".

4. 11 Pennybrook Lane

It's difficult to imagine the scarlet history behind this Victorian terraced house, such is the blandness of its facade. From 1876 until 1880 it was the home of local spinster Miss H_, rumoured to welcome gentlemen of all ages and sexual predilections into her home in the hours after which good folk have long since retired. Believed for years to be a pillar of the community, the truth behind Miss H_ would not be unearthed until the 1960s, when a diary was discovered by workmen prising up floorboards.

The Book of Love – as it was titled – had been kept by Miss H_ unbeknownst to her clientele. By far the most prolific patron of 11 Pennybrook Lane was local gentleman Mr Arnold Rumford, whose name graced the pages of the journal on over 200 separate occasions.

Throughout 1875 and early 1876, Mr Rumford is reported to have requested practices such as "flannelling", "Darwin's Delight", and – to celebrate his birthday – the "old man's bath-chair". In contrast, the final entry relating to Mr Rumford – dated February 5th 1876 – seems somewhat out of character. Lacking the enthusiasm and imagination of previous visits, it simply states "...desultory, lethargic – failed to achieve release". Concerned for his welfare, Miss H_ watched from her upstairs window as Mr Rumford departed the property, "shuffling as if in stupor, as if led by strings, like a puppet, in the direction of the lighthouse – the light from which had taken on a peculiar tint".

5. Wanderer's Cottage

Set back from the road, and concealed by a weeping birch, it's easy to walk past this quaint little house and fail to register its existence. Step into its grounds (a public right of way runs alongside the property), part the mournful branches, and a white single-storey farm worker's cottage will emerge from the purity of a less corrupt age.

Over the centuries it's provided hearth and home to many, its low-ceilinged rooms and modest footprint favoured largely by single folk (widows, widowers, unmarried devotees of God) and, from time to time, the occasional childless couple. Tenants of the latter variety would have included Mr and Mrs Arnold Rumford, resident from 1870 until 1876. Happily betrothed for half a century, the retired couple kept themselves to themselves, hiking in the nearby countryside and strolling hand-in-hand like newlyweds along the harbour. Keen to stay fit and healthy in older life, Mr Rumford would often partake of a late-night constitutional, leaving his wife asleep in bed while he stepped outside to take the evening air. It was a regular, unremarkable occurrence, until February 5th 1876 when Mr Rumford failed to return home. Despite an extensive search, he was not seen again. For months it was presumed he'd been swept out to sea by a freak wave, although the weather on the night in question was reported to have been "calm and still".

The mystery was not solved until April that year, when Mr Rumford's body was found less than half a mile from his house, and, at last, he was declared legally deceased. But it did not bring the peace and closure for which Mrs Rumford had hoped, and she left Wanderer's Cottage soon after, when the circumstances surrounding the location and nature of her husband's ungodly end became public knowledge, and she was propelled into a catatonic fugue from which she would not return.

6. Seagull House (formerly The Retreat)

It's sad to think that this common block of flats was once the residential home of choice for the elderly and infirm of Sourmouth-on-Sea. Renamed by the construction magnate who divided the building into bedsits in 1955, this three-storey Victorian town house provided, in its day, the quiet serenity sought so often in the twilight years.

Perhaps the resident most in need of tranquil surroundings would have been Mrs Hazel Rumford – widow of Mr Arnold Rumford. Present in body only, Mrs Rumford declined to speak from the day she was moved to The Retreat in August 1876, until her death in 1901. It is believed that her silence – born of shame, shock, or a quintessentially English reluctance to display emotion – was broken only once, encouraged, perhaps, by a sense of civic responsibility to warn of the dangers. Overhearing a nurse and servant gossiping about the events at the lighthouse years earlier, Mrs Rumford had startled them both by speaking suddenly of her husband, describing him as a kind, tolerant man and going on to say, "He had his peccadilloes, I'm not naive. But it wasn't those that killed him. It was that damn, wretched lighthouse, poking its nose into folk's private affairs. Towards the end he was obsessed, watching it night after night from our bedroom window".

It was a brief interlude after which Mrs Rumford returned to her mute contemplation of the world, struck dumb by the thought of her husband's remains, discovered beside the other corpses, in the room with the lamp, at the top of the spiral staircase.

7. 14 Main Street

This somewhat mundane three-storey town house would not feature on the heritage trail were it not for the faded mural that adorns its gable end. Thought to have been painted in the 1960s – a decade noted for its gauche artistry – it depicts the Sourmouth-on-Sea lighthouse and harbour, as it would have been in the late 19th century (bleak, oppressive, storm battering the chalk cliffs in the background). Look closely and you will see how the painting draws on local myth: in the lower right-hand corner, Mr Reginald Braithwaite, lighthouse keeper from 1870 until 1875, sprawled on the rocks in the embrace of a "sea-lady", scaly arms wrapped around his neck, green lips pressed against his, bladderwrack draped about her shoulders like "the shawl of the ocean". And Mrs Victoria Braithwaite, standing at the lighthouse door, unseen by her copulating husband, rage and revenge deep in her eyes.

8. 11 The Row

Once a private residence, this unassuming mid-terrace is now an everyday bed and breakfast, host to holidaymakers and, out of season, mostly empty. The property is noted only once in local history books, in February 1876, when its then owner, Mr G. A. Smith, vanished without trace. Smith, a well-known Lothario, was reported missing by his wife on February 15th. When questioned, she told local constabulary that he'd behaved oddly of late, standing in the garden at midnight, gazing – "as if spellbound" – towards the lighthouse.

9. Ornamental Fountain, High Street

Carved by Thomas Arkwright of Holborn, this ornate statue of Eros was gifted to the town by Victorian philanthropist Sir Edward Hall. Hall visited Sourmouth-on-Sea twice in his lifetime: once in 1860, to search the coastline for fossils, and again in 1867, when he gave a talk at the pavilion (demolished c1927) on "Modern Ethics and Morality". Despite a standing ovation, Hall failed to return to the town, stating privately that "the place had left him feeling maudlin, as if unwholesome things lurked in the locale". He later spoke of "the stench that permeates the very soil on which the town is built, like fish but no fish you ever pulled – or would want to pull – from the sea".

It was at the site of the ornamental fountain that Mrs Dorothy Pinchbeck was last seen alive, on March 15th 1876, by a couple who described her as "entirely agog, enthralled by the lamp at the lighthouse, which had taken on a yellow tinge". Pinchbeck would often arrange liaisons at the fountain with gentlemen "believed, almost certainly, to be married".

10. Belle Lane (Descent to the Harbour)

Visitors have described the view from the upper end of this steep and narrow thoroughfare as "intoxicating" and "irresistible". It is the point at which the town is left behind and the ocean becomes suddenly, surprisingly visible. Sebastian Oates, the 19th century poet, described the sight in his 1896 memoir, *The Belles of Helle*, as "...the doorway to evil and romance". Considered an unfinished classic, *The Belles of Helle* was discovered in 1944 in the bombed remains of a bedsit on Lighthouse Rd. More recently, it was displayed in *Sex, Surf and Seaweed*, an exhibition of maritime erotica installed at The Tate Gallery in London, entry to which included a free squirt behind the ear from an atomizer filled with "aquatic pheromone".

Be careful not to lose your footing as you make your way down from Belle Lane and onto the harbour. Sea-spray clings to the cobblestones in the early morning, as if left there during the hours of night. Like delicate perfume it can be both alluring and fatal.

11. A Moment to Pause and Reflect

You are now entering the final part of the trail. At this point, it is worth thinking back over your life, the people you have encountered, the love you have put forth, the love you have received.

If you have been true to your love, your sweetheart, you need not fear. You will be able to turn back, should you wish.

If you have not been true, if your heart has wandered, it is likely you will continue along the trail, toward the lighthouse.

12. Acklam's Apothecary, 2a Harbourside

Pharmaceutical goods to remedy the common cold and assuage various minor ailments have been the business of Acklams & Sons for over a hundred years. Their shop has lost none of its charm since it opened its door in 1870: darkly tinted bottles, weighing scales on the counter, bell over the door that tinkles on entry. Nowadays, it's more likely to be visited by tourists hoping to step back in time than a local housewife needing advice on a verruca.

Stand before the counter and you will be standing in the footsteps of Mrs Victoria Braithwaite, circa January 1876, shortly after her husband, Mr Reginald Braithwaite, official Sourmouth-on-Sea lighthouse keeper, vanished without trace. It was from Mr Acklam's Apothecary that Mrs Victoria Braithwaite procured the ingredients necessary to "mix a potion to purge the town of rakes and hussies".

Precisely which herbs, plants and powders the embittered Mrs Braithwaite asked Mr Acklam to hand over remains unknown, but a similar concoction, listed in *Old Alice's Book of Practical Interventions to Salve the Heart of the Scorned* (1654), includes three parts Essence of Pastor John, two parts Ground Lurin, and a liberal sprinkling of Vril.

13. The Path to the Lighthouse

From the harbourside follow the promontory that stretches out to sea. On windy days the curved walkway is often spattered in saltwater and spume from the rhythmic beat of waves on the rocks below. Note the missive beneath your feet, scraped into the concrete c1900: *The Path to the Lighthouse is the Path to Illumination.*

14. The Steps Down to the Sea

To your left – barricaded for safety reasons – you will see thirteen steps that lead down to the water's edge. High-tide drapes seaweed on the old iron handrails, like matted black hair.

Famously, it is here that Mr Reginald Braithwaite was last seen, on Christmas Day 1875, abandoning both his wife and his post of Lighthouse Keeper, and slipping down the stone steps and into the ocean, to join his aquatic lover.

15. The Lighthouse (Living Quarters)

Enter the lighthouse through the arched door and you will find yourself in what would have been the storeroom, above which, on subsequent floors, you will find the lounge, kitchen, and bedrooms. Period furnishings – cast iron stove, tin bath, nightshirts hung up to dry – help conjure an air of how it might have been when Mr Reginald Braithwaite and wife Victoria lived within these walls. By day, Victoria would have watched her husband maintain the lighthouse, their place of work, their home. In the kitchen she would have prepared food, her husband outside, his eye drawn toward the sea. In the evening she would have watched him scrub his pale skin in the tin bath by the modest fire. And, by night, she would have watched him climb to the room at the top of the stairs, where he would first inspect, and then light, the oil-fired lantern.

16. The Spiral Staircase

Climb the steps to the top of the lighthouse – all 165 – but pause halfway, by the arched window. It is from here that Mrs Victoria Braithwaite would have watched her husband on the rocks below, drenched in surf and slime, allowing himself to be set upon gladly by the whores of the sea.

17. The Lamp Room

It is not the lantern that will draw your immediate attention, nor the view over the ocean. It is the verse, scrawled in the handwriting of the disturbed, on every inch of wall, floor, and ceiling.

> *To the lamp by hand unseen*
> *Illicit kissers shall kiss and bleed*
> *Illumination for their evil deed*

Despite inexperience in such matters, Mrs Braithwaite succeeded in her bid to "bring the lamp around to her point of view". MothWort – simmered on the stove thirteen hours and dripped into the oil of the lamp – proved itself potent, luring the unfaithful from the beds of their lovers, across the moonlit bay and up to the room at the top of the lighthouse, where they each pressed their face to the lamp, immune – in their minds – to the heat. "Like a painting by Bruegel or Bosch," wrote the local magistrate of the scene some months later, "bodies stacked against bodies, skin burnt to the bone, inhuman in this, the final act in their secret lives." Official statistics fail to record the tally of the dead. Historians believe it to be in the region of fifty, amongst which would have been Mr Arnold Rumford, exuding the aroma of the brothel, Mrs Dorothy Pinchbeck, a married man's saliva drying on her lips, and Mr G. A. Smith, his latest conquest forgotten in favour of the lamp…

Observe the plaque at the base of the lamp, dedicated to the men and women who lost their lives in the Sourmouth-on-Sea lighthouse tragedy of 1876.

Exit down the spiral staircase and through the gift shop.

Keepers

by Andrew Hook

*In order for the light to shine so brightly,
the darkness must be present*
– Francis Bacon

Juska

The lighthouse comes with the island. When Juska inherits her grandparents' fortune she scouts locations. Investment banking has left her in good stead regarding properties, financial decisions. Getting away from it all requires an engagement. She engages.

The conversation with her parents is abrupt. With Georgio less so. He comprehends the need for abandonment, after all, this is why he is in her life. Any failure to understand rotates around her need for isolation from *him*. Something even he has been unable to achieve.

She sits on a wooden stool, her ankles tucked behind the footrest. She is already in costume with her brown funnel-neck sweater, its unique crochet pebble-stitch resembling seashells darned through the design. "It's only six months," she says. "It will go in a flash."

Georgio rests the heels of his palms against his eyes. When he removes them, they are moist. "Six months was an eternity until you came along."

She shrugs. She has little time for faux sentimentality. There are lives to be lived. Those unhindered by conventionality. Whilst she has always understood this, her immersion in a corporate world has glamoured for too many years. Her grandfather lived by the expression: *Carpe diem*. Her grandmother: *better out than in*. Both held their own wisdom.

"In six months," she adds, her voice softening, acquiescing to the demands of a small boy, "I'll either be insane or delirious. You won't even desire me by then."

Georgio shudders, an involuntary reaction. He begins to say that he will always want her, that it isn't even a decision he can consciously make, but Juska has tuned out, he can see that in the faraway expression in her eyes, eyes which reflect the bright blue light pouring through the window, as if it were filling her body to the brim. Whereas the blue has leaked from his eyes, in her eyes, the light is contained.

"There isn't even any internet access," he blurts, as if this is the be all and end all.

"Isn't there just," she answers, brightly. "How exciting!"

The island is – inevitably – windswept. When Juska – the refuge giver – steps one foot from the boat her sense of home is evident. Two steps anchor. The Captain has a gruff sensibility, the bonhomie during the two hour journey rough and frank. Now he hauls her suitcases from the deck to the shingle. It's a long way up to the shack which abuts the lighthouse. She accepts his offer to share the weight. Gorse prickles against the thin cotton material of her leggings as she moves from stones to dunes, until eventually this shades into moorland and she sees that the coarse vegetation which surrounds the base of the lighthouse will require cutting back to allow easier access to the entrance.

"You'll be alright here," the Captain says, his thick black moustache peppered with white hairs as if flecked with spume. During the journey he had confirmed the meats and canned food he had stored in the icehouse in preparation for her visit. "I'll return every two weeks, if you wish. More frequently if necessary. Less, if advised."

She nods, distracted by the height of the lighthouse as they near. Walking with her head tilted backwards accentuates a sensation of vertigo. The once-white structure is grey-green, with stanchion-like protrusions of metal near the top bearing rust the colour of atomic tangerine Crayola.

"I won't be alone," she says. "There will be others after me. I've advised them of your presence. They will meet you at the dock when they are ready."

She senses disappointment. She suspects he harbours a fantasy of revisiting her solo; imagining her on the cusp of sexual frustration, borne from unrelenting isolation. Whereas she is aware most lighthouse keepers are driven mad from poisoning not loneliness, the rotating Fresnal lenses floating on a circular track of liquid mercury - facilitating the best zero-friction bearing - creating fumes that gradually overcome reason. The mercury, the culprit. There will be no friction here. Besides, there is the similarity of loneliness and lioness. Despite their familiarity on the boat, she will fight him if needs be.

The shack is basically furnished. The purchase came with no guarantees of habitation, but the workers she has instructed over the past few months have achieved the goals she set. A modern cast-iron fire snakes dark metal up to the roof. There is wood in the grate. A table with four chairs dominates the floor space. The windows are double-glazed. Two sofas are arranged in an L-shape, adorned by cushions made of local material, bright colours interweaving shapes of octopus and sealion. The bedrooms are in the lighthouse itself, but until the restoration is finished she is likely to sleep here.

The Captain touches the brim of his cap.

She watches as he returns to the boat. Then watches the boat reversing into the sea.

Juska sets down her things. She walks around to the outbuilding at the rear of the shack and grabs a scythe. Starting with the shaggy brush at the base of the lighthouse, she moves her arms in a sweeping motion. Makes ready.

Candelaria

Her Italian accent is pronounced, but Juska understands it perfectly.

"My name is derived from the Marian epithet, Maria de la Candelaria. It refers to the Catholic feast of the Purification of the Virgin. Candelaria, itself, from the Latin, *candela*, or candle. A perfect name for a lighthouse keeper, don't you think?"

Juska nods. Candelaria has thick black hair that runs to the base of her spine, a spine that stripped back would in itself resemble masonry blocks dovetailed together in an interlocking pattern, such as those of a lighthouse. Her smile is so bright that it burns. Juska is reminded of a candlewick, held vertical by wax that exudes fumes as fuel when lit; a self-sustaining chain of events that keeps the flame.

Candelaria is one of three who answered her advert. Juska sets her to work on the spiral staircase, a structure which corkscrews upwards through the centre of the lighthouse, tapering until it reaches the Watch Room bracketed by the Gallery Deck. With a stiff brush and an almost unlimited supply of Brasso Metal Polish Wadding, Candelaria winds her way daily, ascending in short bursts of vigour. Her knees retaining imprints from the intricate metalwork that she shows Juska at the end of the day. Overlayed impressions of seashell renditions.

When Juska is on the stairs, Candelaria can sense the vibrations.

She has her own reasons for responding.

"A gap year. A strange expression, don't you think? And in London they say *mind the gap*! Well, I don't mind."

"Have you left anyone behind?" Juska is by the stove, turning a piece of meat.

"Roland. My cat. We should have a lighthouse cat!"

Juska nods, but is dismissive. She likes Candelaria, but she is not without foolishness. Tucked under one arm as Candelaria left the boat, ably assisted by the Captain, was a 4ft x 2ft framed reproduction of Salvador Dali's *Lighthouse of Alexandria*. Such pictures are not easily hung on curved walls.

Candelaria busies herself in the evening with cross-stitch. Her fingers are quick in their movement, the x-shaped stitches and tiled pattern creating a less fluid, boxier image than other types of embroidery. The design is basic. A traditional, white and red striped lighthouse, set upon blue-stitched waves, with horizontal yellow lines jerking from the top as though a child's drawing of cat's whiskers. The rudimentary nature of the image feels at odds with the physicality of the object that stands proud in the dark immediately outside the shack. Juska turns the meat again, fat spattering the sides of the stove. She takes a wet cloth, wipes clean.

When Candelaria had arrived, she was surprised to understand the lighthouse wasn't operative.

"My understanding is that it was decorative," explains Juska, "like that embroidery you're working. Ships don't pass close to this island, but the owners were fanciful and determined. There isn't much written history, however it certainly *can* work. That is the point of my restoration."

Candelaria nods. "Are we going to paint it?"

Juska adds mushrooms to the pan, their meaty colour complementing the flesh. "White. As it was before. Once the outside is cleaned."

The younger woman puts down her cross-stitch. "Is there anything I can help you with?"

Juska deliberates. She doesn't wish to appear mean, especially when it is all for the cause. And Candelaria is working so hard. "Do you mind washing your hands again, the smell of the Brasso..." Whilst there is a low order of toxicity, frequent or prolonged contact could cause defatting of the skin, irritation and dermatitis.

Candelaria understands. She enters the bathroom but doesn't close the door. Juska watches as Candelaria reaches behind herself for her hair, then plaits it quickly in an approximation of her spine, faint residues of the metal cleaner adding sheen. Then Juska hears the water run, and Candelaria scrubs her hands, the coal tar soap facilitating easy movement, her fingers locking and interlocking, twisting and paring tightly against her interdigital folds.

Days pass in a form of supplication. As if within their work they are begging for something earnestly or humbly from the lighthouse itself. Candelaria is over halfway up when she slips a step, yet the curvature of the walls curries an embrace. She is held against the incurve, the bulge, whilst the tin of Brasso clatters downwards, the resultant vibrations creating an orchestral movement for the deaf.

Candelaria stands, intensely aware of the patterns on her knees. She rests one elbow on a windowsill. The glass is dirty but light blurs through it. A compositional picture dictated by the smooth and slimy growth of green algae is backlit by the azure blue of the sea, which in itself bleeds upwards to meet the horizon, becoming paler as it reaches for the stars.

She runs a finger downwards, the glass squealing, but the dirt is outside and all that is achieved is a subtler vibration. A pleasurable squeak.

Ottilie

When the boat brings Ottilie it is almost smashed against the rocks. Bilious waves spite the shoreline. Pebbles thrown and sucked. The noise not dissimilar to the clattering down the stairs. Ottilie lifts her skirts and vaults landside, her kitten heels sinking amongst the small stones as if their constitution were liquid. The Captain ejects her luggage after her, then turns back for fear of being marooned. Ottilie's Samsonite suitcase is damaged at one corner. When she extends the handle and pulls those little wheels behind her she screams her frustration into the rain.

There is a light burning in the shack. Ottilie struggles through the gorse, against the vegetation. When she looks upwards, rain spikes her vision. She wonders why the light isn't lit. There is a battle to be had. Without knocking, she bursts into the shack, her hair dripping water onto the wooden floor. The two women look up from their positions, animatronics jerked to life by her presence. Ottilie uprights her suitcase, leans an elbow upon the extended handle.

"Which one of you is Juska?"

The older one stands. Introductions are made. In the bathroom Ottilie divests herself of her wet clothes and changes afresh. Later she sits by the fire, warming her hands against the flames, whilst Juska cooks and the other woman is involved with some frippery. Ottilie feels aggressively frustrated, as if it were not her idea to respond to the advert, as if she has been enticed here through someone else's whim. This annoyance exacerbated by understanding if she had arrived in clement weather then her experience would be less strained. It is as though the elements are working against her. As a decorator, she is wary of vagaries outside.

At the Lighthouse

After they have eaten, Juska shows her the paint which is housed in an outbuilding. Ottilie nods her approval. Sandtex Trade's water-based X-Treme X-Posure paint, specifically formulated for use in even the harshest of weather, is ideal for this operation.

"It should provide protection for up to twenty years."

Juska nods. "This is why I chose it."

"Then you chose well." Ottilie finds that she has smiled. She cannot be angry for long. And the weather is hardly the fault of these two women, who have already been here for one month and two weeks respectively.

They return inside and weather the storm. She is pleased with the composition of the gathering. The younger woman – Candelaria – is an Italian beauty; Juska exudes Nordic practicalities, and she understands the final girl will be Romanian. "International Rescue," she laughs, letting her French accent go as if it were plucked from her mouth by the wind. She is intrigued by their names. Her own means *prosperous in battle*. She senses the only battle here will be with the elements.

In the Service Room she finds a wooden suspended platform. Thick wire rope is coiled like sleeping sea serpents on the floor; hooks appended at each end remind her of fangs. The height of a lighthouse takes into account the curvature of the earth, so that the higher the light is above mean high water then the further away it can be seen at sea. This is why shorter lighthouses are sited on clifftops and taller lighthouses – like this one – are built nearer the water's edge. She estimates the height of the lighthouse, then the length of the wire rope. Almost fifty metres, she suspects. It is enough. It will have to be enough.

The stanchions which Juska noted on her arrival are there to take the weight. Ottilie savours the horror on Candelaria's face as together with Juska they traverse the Widow's Walk - the narrow platform that provides access to the outside of the lantern room – and loop the hooks around those jutting, rusted metals, then lower the cradle down. Ottilie manoeuvres it top to bottom from

28

the relative safety of the Walk, then descends the newly-polished stairwell and exits the building. The weightless cradle frequently hits the sides of the lighthouse as it descends, but with her weight it should hold firm. Winching upwards, she starts at the top, flexes the bristles on her brush, then dips it into the paint. On first application, ridges in the brick give a fleshy feel to the downwards movement. She sweeps up, and – like brushing fur backwards on an animal – the sensation restores itself.

Ottilie argued persuasively for a pump, a telescopic water-fed window cleaning pole, and an elongated hose. She cannot rock the platform too much by scrubbing. Yet Juska wants outward intervention to be minimal.

Ottilie – ever the perfectionist – crosses her arms. "The algae will bleed through. You'll have patches of pistachio, of emerald, of parakeet."

"Of seafoam," Juska adds. And Ottilie is sold.

She spends sunny days aloft. Her brush with its rhythmic movement a bristling sound that complements the rush of the waves. She is so close to the brick that she respects the tactility. In the unpainted sections, she runs her fingers in and out of grooves, flakes of old paint smearing the tips white.

If she presses her ear to the brick, she fancies she can hear Candelaria on the stairs, can hear reverberations from Juska's scythe against the ever-growing vegetation at the base.

If she presses her mouth to the brick, she can hold a conversation.

Cosmina

She bites down hard on a piece of dry bread. Then realises her mistake and softens it in the broth. The rich texture of the gravy soaks into the substance. When she takes her next bite, juice

At the Lighthouse

dribbles down her chin and she cups her other hand to collect it in her fingers. The black spinel gemstones that adorn the eternity ring around her fourth digit resembling the eyes of crustaceans blinking upwards from a rockpool.

"What made you think Romania was landlocked?" she laughs. "There is the Black Sea. Romania has sixteen lighthouses. Alphabetically from the Capul Tuzla Lighthouse in the North-East to the Tomis Southeast Breakwater Lighthouse in the South-East. And I have visited them all!"

There is a triumphant expression on Cosmina's face that appeals to Juska. It is almost crowded in the shack. Although they only now use this communally. Each has their own living quarters within the body of the lighthouse. Those bedrooms are – like much of the building – now complete. Cosmina has arrived for the most important role. That of maintaining the Fresnal lens.

Cosmina has adopted the recent trend of dyeing her otherwise light-brown hair a silvery grey. The effect is that light appears captured within each of these follicles – those tunnel-shaped structures in the epidermis which in themselves resemble tubular lighthouses – to the extent that it almost appears transparent.

"My grandmother asks me why I want my hair to match hers," says Cosmina, "yet she agrees it somehow makes me look younger."

Juska considers that Cosmina's appearance suits her task of cleaning the lens. There is a reason why Cosmina is the last woman in the process. She watches her easy camaraderie with Candelaria and Ottilie. Together, the four of them are settled in, embedded. Cosmina means order and beauty. Both are reflected in her face, her manner, her composure.

They are talking Georgio, they are talking cats. Cosmina smiled wide when Ottilie admitted her boyfriend was also called Roland. *It is true, he is also a bit of a pussy.* Although Candelaria seems affronted. Cosmina says her man is twenty years her senior, then describes in detail each of his body parts as if she is quoting from a feminist director's version of Jean-Luc Godard's opening to *Le Mepris*.

Yet Cosmina's main fascination is with lighthouses. She shares knowledge that with the exception of seasonal volunteers and educational guides, there are hardly any lighthouse keepers left on the planet. She knows that the UK's last custodian left his post at Kent's North Foreland Lighthouse in 1998 – the same year the US Coast Guard automated the last of its two hundred and seventy-nine federally run beacons. "We are the abnormalities, not the rule," she laughs. She is always laughing. With anyone but Cosmina, this would be an annoyance.

Juska leads her up the spiral, past the Counterweight Well, the Living Quarters, the Control Room, the Service Room, the Watch Room, the Gallery Deck. They enter the Lantern Room. Cosmina immediately runs her hands over the lens, her digits reflected myriadly, as though a hundred fingers are simultaneously caressing. Downstairs, the metal door clangs against the wind and a shudder runs the length and girth of the structure, trembling molecules in glass.

"Beautiful," she says. Juska stands back. Attends.

It is not solely the Fresnal lens that Cosmina will polish, but the windows inside and out. She will walk the Widow's Walk, rag and polish in hand, buffing the glass until birds can no longer see it but everything else can see through. She will work her rag tight around the dioptric prisms of the lens, removing each blemish, each trace of grit. She will fog the cool glass with her warm breath, wipe it clean. She will lovingly burnish the metal ball at the top of the cupola, the device that provides ventilation, allows heat to escape. Cosmina's rhythmic, circular movements will be the crown of their achievement, their accomplishment.

When Cosmina stands on the shore, pebbles between her toes, she views the lighthouse as an entire package: the neatly-trimmed vegetation at the base; the highly-polished metal staircase glimpsed through the windows, adding a sense of rigidity; the paint clinging to the outside, to each undulation of the brick; the reflected sunlight from the lens head, glinting even without power, but with power.

It is then, now their work is complete, that Cosmina questions Juska about the bulb. Asks whether it will be the traditional one thousand watt tungsten variety or a more modern two hundred and fifty watt halogen version. She wonders where Juska has stored it. She has looked in the shack, in the outbuilding, in the Storage Room, even in the icehouse. She expects it will arrive with the Captain, on the boat.

Juska curves a strand of hair away from her mouth, just at the moment that it might become trapped by her lips. "There won't be a bulb," she says. "We don't need one. The lighthouse doesn't need it."

Cosmina looks at her curiously. She remembers the advertisement that she replied to. The one about the restoration of a working lighthouse. Then she opens her mouth to speak, hesitates, and laughs.

Juska

It is a fallacy.

Juska leaves instructions for Candelaria to walk those reverberating metal steps; for Cosmina to repeatedly polish the lens; for Ottilie to ride the cradle up and down the length of the lighthouse, for her fingers to trace the ridges in the brick.

Unseen, she opens the wooden trapdoor set in the base - the one she covered with a rug shortly before Candelaria's arrival - and gently lowers herself, tightly gripping the ladder's rungs as she descends vertical into the depths.

She uses a flashlight to illuminate her passage. The walls are the cool, serious black of onyx, lined as they are with smooth igneous rock. As she walks, the temperature becomes hotter. She pulls her funnel-neck sweater over her head and carries it within the crook of one arm.

After a mile the passage subdivides. She takes the left path, downwards, somewhat steeply, until she no longer requires the torchlight. After another half mile, she reaches a basin.

When she first researched the island, it was the disconnect in the paperwork which intrigued her. When she discovered the passage, she knew she had chosen wisely. On that initial journey, each basin had been empty, with only a residue of what could have been rather than what was. With each subsequent attention the levels in the basins have become measurable, have risen. Now, the basins are almost full, bursting with liquid, molten light. She watches as it bubbles and pops, can sense the surface tension as the liquid strains to be released. Backtracking, she visits the second basin down the right-hand path, where the conditions are seen to be identical.

Quickly she makes her way back up the passage, almost a mirror-image of the structure above it. She dons her sweater, returns the power to her torch.

She ascends the ladder, closes the trapdoor. There is a quote attributable to George Bernard Shaw which states *I can think of no other edifice constructed by man as altruistic as a Lighthouse. They were built only to serve.*

But Juska understands the reverse is the case. She gathers the woman together. Herself. Candelaria. Ottilie. Cosmina. They stand around the base of the lighthouse, extending hands, and although Juska knows that this is a physical impossibility, she imagines their fingers touching, somehow facilitated.

They are four good women.

Their fate is inescapable.

There is a storm coming.

The Zond Tower

by Terry Grimwood

Tumbling.

Anders and me, pressed against the walls of the Luna Lander by centrifugal force. Monstrous versions of human beings in our clumsy white suits. A heavy weight bears down on my chest. Surely my ribs must crack. Surely my lungs must collapse and my heart implode.

Black sky. Horizon. Surface, dark shadowed and unknown. Black sky.

Waiting.

Oh Christ, waiting for the impact. For that moment of agony, chaos and extinction.

I'm screaming because I can do nothing else. My voice is locked inside the helmet.

Now there is the nearness of the surface, felt rather than seen. Ragged, jagged. Cold. Airless. Lethal.

Flimsy craft.

Flimsy flesh and bone.

Moments away. Moments. Moments. Moment –

✻

At the Lighthouse

I wake suddenly, sweat-damp and breathing deep. The room is white, familiar. Delicate silken curtains billow from its huge arched window. The air is cool. Light slants in. Birds sing. The horror was the old dream, which is more memory than nightmare, replayed in all it's vivid terror across the backdrop of sleep.

The crash was a long time ago. All but forgotten.

A long time ago is a difficult concept for me to grasp. Time is a slippery enigma. I sleep when I am tired. I read, walk, work and rest when I am awake. This place brings darkness when I need to sleep. It brings me light when I am awake. There is no need to question or fight.

I simply am.

I am here.

Here is good.

There are occasional troubling thoughts, buried deep, and fleeting like shadows that cross the sun then are gone. I never attempt to bring them back.

I roll over and gather Melanie into my arms. She murmurs my name and I kiss her.

Then I climb out of bed, which is the only item of furniture in this room. Why would there be more? This room is where I sleep. I stretch, then approach the window and push the billowing white curtains aside, so I can stand and stare at the familiar undulating, sun-drenched moonscape that stretches away towards the horizon. The sky is black. I'm on the far side. Earth never rises or sets here.

I don't miss home or my family. I can never go back. I am reconciled to this fact. I am content here. I am cared for. I am fed and kept healthy. I'm not alone either. I have Melanie, my lover.

Music whispers from hidden speakers in the plain walls; soft classical, piano. The notes dance. Melanie murmurs contentedly.

Her hair is dark this morning. I won't know the colour of her eyes until she opens them. They were green when we were last awake together.

"Are you well?" she says sleepily. Her voice is going to be bright this morning, I can tell. Sometimes it's deeper and seductive, sometimes clipped and business-like. Her accent changes and shifts as often as her hair and eye colour. I think I found it disturbing once, but I'm not sure when *once* was.

"Yes," I answer. "But I did have the dream last night."

Night? Was it night? It feels right to call sleep-time night.

Hazel, her eyes are hazel. "That's to be expected."

"Oh?"

"No need to concern yourself, Tom. There's urgent work to be done today."

"What work?" The word unsettles me. I don't know why. It holds an unpleasant connotation, but I can't pin down exactly what it is. I have *worked* here before but can't remember what it entailed.

"You'll know when you need to."

I shrug. If she says I'll know, then I *will* know.

"When I say urgent," a smile, "it's not *that* urgent, Tom." She lies down again and closes her eyes. "Come back and wake me when you're done."

The bedroom door opens onto a corridor, which is bright, and wide. Stained glass windows are set into the high, arched ceiling and splinter the incoming light into showers of green, red and blue. There are other doors to the right and left. I enter the gym. I lift weights then run on the machine until I am exhausted. All the time music drifts from those invisible speakers, always to my taste and always at the right volume. *Stone Free* then *Satisfaction* accompany me through my exercise routine.

I visit the bathroom next. There's a shower, a mirror and a basin. A small cupboard holds a shaver, an electric toothbrush, a selection of toiletries. I need nothing else. I shower then shave my chin and my scalp. I have no use for hair.

Ablutions completed, I stroll to the dining room which is also empty and white but for a simple table and chair. My food has already been prepared. There is fruit and cereal, a jug of coffee, creamer and a mug.

After breakfast, I head back to the bedroom.

※

The crash is a memory even before it ends. There is a heightened sensation of déjà vu as reality fragments into apocalypse. An unthinkable force throws me aside then crushes me with darkness. It is a world of impacts and noise. Everything spins and erupts and disintegrates and flies outwards and inwards in a whirlwind of destruction.

Then: nothing.

It feels as if days have passed when I open my eyes again. I'm supine, my back arched over my life support pack. My clumsy, overlarge suit makes me feel like an upturned beetle. I can see the sky awash with stars. I shouldn't be able to see them. I should be staring at the roof of the lander.

Ah, torn metal. There's a hole.

Something else is wrong. The main control panel has somehow fixed itself to the remains of the roof. There's a reason, but I'm struggling to comprehend – Wait, now I get it. That isn't the top of the craft, it's the front. The roof is…where? I lift my head, look around and realise that the roof is under my feet, which means that the lander is on its side. There's not much left of it. The vehicle's thin metal skin has been pulled apart like silver curtains. I see darkness through the gaps. Night on the far side of the moon.

I draw in a lungful of air. At least my suit's life support appears to be working.

It takes several minutes to move myself into a sitting position.

I switch on the helmet light and there is Anders. His helmet faceplate is smashed and his face, peering through the jagged edged hole, is grotesquely contorted. His eyes bulge. His mouth wide open. I feel deep sadness. He's my buddy and it doesn't look like his was an easy death.

Anders is dead.

But I am not and I have to get out of here.

I crawl through a shadowy obstacle course of debris. There are nests of wires and a dusting of shattered glass. Something is boiling off into the airless dark outside. All I can hear is my own ragged breath, the rhythmic pound of my heart, and the helmet-muffled bumps and scrapes that mark my progress through the wreckage.

I must be careful. Any damage to the suit will be fatal.

When I reach the ripped-open roof, I stop, push my arm outside and rest my gloved hand on the surface of the moon. I'm determined to absorb this moment, to feel it and live it, because I am the first human to touch the face of another world.

Time to move. I crawl slowly through the hole and into the dirty, ashy dust. I can see very little but ill-defined, lumpen shapes which I assume are rocks. The sky, however, is glorious. I cry. I never cry, but right now that dense, glittering, uncountable dome of stars is tearing something out of my soul that I never knew was there. Emotion is not encouraged in the US Navy Airforce, or NASA for that matter.

I take a moment to catch my breath then struggle to my feet. It is exhausting. The suit is too clumsy for gymnastics, but somehow, after a couple of false starts, I manage to stand. I'm soaked in sweat. I'm breathing hard, which is a bad thing because I will use up all my air if I'm not careful –

That's when the truth drives itself into me like a spear to the gut.

It doesn't matter how fast I use up my air. Whatever remains in my tank represents the rest of my life, which means that my future has shrunk to around three hours. No one is coming to rescue me. No one can help in any way whatsoever. This night-dark, alien landscape is my grave. I contemplate the stars again. When the time comes, I want this sky to be the last thing I see. I will lie down, and I will stare upwards and fill my head with beauty.

So, what do I do? Sit here and conserve my air and wait, or walk until I can't walk anymore.

The decision is easy. I'm an explorer. I am the first man on the moon. I am a traveller to new worlds, so I'll keep on travelling.

I survey the horizon.

And there it is.

A long way off, immense, and glowing soft yellow-white.

A tower. A spire that reaches up towards the heavens.

I try to comprehend what I am seeing. A tower on the moon. An artificial structure. Built by *someone*.

Who might still be here.

Now I have a destination.

※

The bedroom is empty.

Melanie's gone.

She said she would wait for me. She was here and now she isn't.

I rush out of the room, call her name. There's no answer, so I set off along the seemingly-endless corridor. I have no idea which way she could have gone or why she would leave me here on my own. I call to her again, and again there is no reply. I stop walking. I feel alone for the first time since…since when? I don't know. I don't understand the concept of *when*.

I must find her.

I open doors and hunt through the countless rooms that line the corridor. Every one is an empty white cube equipped with a wall-sized window that gives sight of the lunar surface. The view is different in each. Some are miles high, so that only the black daytime sky or a distant glimpse of the moon's horizon is visible. An adjacent room, however, might be at ground level and present a vista of jagged rocks and dark-filled craters. I'm disorientated. This place is suddenly alien and frightening. How can I be at the top of the spire and then at its ground floor within the space of a few feet? And why hadn't I seen this before?

The corridor stretches on forever, always in a gentle left-hand curve.

There's no one here.

No, Melanie *has* to be here.

But there's only me.

She. Must. Be. Here.

I'm alone.

I can't be alone. It's not possible for me to be this alone.

❋

I must not question.

I must hope.

There is a structure ahead of me that may be a place where I can breathe, rest and find time to think and plan. The structure is beautiful, graceful and immense. It appears miles high.

It is also familiar and, as I walk, I occupy my mind trying to recall where I've seen it before. A photograph, that's it, grainy and blurred and taken by a Soviet Luna orbiter called…I struggle to recall the name…Zond 3, that's it, back in 1965. The tower was a smudged anomaly that was put down to a camera fault, a trick of light, a plume of dust due to a meteor impact or a gas eruption from inside the moon.

But here it is.

The Zond Tower.

So, was it the source of the pulse and voltage-surge that caused the lander's controls to malfunction and to send it into a spin?

If so, does that make the thing hostile?

Is there an enemy waiting for me there?

What the hell does it matter? I'm doomed anyway.

Every part of my body aches. It takes a lot of effort to plant each boot into the moondust and lift it again. I pray that there are no night-hidden craters or crevices in my path. Breaking a leg or rupturing the suit within sight of sanctuary would be the biggest joke of all in this comedy of unfunny gags.

Christ, this is ironic. I'm not even supposed to be on the moon. The lander's job was to touch down then lift off. In other words, this was a dress rehearsal to find out if it was even possible before letting the world in for Neil, Buzz and Michael's opening night - or calling on Kubrick to make a movie if it proves too difficult to accomplish. That's the rumour. Americans are going to be seen walking on the moon regardless of whether they are actually there or not.

Anders, Lewinson (I guess he's still up there in the command module) and me are supposed to be unsung, unknown heroes. Our story will never be told until some secret file is de-classified long after everyone involved is dead. Well, the secret's a lot safer than they intended because Lewinson will be the only one who makes it home for his behind-locked-doors Medal of Honour ceremony. I guess Anders and me will get posthumous ones. I wonder what they'll tell our wives.

I'm getting closer to the tower and beginning to comprehend how tall it actually is. Its luminescent flanks gently concave as it ascends towards a point. A mast, then, an aerial? Not a building at all? I probably won't be able to get inside and even if I can, what are the chances of a friendly, breathable atmosphere.

Doesn't matter.

It's a destination. It's hope.

It's getting hard to breathe.

※

I know where I can find Melanie. She's playing. She's teasing me. She does that because I like to be teased. I stop running and try to get my bearings. I need to locate the forest. Here, a few doors to my left. One hell of a coincidence, but who cares?

I care.

This isn't right. I wanted to find the forest and here it is. This place can read my mind. It knows all about me. It knows what I want and need and how to keep me happy and that suddenly scares the hell out of me.

I open the door and am immediately walking a path between rows and rows of immense pine trees. Their canopies break the sunlight into dazzlingly beautiful rays that punch down onto the soft, bracken-covered forest floor.

"Melanie!"

No answer. No sign of her. No clue.

There are no wolves or bears in here, but I'm nervous. I shouldn't feel this way. This place is as safe as anywhere, but not being able to find Melanie is unsettling.

"Melanie. *Melanie.*"

No answer.

There is something here, though. Voices, melded into the wind that stirs the branches and cools my face. Familiar voices.

My wife, maybe, although it can't be, I mean I'm here and she's… where the hell is she?

Earth, that's where. Home.

The idea is troubling. This is my home. How can I have another home?

Memories rush in. Forests like this one, cities, automobiles, trucks, the ocean, my house, the woman who lives there, the blue-eyed, Californian blonde who is too good to be true and yet agreed to marry *me*. Jackie, that's her name. I love her. I miss her. I want to hear her voice again.

Her real voice. Not the noise ringing through my skull that masquerades as voices. I have to shut them out. I have to stay sane and concentrate on the job in hand.

I run through a forest under a clear blue sky towards an immense curved white wall, and a door.

And then I'm sprinting, along the corridor, still calling for Melanie. There's no answer. No sign. No sensation of her presence. I can't stay out here. I can't stand the emptiness. That silence, that stillness, that *nothing* is too loud. It presses in. It feels as if it has a personality a soul. It feels hungry.

And there are voices again.

Somehow out of reach because when I stop and attempt to listen, they shut off. As if they don't want me to hear what they're saying -

Major Tom Weller, that is *enough!*

Any more of that kind of thinking and you'll lose it.

I run down those endless damn corridors. I call Melanie's name until I'm hoarse. Then, too exhausted to take another step, I stop and lean against the curved wall to catch my breath.

All the walls are curved.

All the walls are the same.

Every inch of this place is the same as every other.

And why do I never climb? Why is it always horizontal. Why are there no stairs, lifts, or elevators. This is a tower for Chrissakes, all the rooms I've ever visited are on different levels and yet I never ascend or descend. This place is not home.

My home is Earth.

I want to go home.

I hate this place.

※

Dawn is breaking here on the far side of the moon. A glow limns the horizon. Long, extended shadows stretch, finger-like, across the surface, distorted by its undulations and scattered rocks.

There is enough light for me to see that there is a door.

I must make that my focus. I must centre my entire concentration on that door. It's a couple of hundred yards away now. The girth of the tower is titanic, and the door is immense. It's a thin line etched in the surface of the spire's cliff-like wall, a rectangle, softened by rounded corners. A hundred feet high, maybe. Twenty, thirty feet across.

I have no proof that it is a door but it's the only hope I have.

I must stare at it. I must get to it. Straight ahead and straight on.

I mustn't look up because that's madness. The tower is too high for my ape brain to comprehend. No, the door and the door only.

I mustn't stop, even though each step weighs a ton. Every movement hurts. The visor fogs with each panted, gasping breath. I'm lightheaded. I feel dizzy. Nauseated. I ache.

Walk, that's the only thing that might, *might,* save me. Resting will be fatal. I may not make it anyway, but I have to try. I have no idea how much air is left. I have no idea because I've forgotten how to read the gauge on my wrist. I've forgotten everything other than to walk.

One-sixth gravity be damned. It feels as if I am on Jupiter. It feels as if I am forcing my way through the dense icy water at the bottom of the Atlantic Ocean.

Pick up your boot. Plant it into the dust again. Pick up the other boot.

I want to breathe deep, but I can't seem to get enough air down into my lungs.

Keep walking.

And get to that door.

✳

You fucker.

A thought stops me mid-stride.

A realisation. A flash of inspiration.

This tower, this thing, *is* what brought our lander crashing out of the sky. Everything was fine. I can remember it now, as clear as day. Descent almost routine. Each component, each operation, smooth as syrup.

Then that blast of white noise from the radio receiver. The controls went crazy. The steering jets malfunctioned, and suddenly we were upside down and tumbling…

I swing round and slam my fist into the curved wall. It yields a little, so I don't injure my hand. It hurts though and that's what I want; pain. I hope the bastard feels it too.

You killed Anders. He was my friend. You murdered him and you almost killed me as well.

You fucker.

I run back to my apartment. Everything is still here and yet it feels wrong; sterile and fake. The curtains hang limp and the light from outside is the harsh midday sun. The one that burns out of the blackness to paint the lunar landscape - the boring, never-changing, insanely motionless landscape – a dazzling grey-white.

I yell in frustration then swing about and wrench the cover from the bed before grasping the frame from underneath to tip it over. I scream and rant and kick and tear.

The tower is silent and still.

It listens though.

Oh yeah. It listens.

※

The door opens.

I'm crawling now. I want to lie down, to sleep. I want to rip off my helmet so I can breathe. I need to *breathe*.

No. No. No. I can't do that. There's still some air in here. A tiny puff of life. One more lungful.

I haul myself over the stones and dust, no longer concerned about damaging the suit.

I crawl to the threshold. Every movement is forced on *this* me, by some *other* me that is determined to survive no matter how much it hurts.

There is light, soft and white. I haul myself onto a smooth floor. Symbols are engraved into its surface. No language I know. I don't care. Once inside, I curl into myself and lie there as the door slides shut behind me. There is no clang or vibration.

A breeze tugs at the suit. I attempt to draw breath but there is nothing. I strain at the vacuum and try to suck some miniscule wisp of air into my lungs. My ears ring loudly. I'm dizzy. Panicked I claw at the helmet. I'm almost too weak to release its seals and remove it.

I breathe.

I pant and gasp and taste cool, sweet air. I roll onto my back, big and clumsy in the suit.

I breathe.

The inner door, which is much smaller than the outer one, slides noiselessly open. I don't pay much attention to what lies beyond. I simply look up at the oddly curved ceiling of the airlock chamber and weep because I'm alive.

After some indefinable period, I have no idea how long because time has lost all meaning, I roll over onto my hands and knees and gaze at the tower's interior. The beauty of it makes me weep again. My emotions are close to the surface. I've flown all kinds of fast, dangerous, vicious beasts and landed them on tiny floating runways bobbing around in the endless ocean. I've fought for my country and almost died for it in the process, so I don't cry easily, but this, here, now. This shatters me.

I see an immense curved stairway of gleaming metal and what looks like marble. It sweeps up to a gallery lined with open archways that must lead deeper into the building. I see a vast domed ceiling that consists entirely of stained glass that refracts the light into a million brilliant colours. There is a chequered marble floor. Plants hang from the gallery like lush green waterfalls. Others bear fruit around a pool and a fountain. The temperature is temperate, pleasant.

When I finally struggle to my feet, I notice a marble table by the entrance, a jug of water and a glass. I drink. The water is pure and cold. Music drifts. The Byrds, *Going Back*. A favourite. How the hell do they know? It's as if I'm expected and everything has been prepared for me.

"Tom?"

Startled, I turn to see that I'm not alone. A woman is descending the stairs. She is tall, exceptionally so, and slender. Her hair is blonde, her eyes blue. She wears a skin-tight suit, the same grey-white as the walls. Her voice is deep. I like her voice.

"Melanie," I say and have no idea where that comes from.

"Melanie." She appears to ponder the name, then smiles and nods. "Yes. I am Melanie." She waits on the lower steps, her hand extended. "I'm happy to see you, Tom. I hope you're happy here."

Some cloud of unease slides over my contentment, but it doesn't last. I *am* happy here. Why wouldn't I be?

A new song, *Moonlight Drive* by The Doors. Another great number.

I hold Melanie's hand. She says, "I'll take you to your apartment."

I'd like that.

This place feels like home. I already find it hard to remember how long I've been here.

This is Heaven.

❇

This is Hell.

I kneel on the floor of my bedroom. I hug myself and rock because it is the only way I can keep it together. I'm alone here. Utterly, completely and entirely alone. The vastness of it, the reality, the truth, the horror of it bears in and crushes my will. I don't know how long I've been in this prison. I've been buried alive. I'm clawing at the coffin lid. I'm screaming and shrieking and pleading for release, yet there is none. No one, not one human being can hear me or knows where I am.

I've fouled the room. My filth is daubed over the walls and the splintered remains of the bed. The stink of it nauseates and is but a trivial discomfort in comparison with my loneliness and exhaustion. I have stamped and smashed and torn and now I can barely move.

If I could find the airlock I would step outside and after a few, agonising seconds, be released into oblivion. But there can be no oblivion. Only this endless, timeless, eternal *now*.

❇

The ship, a huge, dark vessel whose flanks slide against the walls of time and space as it carries cargo from the rim to the galactic heart, detects signal-scramble from a nearby planet. The signals indicate sentient life. The ship's systems alert its pilot, who prepares to divert. First contact is mandatory if the conditions are ripe for such a meeting.

Wait.

A stronger signal interposes itself between the vessel's receiving station and the audio-visual-data tangle emanating from the blue-green planet.

There is a lighthouse on the planet's solitary moon.

Its signal is a warning.

Change course. Ignore the noise, it says. These lifeforms are apes who transform fear into violence. They are self-destructive and murderous. See for yourself. We have a specimen.

The pilot absorbs the quantum-entangled data that swims in the lighthouse's beacon and *becomes* –

- a creature that cowers in the ruins of a room befouled with its own waste. That finds terror in the silence and isolation. That rages and snarls and yearns to kill that which it believes to be the cause of its suffering. That is animal, instinct, reflex, barely out of its cave and still afraid of the dark outside.

Repulsed and unnerved, the pilot withdraws and executes an emergency course change. The manoeuvre is a sudden twist of the ship's fabric that disrupts adjacent gravity waves and causes a momentary freeze of space-time that extends as far as this solar system's innermost gas giant. The ship then climbs away from the dangerous blue planet and its moon and, an instant later, resumes it progress towards the galactic heart.

※

I wake up suddenly, sweat damp and breathing hard. The room is white and familiar. Delicate silken curtains billow from its huge arched window. The air is cool. Light slants in. Birds sing. The horror was a dream. An old dream of loneliness, which is more memory than nightmare, replayed in all its vivid terror across the backdrop of sleep.

I roll over and gather Melanie into my arms. She murmurs my name and tells me to rest. There is no work for me today.

I kiss her.

I am content.

I am here.

Here is good.

There are occasional troubling thoughts and memories, buried deep, and fleeting like shadows that cross the sun then are gone. I never attempt to bring them back because there is no need.

The Sirens Are Calling In

by Rory Moores

You were always told to never follow them. Your parents, grandparents, cousins and friends, all told you they were dangerous, that they would get you into trouble.

You were also always told to stay away from the lighthouse. Its presence had haunted the town forever, but no one could tell you why.

Now, you are awake in your bed, staring at a face that is pressed against the glass sliding door that overlooks your garden. They beckon you with their finger. They motion to the light in the distance, forever spinning in the night.

Their eyes grow wider and wild. Their sclera gleams and reflects the full moon. They tap again and again on the glass.

You press your finger to your lips and wave your hand to silence them. You look over to your partner, they are deep in a peaceful slumber. They will not wake, you are certain.

You slip out of bed, covering your nudity as you search the floor for yesterday's clothes. Outside, they turn away to give you privacy. They are many things, but they are aways respectful; you never feel uncomfortable in their presence, not in that way at least.

You are dressed now. Your sneakers are in your hand. You tiptoe to the door, careful to avoid the one floorboard which always creaks. You look back at your partner as you unlock the slider and open it; they do not move. You are struck with pangs of love and lust at their intense beauty and you resist the urge to wake and kiss them passionately as you step out into the cool night air.

You shut the door. You face the one they warned you of.

They smile at you with perfectly crooked, radiant teeth. Behind them red and purple flowers dance in the breeze. You are blue now; blue and calm.

They hold out their hand. "Come," they say.

You take it.

"I am the mountain."

You nod. You walk together in the dark.

✺

The dog ran down the hill, chasing three sparrows. You followed behind. Your lips and teeth stained black from the blackberries you had been picking and eating from the bushes that used to grow wild back then. Behind you, the lighthouse stood proud at the top of the hill.

They were with you too. They swung a large stick, hitting everything they walked past. They stomped on ants and snails.

"Stop," you said, tired of the crunching of shells and the mass death of molluscs.

"Jesus talks to me," they replied.

The sky was filling with rolling, dark grey clouds. You pointed to them. "It's going to rain soon."

They nodded. "I am the rain. I am God's tears."

You were red, then.

✺

They touch the brown and wispy seagrass. Their hands change its colour to green and yellow.

You walk on, inhaling the sea air. Above you, the stars pulsate and twinkle, becoming clearer as a cloud blankets the moon. The stars then vanish too, blinded out by the passing lighthouse's lamp.

"I've lost my lover," they say. "They have fallen, struck down by Apollo's disc."

You grimace as you remember. You spit on a flax bush. It turns brown.

※

You watched from the bank, staring at them as they frolicked. They chased and tackled each other to the ground. They rolled and kissed on the dry, dusty earth.

"I am the sun, you are the moon," one, or maybe both of them shouted. You could barely tell them apart when they were together.

A bird: a pīwakawaka, flitted above your head. It dipped down, closer and closer to you. You reached out and snatched it from the air. You squeezed it tight. It turned black and you released it.

You heard screaming.

※

"Why have you come tonight?"

They don't answer.

"They said you had gone away. I thought you were gone."

They ignore you. Instead, they laugh and point to the path leading up the cliff to the place you were always told to avoid; the place you've stared out at everyday for the last five years, but which you have never returned to…

"I am the lighthouse. I am the homecoming."

"Stop it," you shout at them.

"I am the fire. I am the water."

You collapse to the ground. You roll on to your back. A meteor shower lights up the sky and in turn your face. Your eyes glimmer golden.

※

You were lying by the fireplace with a belly full of bolognese. The television was on, the reception was bad, every now and again someone would stand and adjust the bunny ears.

"'That's it," you said when the picture became clearer.

There was a knock on the door, stern and authoritative. You looked at them. They avoided your gaze. You stood to answer the door. You were stopped by a family member, they held you back as someone else went to see what the commotion was.

The door opened, then a gasp.

"Are they home?" the authority asked.

There was a mumbled conversation and then someone entered and took them away. Everyone in the room started to cry.

Your heart was grey.

※

The meteor shower has finished and the night is alive. Moths and insects flit around your glowing face.

"I am the vision, I am the cavern."

You smile, no longer disturbed, no longer confused. In the distance you hear laughter and clapping, singing and dancing.

They look back at you as you start up the path to the disused sentinel who guides the ghosts of the past home. You pluck a white flower as you stroll. You wave it in front of you, sending its pollen through the air. You breathe in its scent.

✸

You ran and ran and ran and then ran some more. Heaven opened up and the tears of the gods mixed with your own. The world was grieving them.

You turned from the roads and into the hills overlooking the sea. The lighthouse was pulling you, they'd always talked about it so much and now you were compelled towards it. Up the winding path you went as the rains got heavier. Higher still, battered by wind and crippled by the ever-expanding hole in your heart.

You reached the lighthouse.

As always, the lantern was on. It had never been turned off, even after the lighthouse was decommissioned.

Its door was ajar, you could hear the clicking of the turning lens. You pushed it open and were hit with the stench of mildew, rot and piss. It was dark inside. The steps were slippery. Red, violet, white and orange flowers grew from cracks in the wall, coiled their way around the railing. Their colours grew more vivid as the darkness faded to a twilight glow in your ascent.

You reached the top. You looked out the window at dark clouds gathering in the distance, lightning flashing out at sea.

The lamp revealed the jagged rocks protruding from the choppy, foamy seawater.

An overturned desk with enraged red writing scrawled on its underside caught your eye.

I killed them. This is my fault.

It was their writing…

※

They guide you through the crowd of singers and dancers. They wear masks adorned with feathers and antlers and fishbones. One spins in front of you, their naked body covered in seaweed.

"I am the return, I am the ascent."

"Why do you say such things?" you ask. "What is all of this?"

"Ascension," the crowd of revellers chant. They lift up their masks and kiss each other. They hold each other tight and spin in circles.

You look away, embarrassed by the sight of an old, naked, sagging white body, their identity hidden by a poorly made mask.

Exploding fireworks light the sky in a neon pink dreamscape. You feel yourself turn pink as well.

"I have arrived, the lover has returned!" they yell, standing at the lighthouse's entrance.

The masked revellers cheer, some take each others hands and skip away into the night.

"You are the answer, I am the question. You are the omega, I am the alpha!" they say to you, peering into your lost soul with piercing eyes.

You sigh. You gaze down at the grass. It sways with the wind. It moves in deliberate patterns that sweep around you, before weaving through the thinning party. Glowing geometric patterns float up from the ground, they hover and spin, then fly towards the lighthouse.

They are still standing there. You make eye contact.

"Will you come? Will you climb to the lamp on the hill with me?" they ask with outstretched arms.

You nod.

※

They called it the rock game and the three of you always played it on Saturdays. You would take as many stones and small rocks as you could carry from the quarry, down the bank, and to the open grassy field. A large boulder sat in the centre of this unused space. You would measure out ten large steps away from it. Then, you would take turns throwing your stones and rocks, trying to bounce them off the boulder to hit the fence in the distance. The winner of the game was either the first to hit the fence, or whoever's rock fell the closest.

They were playing the rock game without you the day that you caught the pīwakawaka. Something went horribly wrong.

They told you it was an accident, that their rock recoiled and hit them in the face. They told you the angle, combined with where it struck them, would have killed anyone instantly. They told you this at the lighthouse, through the messages scrawled on the desk and in a note stuck to the wall. You shivered as you read.

It was an accident, they had written. *It was accidentally on purpose,* it said further down.

You looked back out to sea. A ship had appeared. It was struggling through the violent swell. It was ignoring the light! Ignoring the guidance and the lifeline being offered.

The ship struck a rock. It swayed and tipped to its side. The containers it was carrying slid off and tumbled into the sea. You thought you caught glimpses of people diving overboard to a certain death.

You stepped back and realised they had been behind you this whole time, hovering over you like mist. You felt them brush past your neck as they turned with the light.

You were drained of all colours.

✵

They beckon you to come inside. You understand now, you always did but you needed this night to finally accept reality. You chase after them as they disappear into the lighthouse.

You step inside, the flowers from your last visit now dominate the interior; hyacinths.

You race up the stairs. Each step is covered in slippery moss and coiled weeds. It smells like the forest floor, musty and alive.

You reach the top, where the light shines on forever and ever. Has someone been maintaining the lamp, all these years? Or is the bulb inside invincible, impossible to break and extinguish? The answer does not matter, because you are alone.

They are gone.

They've been gone for a long time, appearing only in the caverns of your mind, in your visions, in the lighthouse.

"I am the lighthouse," they said. And, they are. They exist here and now as a knotted rope.

The Lighthouse at Addenbay

by Pete Sillett

"Bet you can't find the Lighthouse at Addenbay" the note read. I looked down at the now crumpled piece of paper in my hand and sighed. I hadn't heard from Joseph in nearly three years. Not since a few months after the divorce. It had been relatively amicable, despite a few cutting remarks on both sides, but we had each continued on with our own lives after the final paperwork had been signed, he as a travel writer of medium repute, and I as a part-time lecturer in maritime history.

And then, out of the blue, devoid of context or pleasantries, came this single-sentence taunt. I'd initially assumed that it was intended for someone else, that some fluke of an application opening had resulted in him sending the message to me instead of the anticipated recipient. I ignored it for a week. After seven days of 'Addenbay' floating in and out of my consciousness, I relented and typed the name into a search engine. It was a small coastal town, not much to distinguish it from the myriad of other small UK coastal towns that had fallen out of favour in the last few decades. I could think of no logical link between the place and myself, or with Joseph. I'd certainly never written or read about Addenbay, and I don't recall it ever appearing on his travel itineraries.

There was something about the sentence – the flagrant outright challenge that piqued my interest. Our entire relationship had, in fact, been founded upon taunts and challenges. Our first kiss had been the result of a lost bet, an outcome that each of us had not-so-subtly swayed, and most of our marriage had been structured around playfully setting one another impossible goals to push our professional boundaries. 'I bet you can't visit all the family-owned pubs in Shropshire' had given rise to a book that had gained Joseph some significant attention, while 'I bet you can't find any evidence that the Mary Rose was sabotaged' had led to a notorious conference paper delivered by myself. The more I thought back to our relationship, the more I felt that the sentence *had* been meant for me, and that it *was* a challenge. Joseph, it seemed, was confident that there was something in Addenbay that would engage me.

So it was that fifteen days after receiving his message, I was standing in Addenbay High Street, the sea-infused wind whipping harshly at my face, clutching a scrap of paper with a list of hotels, bed-and-breakfasts, places of local interest and Joseph's obnoxious taunt. It surely says a lot about a person if eight words from a largely forgotten ex can inspire them to book annual leave, throw together a week's worth of clothing and toiletries, and head down to a dingy little town that they had never heard of. I really needed to find a boyfriend.

※

It was out of season. Being a coastal town, almost all its businesses were those geared towards tourists and holidaymakers and here, in mid-February, with breath hanging in the air like unquiet spirits, Addenbay High Street was decidedly empty. I was, in fact, the only person in the immediate vicinity. A gust of sea air hit me in the face and I pulled my coat collar up to form some meagre barrier. I took a deep breath and headed down the street. On my right, a row of shops and houses stretched up and away in front of me, slowly curving left in line with the coast. To my left was the beach; grey and forlorn, the sand and pebbles looking as if the energy had been sucked out of them. Beyond them, the waves smashed furiously into one another whilst tiny specks of seagull wheeled about madly, diving towards the water below. For a good five minutes of walking, I did not see a single open establishment. There were ice-cream stands, sweet shops, cafes, arcades, and fishing supplies – all with doors locked and windows barred, the occasional panels of smashed glass on the pavement were smoothed by the erosion of sea breeze. The rust and salt over most of the signs and bolts indicated that many of the places had been shut up since the end of August. Clearly Addenbay was a town that only came out of hibernation for two or three months of the year.

    I crossed the road and walked the beach side. Sand and stones had gradually encroached upon the flat surface of the pavement, evidently moved along their way by high winds and higher water. I looked to sea, absent-mindedly watching the seagulls battle each other for whatever prize was just below the surface. On the horizon, a cargo ship drifted slowly across the hazy line that just managed to separate sea from sky. It seemed as though they were one and the same, that the dark grey clouds were merely the upper lip, and the roiling waves of slightly darker grey the lower lip of a gigantic mouth. At any moment, the tiny ship would be consumed, licked away without a second thought by the appetite of Mother Nature. I was struck by a sense of extreme isolation. Even though there must surely have been some residents not a hundred meters from where I stood, perhaps even watching me curiously from behind netted curtains, as they sipped tea and pitied my slightly soggy form, I felt that the crew of that distant cargo ship was the closest human contact for miles. It was with a faint sense of mourning that I watched the black rectangle disappear in the distance, finally engulfed in the monochrome mouth of the horizon.

I blinked and realised that I had probably spent twenty minutes slowly trudging along the pavement, watching the cargo ship quietly fade into oblivion. I looked to my right and saw that indeed the High Street had become very different. While there was still a pervading sense of emptiness, the nature of the building fronts had changed. While further down the road, the shops were all tightly locked up, waiting for their next resurrection in another four months, these building facades were well kept and inviting, albeit whilst still conveying the same sense of vacancy. Vacancy, as it turned out, was an appropriate word, as I realised that these buildings were predominantly hotels and bed-and-breakfasts. I smiled with relief, glad that I had accidentally stumbled upon the very thing that I was looking for.

I peered at the signs that adorned the front patios and gardens of the buildings, stating the names in gold and ornate fonts. I looked down at my scrap of paper again; my list started with the cheapest first. A few doors further along the road was the Farnchester Hotel, which had eagerly stated on their website that rooms in the off-season were well kept, well heated, and extremely cheap. Doubting, but optimistic, I walked up to the entrance with its large archway that had been designed to evoke grotesque art. A sneering face with strange branches growing out of its mouth looked down at me. A large dark green double-door was in the centre of the archway. A similarly decorated doorknocker leered as I approached and used it.

After a minute or so, I knocked again and heard the sound of thumping and muttering. The door jerked open inwards, and a balding man with a thin moustache and a surprisingly bright sparkle in his eyes smiled at me apologetically. He pointed up at the archway and I saw that just below the grotesque face was a black screen of a motion sensor device. He told me that the weather, for whatever reason, seemed to play havoc with the automatic door.

I smiled politely at his small talk, but he remained blocking the way. I coughed and made a slight movement towards him. His eyes widened and he apologised, having assumed that I was simply asking for directions. Apparently, there was no-one at the hotel barring the owner – who I took to be the man in front of me – his wife, daughter, and father. But he was eager for out-of-season patrons and welcomed me in.

As if to punctuate his point, another freezing gust of violent wind almost pushed me into him. He laughed a little and stepped aside, showing me into the foyer. It was cosy if a little bland, with white wallpaper and a light blue carpet being apparently consciously undermined by several huge and inappropriate vases that were so garishly decorated that they looked like they belonged in a pantomime. In them was a selection of greenery, from holly bushes to spider plants, implying a fairly haphazard approach to botany. Noticing my stare, the owner shook his head as he walked over to the front desk. He explained that the interior design was the result of his wife's idea of 'classicism' and took it as evidence that the old saying was true: ignorance is bliss.

I smiled again, genuinely this time, as I approached the desk. I put down my bag and removed my coat and realised for the first time how comfortable the lodgings appeared. The heating was on and, despite the size of the foyer, it had the feeling of a living room. I signed my name and paid the amount for a stay of six days in a standard room on the fifth floor. He led me over to the lift. As we entered, I almost asked him about the lighthouse but thought better of it. Given the inherent challenge of Joseph's note, there was no way that simply asking a local would yield the answer. There was obviously *something* about the lighthouse that I was as yet oblivious to. Rather than risk making myself look a fool, I kept the conversation away from it. We rode the lift in silence, until we reached the fifth floor. The man deposited me outside a room, number 590. I furrowed my brow, as surely there wasn't enough space on this floor for ninety rooms. Again, the man responded to my unasked question. He told me that his wife had made the decision, making the place appear bigger and grander than it actually was. The same was true of the interior, he warned me, where a fondness for mirrors had gotten the better of her. With an apologetic eye-roll, he opened my door, dropped the key into my hand and headed back to the lift.

❋

In truth, I hadn't realised just how tired I was. The sea air had completely knocked me for six, and I was scarcely in my room three minutes before I collapsed on to my bed with a heavy sigh. My bag and coat sat by a wardrobe, I could unpack later, and I casually cast my gaze around the room. The man – and it was only once I was in the room that I realised that I had never asked his name – had been right about the mirrors. There were at least ten of them strategically placed around the four walls. In fairness to his wife, they did make the place look bigger, but considering the cost of mirrors I wondered whether similarly decorating all of the rooms might have been something of an unnecessary expense.

Determined to not fall asleep that afternoon and then slip into a cycle of day-sleeping and night-living, I heaved myself up on to my elbows. I retrieved my phone from my pocket and did an internet search for 'Addenbay Lighthouse'. I was unsurprised to find it yielded no results. I tried several other options, including a list of lighthouses in the immediate area, and memorable landmarks of Addenbay. Nothing of any relevance came up. I dejectedly scrolled through the fifth page of results, contemplating that *obviously* Joseph had sent me in search of something far too obscure for the internet to know about, when I happened upon a result that at the very least contained 'Addenbay', 'Light' and

'Sea'. It was a now-defunct message board, according to the visitor counter on the page I entered, it had not been updated in seven years.

The relevant passage was a lengthy post by someone claiming to be a 'Hunter of the Weird', who had scoured the British Isles in search of undiscovered creatures and bizarre phenomena. Despite its overly self-congratulatory tone (the person had *very nearly* proven the existence of the Middlesex Devil Dog, but for the minor detail of the lack of any solid evidence whatsoever), I found towards the bottom a mention of an unexplained optical illusion that occasionally appeared at Addenbay. Apparently, there had been accounts – or more accurately *an* account – of someone witnessing a blinking light on the outcropping of land just east of Addenbay. It had been spotted on three consecutive nights and then ceased. That was all. However, this was enough for the Hunter of the Weird to conclude that there was clearly some supernatural or otherwise unearthly singularity to be found at Addenbay. After reeling off a list of increasingly absurd explanations – ranging from UFOs to Faeries – they eagerly concluded that the only way to know for certain was to visit Addenbay themselves and discover the truth.

A cursory search of the site showed that there were no further updates on this and whether or not the Hunter of the Weird ever came to Addenbay was a mystery to be left to the ages. I was faintly annoyed. I was concerned that *this* tiny speck of ghostly gossip was the entire foundation upon which Joseph's message had been built. Had my annoyance been fanned any further at that point, I might have stormed out of the hotel, taken the train back home, sent Joseph a long and angry message with a bill for the hotel room attached, and never given the trip another thought. As it was, I was mildly irritated, slumped onto my back and against my better judgement drifted into a sleep that, in retrospect, changed my life in the most fundamental way possible.

※

At the Lighthouse

I was conscious of the sound much earlier than I was conscious of being awake. Perhaps I had incorporated the sound into my dream, and so when I slipped from one state into the other, the whole process became blurred and disorienting. There were actually three sounds that alternated in their volume and prominence in my perception – the first two were ordinary enough for the location; my window rattling as the wind beat against it, and waves crashing on the shore. The third sound was the most inexplicable. At first, I thought it was singing. After I had fully regained consciousness, I dismissed the initial assumption. It wasn't singing in any traditional sense, as it sounded nothing like a human voice. But it was melodic and was not suggestive of a man-made instrument producing the notes. A clumsy comparison would be whale song, though it was in no way similar. It almost sounded like a gurgle or buzzing, with a lyrical quality to it. It was often drowned out by the rattle or the waves, but was nevertheless there beneath them, continuing on in its strange musical journey.

I was so concerned with deciphering the sound that my sluggish brain had not even processed the visual phenomenon occurring around me. It was dark by this point. I checked my phone and discovered to my surprise that it was 3am. I had not drawn the curtain when I arrived, which is why I was able to make out, glinting in the score of mirrors that hung on my walls, a distant flashing light. I immediately jumped up and headed over to the window. My head spun at the shift in position, but I held myself steady on the window ledge. I looked out towards the east and saw the unmistakable blinking of a lighthouse. I realised that Addenbay was completely dark. I could barely make anything out from my position and, bracing myself for the icy wet wind, I opened the window so I could lean out. I gritted my teeth against the cold and checked left and right, up and down the High Street, but there was definitely no visible light from any of the houses and no streetlights were lit. I looked towards the blinking lighthouse again and caught the strange melodic sound on the wind. It was clearer now that the window was open, but remained faint, distant.

Well, I thought to myself as I closed the window and wrapped my arms around my body, *there* was the bloody lighthouse at Addenbay. Mystery solved, such as it was. Joseph could go hang. I sat on the bed, pondering the darkness outside. I thought about the rows of locked up shop fronts and concluded that there were very few actual residents in Addenbay. Probably, the shops were run by temporary staff hired exclusively for the summer months and owned by people who lived far away in big cities and barely even saw this place. Likewise, aside from this hotel, most accommodation would be closed for much of the year. I estimated, given the size of the town, that maybe only a couple of hundred people might be living here all year round. Barely a village's worth of population. Therefore, what would be the point in spending council money on street lighting that nobody was going to benefit from? Better to leave it off, at least during the dead hours of the early morning. Satisfied with my concocted logic, I laid myself back down to sleep. The strange music continued to drift in over the wind, and it seemed to me that it was rather mournful.

I awoke again four hours later at 7am. Feeling groggy from oversleep as well as famished – I had fallen into my first nap before I had eaten any dinner – I traipsed down the hallway to the lift. On my way to the ground floor it occurred to me that there might not be any breakfast served, given that it was off-season, but I was relieved to discover that a modest breakfast bar had been laid out. I was so relieved to see food that at first I did not notice the lack of people in the dining room. After I had finished half a grapefruit and poured myself a coffee, I peered around and saw nothing but empty seats and tables. I craned my neck to see if I could see the foyer, hoping to catch a glimpse of the owner, but I was too far back in the room to see beyond the doorway.

Then a door opened leading out to a kitchen and he entered, carrying a plate of bacon. He smiled and asked if I had slept well. I lied and told him that I had. Now confident that the lighthouse was a very real, though strangely undocumented, building at the edge of the town, I asked the owner about it. He looked confused and told me that the closest lighthouse was several miles in the opposite direction to where I had claimed to see the light. I was intrigued to say the least, and immediately created two suppositions in my head: first, the lighthouse had been a dream (and it was at this point that I also remembered the singing, which had indeed given the whole thing an oneiric quality), or second, the lighthouse was not a purpose-built council-sanctioned lighthouse, but some kind of amateur construction that had gone unnoticed in the largely empty nights. Given the context of Joseph's note, I went with the latter.

The owner began to clear my table and I noticed an infrequent glint coming from his wrist. A small piece of crystal or glass, eroded at the edges like a pebble, appeared and disappeared beneath his sleeve. Assuming that it was some kind of bracelet or keepsake from the shore I asked him about it. He became quite flustered and, deducing that I may have offended him in some way, I turned the conversation back to the matter at hand. I queried whether or not any travel writers had come to Addenbay in the recent past. I did not trust Joseph for one minute, and immediately suspected that he was setting up some elaborate prank. The owner gave a noncommittal shrug and said that generally speaking only a certain kind of person came to Addenbay. I decided not to question that cryptic response and instead asked the best way to reach the coastal outcropping where I thought I had seen the light.

Taking the owner's advice, I hopped on to the number 36 bus towards Grawford. It was surprisingly full, in that there were more than three people on board excluding myself. The journey was uneventful, and I spent most of the time staring out of the increasingly foggy window, trying to tune out the bickering between an elderly married couple regarding the price of red cabbage. I felt a slight twinge of jealousy, that the two of them at least had someone to bicker *with*. The bus took us through several small backroads that one would have thought were too obscure for a bus route, but at several points we stopped and more people boarded. I noticed many of them glance at me, identifying the outsider with the keen senses of a xenophobe. With each turn the incline grew steeper, gaining height the further inland we travelled. I glimpsed the sea between houses as we passed by, looking more settled though no less grey than it had the previous day. Drizzle fell on the window and, combined with the condensation within, eventually made it quite impossible to see anything at all.

After a little over twenty minutes, the driver called back to inform me that I had reached my stop. I awkwardly thanked him, feeling self-conscious in front of the local community, and stepped off the bus. The cold hit me hard, having taken for granted the heat on the bus, and I pulled my coat tight around me. I was as close to the middle of nowhere as one might wish to be, and as I watched the bus pull away down the country lane, I surveyed my surroundings. On one side was a vast expanse of rolling fields, though there was no indication that these were owned by farmers or even frequented by casual walkers. The grass was tall, nearly up to my waist, and undulated in the wind. The effect was disquieting as it felt like I was again staring out at the sea. I felt, too, as if there was unseen wildlife in the grass, watching me curiously. On the other side of the country lane was the outcropping that stretched some hundred yards away before dropping as a steep cliff down into the water below. There was no indication at all that there is, was, or would ever be a lighthouse there.

Perplexed, I marched away from the waves of grass towards the outcropping, hearing the complimentary hisses of waves far below and blades of grass brushing against one another. I focussed on the ground, searching for some sign of recent human activity. After twenty minutes I did not find so much as a cigarette butt. Having been at least partially prepared for this disappointment, I pulled out a pair of binoculars from my coat pocket. It was possible, after all, that I had misjudged the direction of the lighthouse from my hotel room and simply come to the wrong place. I scanned the horizon, looking back in the direction where I had come on the bus. I could see – though only just – the row of hotels from whence I had set out. It took a moment, but I was able to discern with reasonable confidence which window I had leant out of the night before. Again, I mentally worked out the angle in relation to where I was and where I had been at 3am that morning. There was little room for error. I was definitely in the right place. If not the exact spot, certainly close enough that I should be able to see the source of light from here.

I heard the sound of an engine and turned to see a bus heading towards the town. Disappointed that I had not gotten any further in solving the mystery but determined to not stand around on this outcropping for another half-hour unnecessarily, I waved my hand at the bus and boarded.

※

I awoke that night in much the same manner as I had previously, slowly becoming conscious of the audio and visual stimulus in my room. Again, I could make out the dim flashes of light in the mirrors. Again, I could hear the faint sound of melancholic singing on the wind. Perhaps spurred on by the day's earlier disappointment, I jumped out of bed and looked out of the window. There was the same rhythmic movement from left to right of the lighthouse beam. I was certain now that the light emanated from the spot where I had stood not eighteen hours previously. Without thinking, I began to dress.

I felt like I was being played for a fool and was determined to put an end to it. I would head up there myself whilst I could still see the light's position and find whoever or whatever the source was. I put on my coat and left my hotel room quietly, not wanting to wake anyone else. It occurred to me whilst I headed down to the foyer that I was going to look highly suspicious leaving the hotel at 3am with no particular justification other than to look for a lighthouse. Thankfully, when I reached the ground floor, I found that the night porter – an old man who must have been in his seventies – sound asleep in his chair, with the radio quietly playing Brahms.

I gently opened the front door and stepped out into the pitch blackness. I understood immediately the folly of my actions. Addenbay's lightless streets would be impossible to traverse successfully without stumbling into some form of obstacle or perhaps undesirable person. As if to spur me on, or maybe mock me, at that moment the beam of light flashed directly at the hotel. I glared in the direction of the outcropping and stepped into the road. I crossed over to the shore side of the pavement, using the reflection of the light on the waves as some vague guide of my whereabouts. I continued down the pavement, walking with purpose, before another thought hit me. Following this pavement along the shore would take me down the beach *below* the outcropping. I would need to take the bus route in order to reach the top where the light-source was surely standing. This second thought knocked the wind from my sails considerably. I knew full well that I would not be able to successfully follow the maze of backroads and lanes that the bus had taken, particularly when I could barely see my own surroundings.

But once again that light hit me square in the face and spurred me on. I took a right at the first juncture where I thought the bus had taken me and found myself plunged into even thicker blackness. Although I could still hear the sea well enough, I could now only glimpse it between the houses as I headed up the incline of the road. Perhaps it was at that point that the last of my adrenaline was spent, as I was hit by how vulnerable I was. I was as good as blind, did not actually know my surroundings, could easily take a wrong turn and end up in the middle of a field with no chance of being discovered by anyone. I then thought of what might happen if I *did* manage to find my way up to the outcropping; picturing myself there, alone, with that hissing and undulating field behind me, confronting whatever odd person had decided to set up a light in the middle of nowhere. I decided that I should turn back and return to my hotel room. That room, with its many mirrors and rattling windows, suddenly seemed very appealing indeed.

    I spun 180 degrees on my heels and headed back down the road. Or at least I *thought* I had turned 180 degrees, but after ten minutes of walking and not finding myself any closer to sea level, I determined that I was inexplicably still heading *up* the incline. I caught another glimpse of the lighthouse beam through the breaks between the houses and heard the sound of the sorrowful singing. I got the impression that the light was moving in time to the sound, that with each rotation of the beam across the sea, the singing grew louder and fainter depending on the direction. The feeling of isolation and loss hit me hard. It was almost as if my immediate situation brought into sharp relief the current state of my life. I very much wanted to be back in my room, with a closed window and curtain separating me from that beam of light.

    I probably wandered the streets of Addenbay for forty minutes before I managed to find myself back on the shore pavement of the High Street. I practically ran to the hotel and, without casting a backwards glance towards the outcropping, I gently opened the front door and stepped into the foyer. My adventure, though feeling like a lifetime to me, had only been a peaceful hour of dozing for the old night porter and I found him in exactly the same position that I had left him. The only difference was that Rachmaninov was now on the radio. I entered my room feeling an overwhelming sense of relief. I could still see the blinking of the light multiplied in the mirrors, so I headed over to the thick heavy curtains and pulled them shut. In the darkness – a much warmer and more secure darkness than the one I had just stepped in from – I laid myself down in my bed and slept. The last thing I remember thinking before drifting off was that I needed to be better prepared for tomorrow night.

※

The following morning, I awoke with a sense of grim determination. I was going to be prepared tonight, so that when 3am came and that sad musical noise and unrelenting light drifted over from the outcropping, I would be able to head straight there without delay. I caught the number 36 bus and this time stayed on until I reached the next town of Grawford. Although considerably smaller than Addenbay, it was a bustling metropolis in comparison. Despite the cold rain beating down on the streets, there were dozens of people out and about, shopping or socialising. I took out my phone and checked the address of the business I was looking for: Grawford Motor Rentals.

    I did not generally like to drive if I could help it, as I found the experience to be stressful and irritating, what with all the other less conscientious drivers on the road. But this situation called for thinking outside of the box. I would rent a car, learn the road turning to take me from the Farnchester Hotel to the outcropping and – as soon as my eyes and ears indicated that the time was upon me – I would head up to the location of the lighthouse and put the whole mystery to bed.

    I spent little more than ten minutes in the building, as I was only concerned with whether the car had four wheels and an engine. Everything else was an unnecessary luxury for my purposes. I suspect that the young man who sorted through the transaction with me thought that I was planning to rob a bank or something similar – though clearly wasn't being paid enough to bother pursuing that particular line of enquiry. I drove the car away from Grawford slowly – it had been close to eight months since I had last driven at all, and the winding and bumpy back roads that lead to Addenbay were more work than I had bargained for.

On my way back I passed the outcropping. I decided to pull over to investigate, now I was no longer beholden to the whims of public transport. I could comb the area at my leisure. I parked the car on the side of the road, by the open field of long grass so as not to obstruct the bus when it came through, and got out. Again, I was struck with the paranoiac sensation that there were eyes watching me from the long grass, but passed it off as my overactive imagination, exacerbated by my blind stumblings the night before.

I walked to the edge of the cliff, again with my eyes cast downwards, looking for any clues as to the identity of the lamp-lighter, or indeed unearthly singer. After a few minutes, my search yielded a result – a small shard of glass, worn at the edges but still clear and slightly convex. This at least was evidence that *something* had been up here at some point. As I turned back towards the car, I caught a glimpse of movement in the grass. I took a sharp intake of breath but by the time I had done so the thing that I had spotted was gone. It seemed for a split-second that there was a glint of something, like glass reflecting the sunlight, two spots of light peering out from the long grass. I cautiously trod over the road to the field and stood at its edge, awaiting some sign of movement. Other than the slight undulation caused by the breeze, there was nothing. My imagination briefly coerced me into believing that I could hear whispering behind the faint hiss of moving grass, but in truth I could not distinguish any other sounds.

As I drove back, I made a point to remember the number of turns and forks in the road that linked the hotel to the outcropping, so that there would be no chance of my getting lost when I returned to finally unmask the lighthouse's origin. Satisfied that I could repeat the journey, in reverse, and in the dark, I pulled up on the road several yards down from the hotel and parked. I didn't want the sound of the engine to awaken the night porter later.

By this time, it was late afternoon. I had eaten in Grawford and so I made my excuses to the owner that I would not require any dinner. My plan was to go to bed early, to ensure that I would be fully awake and prepared later when the lighthouse next lit up. I decided that I would not undress, and instead simply removed my coat and shoes and laid myself on top of the bed. I opened the curtains – still shut from the previous night – and saw the sun setting on the horizon. It was the first clear sky I had seen since arriving and it gave me a strange sense of hope.

※

I do not know how soon I fell asleep, but I know that the dream crept up on me very early. There was nothing clear or distinct about it, just a pervading sense of emptiness. I was surrounded on all sides by void, and that there was nothing that would allow me to escape it. I attempted to traverse the space but lost all sense of distance or perspective. I couldn't distinguish between up or down, forward or backwards. And then, all of a sudden, as if a spotlight was switched on, Joseph was stood in front of me, some fifty meters away.

I felt a sensation of nausea in my stomach. I was convinced that he would vanish as quickly as he had appeared, leaving me floating in the nothingness. I looked up into Joseph's face and he began to sing. It was not in English, nor indeed did it sound like any kind of song sung by a human being. It was a strange, melancholic melody that sounded in equal parts like whale song, buzzing and the bubbling of boiling water. My head began to spin as the singing grew louder and louder…

I awoke with a start, just as the flash of the lighthouse beam reflected off my mirrors and on to my sweat-drenched face. I could hear through the window the faint sounds of the singing drifting over the sea. I was more disoriented than I had hoped to be at this point, but I quickly rose to my feet and prepared myself. I looked out towards the outcropping and saw the slow and steady movement of the light's beam as it moved left to right across the water. I hurried down to the streets below.

I quickly paced to where I had left the car and took the keys out of my pocket. When I turned the engine I was struck by how terribly bright the headlights were. If I drove up to the outcropping with them on, the lighthouse keeper or whomever it was would see my approach and perhaps make an escape. On the other hand, I did not like the idea of driving through those back alleys without some kind of illumination. I got out of the car and scurried across the road to the shore side. I looked across to the outcropping and saw the beam faced out to sea. I grabbed two handfuls of wet sand and pebbles and headed back to the car. Smearing the sand over the headlights, I was able to dim them to a hazy blur, enough to make out maybe five or six meters ahead of me.

I was aware that this was highly risky, illegal in fact, but I was so determined to solve the mystery of the light and singing that I felt that it was worth the risk. I drove slowly and deliberately, alternating my focus on the road in front of me and the light on the cliff. I rolled down both windows and braced the cold so as not to risk the windscreen becoming steamed.

After half an hour, longer than the journey had taken on the bus, I neared the point where the road turned away from the last of the houses and gave way to the open expanse of field and cliff. I still glimpsed the light from behind the houses and trees. I switched off the headlights altogether and slowed the car further.

I rolled almost silently around that final bend and realised that I was holding my breath. I could hear a sound.

It wasn't the singing, though that was still apparent on the wind. Rather it was another, quieter sound beneath the singing, something akin to a subdued chattering. I don't mind admitting that I was scared. I am an academic by nature and the most conflict that I dealt with took the form of having to occasionally admonish a student for plagiarism. But I had to know the truth. I had to know what it was that Joseph intended me to find and, perhaps, understand why he had sent me to this cold, empty place.

I steadied my nerves and quietly opened the car door, conscious of the sound of the clicking in the cold night air. Thankfully, the waves, wind, singing and chattering seemed to muffle out the noise of my movements. I crept slowly to the top of the road, to the point where the bend would reveal the field, the clifftop, and the lighthouse. My heart was pounding and the voice in the back of my head debated the wisdom of my actions, urging me to return to the car and drive back home. I was a meter from the turning now, with the singing and chattering louder than I had ever heard it. I made my mind up to simply peer around the corner, hugging close to the wall of the disused barn that currently blocked my view of the light.

I breathed in deeply and pressed my face up close to the stone wall, then very carefully moved my head to bring the lighthouse into view. I knew immediately that it was no lighthouse. It was still pitch black, the only light source being the thing itself, but it was clear from the outline and the brief illumination of its moving contours that the thing sat on the edge of the cliff was no ordinary manmade structure. It writhed and undulated, like an underwater creature, a gigantic sea anemone with frond-like tentacles waving. However, it was more terrifying than that, there was something that my unconscious mind was trying desperately to shield me from. A shard of light illuminated a face and there were no more protective measures that my mind could use. The thing was a hulking mass of human bodies. What had looked like tentacles were arms, twitching and swaying in time to the singing. The faces within the structure were open-mouthed and the sound of sorrowful singing was emanating from most of them. A few were quietly talking – I couldn't tell if this was amongst themselves or an insane babble to the night air.

But the thing that struck me most about the flesh structure was the sense of *intention*. I could see now that the beam of light that shone out over the sea was emitted through an opening made in the bodies, a kind of tunnel created from torsos wrapping around one another to form an alcove. There were shards of reflective glass jutting out of skin. This did not appear violent, rather it seemed natural, like scales on reptiles or petals on flowers. These shards were angled in a particular way, to steer and maximise the reflection of light towards this central tunnel, which then refracted the collective beam outwards across the surrounding landscape. The source of these multiple light beams were the eyes of each of these faces.

It dawned on me far too late that I was able to make out so much detail because I had strayed from behind the building and was slowly trudging towards the thing with surprising steadiness. I thought about the empty streets of Addenbay and the lack of lighting outside, the careful placement of mirrors in my hotel room to refract and reflect the light of the lighthouse, and the unsolicited and enticing challenge from Joseph. What had started this process? Who had been the first person to sit atop this cliff, casting their light out across the sea, inviting others to come and join them, to warm the cold nights and light the dark abyss with human contact? When had Joseph first come here and how did he send his summons to me? Had he hoped that I would find him again, and join him in this strange blissful state? I was merely three feet from the base when I saw a familiar face peering out. The hotel owner was embedded within several other bodies, his expression not entirely dissimilar to the grotesque face that adorned the entrance to his hotel. Short beams of light emanated from his eyes, hitting the glass plate, which refracted the beam upwards.

Perhaps there was the answer to some of my questions. Perhaps the people of Addenbay could lead normal lives during the day, and only came together in this bizarre orgy of sombre communion at night. I looked up at the thing, tears welling. I could see an all too familiar face, maybe ten foot above me.

I *did* find the lighthouse at Addenbay.

The Keeper

by Ariel Dodson

Started journal today. There seems something oddly juvenile about it, as though I were still a schoolboy observing and reporting on my fellows and masters. But I am no longer a schoolboy, and there is no one here to observe. No one but the gulls, the sea, and the occasional vessel that it is my job to protect.

And protect them I do. I don't want them to come any closer. I have left all that behind. And others just remind me of the accident.

I prefer to think of it as that. It is easier for the soul to bear.

That is why I will have no dates in this journal. Nothing to remind me of what went before. Just the endless blur of day after day.

They are long here and strangely silent, even with the constant roar of surf and seagull cry. And that is how it should be.

A line only will separate the entries. A line, like a bar. Like the bar of the horizon that I see always in the distance, reminding me. Mocking me.

But enough of that.

I have been here six months, although it could easily be longer. A lonely lighthouse, with its light burden of remembering the lamp each evening.

Some would say that I have made my own prison. But there is a freedom in solitude. I need no one, and no one needs me. No one, that is, save those in the occasional vessels.

I rarely venture out. There is no need. Goods are brought to me on account from the village, and my small affairs are easily taken care of by post. I leave the letters with the groceries box and trust that they are delivered safely. There is nothing for anyone to pry into – I make sure of that – although I wonder sometimes whether suspicion has already raised its sniffing head.

I see them sometimes from my tower above – the boy or the young man, who alternate the grocery despatch between them. They are nervous, twitching with that unmistakeable anticipation of stories to be dug out; that restless thrill that plagues the curious or bored like a rash. Histories to be exhumed, no matter how painful or unpleasant. And always someone else's, as if they are the self-appointed archaeologists of the living.

I do not see how they can have heard of mine – I have been so careful – yet still I feel the sense of hope gathering, drawing in like a winter's evening. A fearful hope, fed by nothing more perhaps than my decision to take this isolated post at the margins of their village; a post none of their own ever cared for.

But it suits me. As long as I am left alone for my memory to be picked clean and bare like those many bleached bones beneath the sea that is now my only companion. The sea cleanses all things, strips them naked to the frame and then begins again. Sometimes I feel that I am turning into something strange and beyond myself; old, older even than those dark grey depths which pound below; those depths which some day I shall know.

They remind me of me; those youngsters bearing the wooden parcel of eggs and beans, milk and cheese, which they leave in a small cove of rocks by the tower door. They stand for a few minutes after dropping it, raising themselves with a grunt and stretching their strong, young backs to meet the brace of brisk sea air. I, too, was like that once, although it is hard to believe now.

Even for me. Yet once I was so, strong and young and curious, and with all of my future ahead of me.

They wear soft shoes and dare to creep a few steps by the door, the temptation to peer through the nearest window almost too great to resist. But their courage fails them always and they slip away quickly, giving a sharp rap on the door before treading lightly across the rocks to the safety of their people.

They never look back, and the sea foam laps their footprints away as if they have never been. I wonder what stories circulate about me in the cottages and taverns of an evening. Practical or fanciful? And could anyone possibly know? I think not, or I am sure the constable would have braved my door before now.

Strangely, I like to see them come, although I resent the intrusion. I see myself in them, the self I once was, and I hope that the paths they choose going forward treat them well.

I chose badly.

⁕

The weather has been fine of late and almost unbearably hot, with a heavy, hovering haze hanging over the horizon. It is mesmerising to view, and I feel myself growing lost within it as I stare, lost to the point where I might forget who I am and why I am here by the time the season turns once more.

If only it were so.

The sea is calm with a glassy shine; deceptive, as though I could walk upon it without danger of sinking. Not much threat to the seafarers today. I feel as though I should be able to see to the bottom and glimpse the mysteries of the deep. But the waters are inscrutable as always, despite their inviting glow.

⁕

I have made a friend, although not in the way you may think.

A grey seal, bobbing amongst the waves, with a head so slick and sculpted that I mistook it for a man. I wonder what it is doing so far from its colony, for seals are rarely seen in these waters. Has it been caught in an unexpected current and thrown off course? Or has it been banished for some reason, ostracised by those it should have trusted? Been able to trust?

I felt it was sizing me up in those first few days, trying to decide where I belonged. My heart lifted when it finally swam closer, something I have not been able to say in many a day. It is nice to know that it is there, that there is another life nearby to acknowledge my own, and one that is no threat, for it is as silent and remote as I.

Poor creature, I wonder what its story is. Strangely I feel a kind of kinship towards it, as if we two should be able to trust each other in our mistrust of those who dwell beyond this isolated finger of land. We are both alone, both silent, both surrounded by sea and air.

I hope it stays. It has given me something to believe in again.

※

The seal is still here. I do not feel I have the right to give it a name; silent and solitary as I am, it deserves also to retain its wildness, its anonymity, its control of itself.

And yet I am glad it is there, as indeed I think it feels of me. It has come as close as the rocks now, and sometimes I see it sunning itself, stretched out and lazing, or resting on the gentle curl of a wave with its tail folded over its belly like a dog asleep by the fire.

The Keeper

I have begun to order fish with my groceries, and leave a little out so that it knows it is welcome, but not enough that it will grow dependent. That is not a good idea for anyone, and I am the first to admit it. Sometimes I feel I can't even be sure of myself.

Its herd has never appeared and so we muddle along silently, the seal and I, in perfect companionship, with just a few squalling gulls added in for good measure. I feel clean with just the sea and the sky and the wild things, and am pleased to have dispensed with people as much as possible in my situation. People only bring in the negativity – the anger, suspicion, jealousy – and the fear.

No, we plod along well together, we two separate creatures, and my mind darts back sometimes to the stories I enjoyed as a boy; tales of adventure with sailors stranded on deserted islands or blown off course by magical events which took them to even more magical places. Sometimes, I recall, they were sent a wild creature as a companion, and I like to imagine that this may be mine.

Perhaps it is just possible that something – some greater power – has taken pity on me after all.

※

I don't understand it.

For the last few days I have seen it, dark and motionless; ominous, like a warning on the waves. It is distant, just skirting the periphery of my vision, but near enough for me to know it.

It is a boat.

Large, and somehow ancient looking, although perhaps that is just my imagination; a boyish delight in the unexplained surging up from long forgotten depths. But I am a boy no longer, and the man I am now takes no joy in a mystery. There is too much that could be uncovered.

※

At the Lighthouse

It remains. Still dark, stationary, and driving me mad. The weather continues to be fine – no danger to a vessel at all in the day – and I light the lamp religiously as the dusk falls. A slow dusk, grey and creeping, settling over the sea like cobwebs. Like webs over my thoughts.

A strange fancy comes over me to ask the seal to scout for me – as if it could understand – but I have not seen it for a few days. No doubt it is out on one of its hunting trips.

That, of course, is the one difference between us. It is still free.

※

There is a storm coming.

I can feel it, taste it, like the bitterness of iron on the tip of my tongue. The sea is restless, endlessly choppy beneath a reddening sky, and I stand my guard. Something is about to change. The sailors must have felt it too, out there, in the dark boat, for it has gone, sailed away in the night.

Sometimes I am not sure if I imagined it. But I am glad. Something about it felt wrong; personal almost, as if it was watching, waiting for me.

I am being foolish. It could have been anything. Vessels anchor for all sorts of reasons. And I doubt even the best telescope could have seen more than the movement of a figure at that distance. It doesn't take paranoia long to make itself known in isolation. Though it is preferable to the alternative.

I do wonder what has happened to my seal friend. It has not reappeared, and suddenly I feel terribly alone.

※

Still no sign of the seal or the storm, and I am tired of the latter's brooding. I feel angry at the stagnancy, crippled with waiting. It has been four days now.

Yesterday a great crash shook the building, and when I investigated I found the remains of a gull clinging to the great window that holds the light. I cleaned it as best I could, half hanging from the sill with a scrubbing brush in hand. The rest must have dropped into the waves below; a welcome meal, I've no doubt, for something.

I have never seen that happen before, although I know birds do fly into glass at times. Poor thing. Perhaps it was blown into it. I was nearly blown out myself, gripping the sill with my knees so tightly that they are strained and bruised. Like the sky.

It is crimson now; a dark, broody, bloody colour above me, as if it is waiting for something, waiting to pounce.

I am braced; alert and ready for a storm that does not want to arrive. I have never known this before. It makes me uneasy.

※

Those damn kids.

Evidently I am not the menace I once was, for they have grown bolder now, rapping on the door and bounding over the rocks like young goats. Laughing. It grates on my ears.

Sometimes I hear them even when no delivery is due, and yesterday I found that my grocery parcel had been broken into; the eggs smashed outside the door, the milk missing. I no longer order the fish.

I scooped in the remains quickly, leaving the shattered eggshells for the sea to wash away. Needless to say, the innards were long gone, gobbled up by the gulls, no doubt, if the boys hadn't got to them first.

What does it mean?

That they have decided I am no harm after all, and so an easy target for torment? Or have suspicions grown so that this is a warning – a message to get out? I have seen no one to be able to judge, but I am increasingly vigilant, and yesterday took my long unused gun from its wrappings. It is ready, should I need it, as am I.

The threatening storm still hangs heavy above, and a headache is encroaching. My eyes feel red and glazed, like the sky. When will it break? The sea chops and flares as though angry, as if it wants to spit something out, something that disgusts it. The old stories say that it is never in vain. That what the sea gives it must take, and so on. I can believe it; the churning waters seem like a huge, gasping beast which cannot be tamed yet must be placated as best it can. Something has upset it. Something is wrong. The air is growing electric, a palpable tension, and I keep my hand at the ready for whatever action is needed. What will it spit at me, I wonder? What is it trying to tell me? My head pounds with a message I cannot interpret and it infuriates me.

❋

My seal friend is dead.

I found it yesterday, dashed brutally on the rocks by the side of the lighthouse. I don't understand. Seals are so intelligent, and this one knew the terrain.

Where has it been, I wonder, and what can have caused it to brave these waters now, when it had obviously found somewhere else, and the pitch and roll of the waves are so deadly? The storm is imminent – it must be – and yet my friend strove out here for a reason.

The Keeper

I would like to do something for it – bury it somehow, or just remove it from the rocks, but I cannot reach it beyond the crashing waves. They are almost halfway up the building.

I now wish I had named it. To distinguish it, dignify it. Another wild life ripped away to where?

※

The seal is gone, torn away, I presume, by the waves, for I have not seen another creature large enough to do so, were it even so foolish as to try. The waves climb the side of the lighthouse, even higher today, as though determined to drown it and all within, and I hear the wind wailing eerily outside, as though seeking an entrance.

The storm is swelling, ready to vomit its worst tonight, I am sure of it, and I will be ready. The sailors need me tonight more than ever and, come what may, that light will go on.

I shall stay by it, I think, for I feel glad of the company of something. My isolation grows demanding, I fear, and my eyes are beginning to play tricks. For a moment this afternoon I thought I saw my old friend bobbing out there in the waves, sleek and sculpted like a man's head. But the seal is dead, and no man would be foolish or desperate enough to dare the sea in this mood.

※

The storm has hit.

Nature – or whatever greater power lurks behind it – is angry, and is displaying it in full force tonight.

The lighthouse is solid, resting in its base of rock almost as if it had sprung independently of mortar or mason's tools. It was designed to withstand such weather. And yet still I feel buffeted, as though the power outside has targeted me and knows I am in here. My head seems to rock with walls, swaying and trembling, despite knowing they are as still and sturdy as ever. Am I going a little mad?

It is unnaturally dark in here, although I checked on the light not a quarter of an hour ago and it was beaming steadily as usual. Still, I had better make sure. I want no more life on my hands.

※

It has gone out.

It has gone out and I know not what to do. I have never known this to happen before. The flame will not strike, the oil will not light, and the jagged teeth of the rocks below are dark. If I were superstitious I would be convinced that some malevolent force was at play. Perhaps I would hang some mountain ash or juniper, or even a cross.

But I am not superstitious. I do not allow myself to be, for madness lies in that direction. And yet, I know not what to do. I do not worry for myself, and I maintain that claim to the core of my being, but for those who depend on me.

※

I have done it, and a light shines brightly again from the tower window. Or rather, numerous lights, for I am having to rely on the many gentle glowings of my lamp's smaller cousins. Candles, of course. Every candle I could find, inching, groping in the dim light of one small wax halo until I had collected a box worth of all sizes and shapes, along with every receptacle in the place capable of holding one.

A good spirit, if I believed in such things, must have been with me as the match fire took hold and the wicks of each began to shine merrily, like saucy little tongues poking a dance at the roarings of the tempest outside.

It cannot enter, and I can take my time staring it in the face from behind the staunch panes of glass.

And yet it makes me uneasy. I can see my reflection staring back from the dark mirror of glass, echoing the blackness beyond. I am surrounded by the candles, my figure motionless amongst them like a painting, my face white and blank. I resemble a corpse, as though I am the centrepiece of a wake fashioned and executed by myself.

I leave the room quickly, after a final check that all is flaming and stable. It does no good to think like that, and I wish the image hadn't arisen in my head, like some dark buried thing dislodged and brought afloat by an unplanned action. An accident. It's a convenient word.

I remember suddenly a half bottle of whiskey, lying at the bottom of a drawer to resist temptation. I feel it would do me good tonight. Bolster the strength and the courage, for I have a feeling I will need them both in great measure for what lies ahead. That image – my eerie reflection in the candlelit glass – felt like an omen, and I cannot shake the thought that I am to be put to the test in some violent way. The wind howls feverishly, and I am reminded of the tales told to me by my Irish grandmother of the banshee; the fairy woman, warning of death. But it does not sound like a woman out there, nor a beast. It is something beyond us here on this earth; some great, bleak, elemental force with no mind or soul, but with the ability to leave a terrible destruction in its wake. So terrible, that nothing is ever the same again.

And maybe that is for the best.

※

At the Lighthouse

I have been to check on the lamp room several times, and all is well. The mugs and jars hold and the flames still burn. But I avoid looking at the glass.

I have come downstairs to find a book. Perhaps I can manage to read a little in the quiet light afforded by the one meagre candle I have allowed for myself.

Damn –

※

It has come.

Last night, when my candle blew out and I groped for the matchbox that I was sure I had left on the side, I heard a bell ringing somewhere in the din of the storm. It sounded like something in distress, and I prayed that if it were a vessel it would see the light. If the light was still flaming, for I still know not what caused my candle to die – the building is as tight as a drum.

My fingers rested on the cardboard flap of the matches and I used the wall to strike one, unwilling to lose grip of the precious candle stub in my other hand. Perhaps I could see from down there – there are windows on this level and I preferred not to face the light upstairs.

The wick caught, and my eyes turned to the window to meet the face squashed against the glass, watching me.

I dropped the match, my yelp mingling with the cries of the storm beyond. All was darkness, and God help me I would rather it remain so than see that again. Was it still there? There are no curtains at the windows for they face out to sea, and I feared that I could still see the shape before me, clinging to the glass as if for preservation. My heart crashed louder than the noise outside.

And then I saw something move. I dropped to my knees and the candle fell, but the lightning anticipated me, the figure visible again for a fleeting second, hands pressed imploringly, great meat hook hands, and a crooked nose with a scar running down one cheek beside it.

I know that face. Dear God, I do. Why do I know that face?

My hand trembled as it rested finally on the stub, while my other hand inched in a palsy until it once again located the matches. My heart seemed to stop with the strike. But the window was empty.

The figure had gone and I knew not whether to be fearful or relieved.

And yet –

There was a movement outside; a darkness on the darker surge of the waves, a sleek, rounded shape that for a moment I mistook for the seal.

It could not be – he must have slipped and fallen in and I cannot wrestle with doubt; I took on this duty with good conscience and I must carry it out. If help is needed then I must answer. And I have little satisfaction in fearing the omen to be true.

The gale nearly lifted me as I tentatively opened the door, the wood ripped from my grasp and hurled back to the stone wall, battering back and forth on squealing hinges. The rocks were lethal, glistening in their jagged smiles and slippery with seaweed, and I do not know how I managed to hold on when the wave crashed over me, choking me, trying to suck me down. Yet I held and I saw him in the freezing water, clutching desperately for a grip on the heartless stone. How is it that a seasoned navigator like the seal did not make it, yet this man – this creature – has? I cannot question the power of the sea, but if either of us were to have a chance at survival my action need be swift, and I curled my foot around a crevice of rock as I stretched forward into the gale and the storm and reached out my hand.

He was heavy, heavy with a life-draining, strength-sapping heaviness, and it took all my power to drag him from the clutch of the icy waves and onto the rocks. He did not seem to be aware of what was happening, and his strength argued against mine so that we were almost wrestling, out there in the midst of a storm that felt like the end of all days that have been and are to come. The water had torn all from him, and it was hard to find a grip as I attempted to pull him back towards the house, so wet and slimy was he from the throat of the sea. He was glistening with it, like a newborn babe vomited up from the depths. It put me in mind of my sister's child, for she was delivered many years ago of a babe begat in circumstances I care not to think upon or repeat. But I remember seeing the child carried out, shining and slick still in its covering of birth sweat. It was dead, as though it knew it had not been wanted, and yet its sticky coat of mucus glowed in the dull light like a little beacon signalling of hope to be lost and faith to be buried.

It was as if I was grasping water.

Yet at last something in him gave and somehow we were inside and the door had shut out the shrieking forces beyond. He collapsed to the floor, a shivering bundle of flesh, and I covered him with my greatcoat, leaving him in the dark as I grasped the candle to head upstairs and check on the light. And to fetch a slug of whiskey for us both while I determined what the sea had brought me.

※

He says little.

His silence unnerves me, although I can't deny that I prefer it to the thought of idle prattle.

Where has he come from, I wonder, and what is he doing here? Washed up from a shipwreck? But he does not have a sailor's hands, and I have seen no vessels lost on my watch. I can be proud of that.

And I know his face.

Strange to say, for I also know that I have never seen it before, and I cannot place it. If he knows me he gives no indication. But then, he gives little indication of anything. Perhaps he is just grateful to be alive.

Yet it bothers me, for it is the sort of face one should not easily be able to forget. Harsh and clumsy, with a large cauliflower nose and thin, crooked lips, the scar accentuating their awkwardness somehow with its ugly red line. It runs from below the left eye to the chin, and may partially account for his squint. It has not been stitched well. Like my own.

The dome of his head is completely round and bald, save for the rising stubble of unshaved hair. I am reluctant to offer him my razor. No wonder I had mistaken him for the seal.

As I said, the sort of face one should not be able to forget; yet somehow I have, and would rather do so again, for I know not what to do with him.

It was weeks before he was on his feet, feverish with his experience, although letting surprisingly little slip, even during his delirium. The morning after the storm was like looking at another world, although nothing was actually different. Various bits of flotsam drifted on the waves, blown or dragged no doubt from the shore or from any nearby vessels. But there were no further lives to rescue, and the sea and the skies were as blue and shining as if the previous night had never happened.

Oddly also, the lamp was working again. I tested it as soon as he was sleeping, and cannot understand what happened. I must keep my eye on that. The candles were all out, but they held when needed and they had done their job, for the rocks remained clear and smooth and spattered only with their own sea slime. I must remember to order a new boxful from the village.

I heard him cry out several times then, as I was gazing out to sea, although I could not decipher the words. Some god or goddess must have been watching over him that night, for I find it impossible to understand how a person could have survived the waves in that storm. It is just one of many puzzling things. Now he has recovered he feeds as though starving, and my meagre grocery order must increase by double. But he will not go.

The first day, when he recovered, he stood there saying nothing, his back to the door. Not a question or a thank you; just that shifty probe of a half glance which may or may not be due to the squint. I asked him what his plans were but he refused to answer, choosing instead to stand and stare at me expectantly. It is not a language barrier, for the few words he has spoken since are English and his accent is as familiar as my own. Then what? What does he want from me?

I will set him odd jobs to do around the place, for he must earn his keep. But I am unhappy about it. I fear he has an agenda. I can sense him watching me.

✻

It is an odd situation, to be living life alongside another but without companionship. It is like living with a shadow of oneself.

He has taken to the odd jobs, without complaint and as if he has been undertaking them his whole life, but still he remains largely silent and strangely unappreciative, as though *he* is the one doing me a favour and begrudges it.

It is not as though he cannot find the words when needed; yesterday I saw him talking to the delivery boy in what seemed a long and earnest conversation. But he said not a word to me.

I cannot help but wonder what passed between them.

✻

The Keeper

He has dragged me into his game and now there are two of us, watching, waiting, eyeing each other from the shadows like cornered cats. I don't know what he wants from me, but I can feel the need gnawing at him like an endless hunger. And gnawing at me.

I must watch him, close and closer. And yet he always seems one step ahead. I have begun to notice his presence encroaching upon the place, without my authority; tasks I have not commissioned him to engage with, jobs completed that I have not requested he do. Those that require the knowledge and judgement of my position. If I should lose this post I know not where I can go. And yet I cannot catch him at work. When I confronted him the other day he merely gazed at me blankly, with a mocking in his eyes that suggested he thought I was mad.

Sometimes I think he may be right.

❋

Have I solved the mystery of his conversation with the delivery boy? Yesterday the parcel was left, as usual, and when the boy departed I fetched it in, quickly and without glancing around. The boy had lingered – I know not why – and there was a mocking, proprietorial glance in his eyes as they surveyed the lighthouse – travelling over it, searching for something.

Perhaps me? But what could he know, what could any of them know? And yet the fears wrestle and twine like eels in a pool, brushing, tickling, in an empty, silent laughter. And always at me.

The boy wants something. I can feel it. And I must now add him to my worries – watching, waiting – like the other, of whom

At the Lighthouse

there is no sign. Did he do it on purpose, I wonder? Hoping that the boy would see me, would jump out even and jeer, or stare at me accusingly?

I know not, for he squats somewhere inside, watching me no doubt from those deep, blank eyes. Watching and waiting, like me.

I unpacked quickly, almost just as quickly repacking, for these items are not mine; my plain, wholesome fare discarded instead for cakes and meats and several bottles I know I did not request. I recognise them though, precisely because I do not touch the stuff. Not any longer. Not since then.

And yet there is my bill, written out neatly and attached with the order signed at the bottom in my own hand. It is not my doing, and I do not remember authorising such a thing. I would not authorise it. Could it be that he has learned to imitate my signature? And if so, what else has he done with it?

He is lurking now; somewhere inside, watching me I have no doubt, and plotting his next move.

I cannot let him make it. I must regain my ground. I *must* find out.

✺

I am writing in semi-darkness, for the light has been extinguished for the second time this week. He is under strict instructions not to enter the lamp room, but I know it is his hand – I found the wick snipped to a point beyond repair and I have again had to write for a replacement.

In the meantime I have relit the candles that saved me last time – the night when *he* arrived – although there are less of them now and I know who has taken them. Yesterday I saw several bobbing on the waves, mocking me, it seemed, as they floated out to sea.

Why would he do such a thing? Is he a sailor with a vendetta, that he would put so many lives at risk? Or is it, as I suspect, myself that is the target?

I have deliberately left the lamp room unattended, and have secreted myself in a small niche off the stairs from where I can view the entrance to the room unobserved. There is no reason he should know of it. It is well hidden and I have never revealed it to his eyes. If I should catch him, then I should have reason to take action. One life to save many. And this time I should be justified.

❋

I *cannot* catch him.

It has been three nights now. The new wick is not expected for another week, and the tallow burns low on the remaining tapers.

He is still here, for the jobs are still done, although I notice that his initial enthusiasm has waned and I have had to redo several of them. The nights continue to draw in and the lights must be aflame earlier each evening. I thought I heard him before me last night – a footstep on the landing ahead of me, the click of the lamp room door – and I thrust it open wide and fierce in triumph. He gazed back, his face just as gloating in challenge, but when I reached for him he wasn't there, and I realised it was merely the reflection of the light in the window once more. We are not unalike, I admit.

What do they see when they look in, I wonder? The sea birds? The wind and waves, or any sailor with a telescope out there beyond the rocks? Him or me? And which one is it?

❋

At the Lighthouse

It has happened.

Happened at last, and I feel only numbness.

The delivery arrived yesterday, and with it the new wick. I installed it immediately and will sleep in the lamp room from now on, for both my own safety and its. There was a note with the groceries, pinned neatly to the back of the bill which once again reflected my own order. It was simple and direct and written in a handwriting I recognised, for it is the same as the sign on the order. My own.

I KNOW

But how? How can he know? And what?

If it is what I fear then how much does he know? And what does he want from me?

I cannot place him. I *cannot*, although his familiarity is as strong as the recognition of my own face. Can it be that and nothing more? I have remarked before that we are not unalike. But I do not know him, and I have no brother or distant cousins that the similarity could be attributed to. My sister's child died, and could not look that age even had it survived.

Then who, for the only other who could know – who could hate me like this – is dead. I know it for certain, for I was there.

Perhaps it is a hook – a fishing line to see how I react and to assess whether there may be any gain. To some, a post as isolated as this is all the proof they need that a person has something to hide. Perhaps he actually knows nothing at all. *Nothing*. And what is his secret, I wonder. Concealment is part of human nature, and many wish to throw the light on to another in order to shade their own misdemeanours.

I saw him yesterday, standing on the rocks, grimacing. He seemed to be mouthing at the sea, and I saw him throw an item in – something small and shining and too quick for me to register. There must be some reason he insists on remaining here; something beyond just tormenting me. Has he deserted a ship? I must watch him ever closer and must stay nonchalant. That is the only reaction he shall have. He knows *nothing*.

※

The lamp is out and I know not how long it has been that way.

I remember very little except making my way to the lamp room to investigate and the congealed pool of sticky substance on the stairs; slippery, so slippery and treacherous that I fell – I think it was candle grease.

I am always so careful. I know it was he who has done it. I know now that he has a plan for me, that his plea at my window that storm-torn night was no coincidence. His features racked my brain after I fell, toppling to the bottom of the stairs, landing in a crumpled heap and lucky to have suffered no more than a swollen ankle and a splitting headache. I must have blacked out, for the next thing I remember is awakening in my own bed, a welcome tumbler of half drunk whiskey at my side.

He could have finished me off then and there and I would be none the wiser. I don't know why he has not, but it is obvious that there is further to come in his little game. My dreams are filled with his face and yet still I cannot place it, still he eludes me.

I know not where he is, but I must drag myself up; I must rekindle the light, for if that were to die altogether there is no hope for any of us.

He is not to be trusted.

※

It will not light.

It seemed like hours, pulling myself up the stairs, my injured ankle trailing behind me like extra baggage. I am vulnerable here, and my journey upwards has been lengthened by my attempts to crawl into the shadows at every distant noise. I can hear him; the sounds of his existence, the very expectancy of his breath echoes throughout these cavernous chambers like a chorus, and yet I cannot place their direction. If he were to appear before me, or come from behind, I would be completely at his mercy. He is toying with me. My end will not come so easily.

I waited outside the lamp room for a few moments before entering, and I must admit the repeated slugs from the flask of whiskey in my pocket came as no small comfort. I could hear nothing beyond but the moan of sea and sky, and when I finally opened the door I found the room empty.

Not unchanged though, for he has been busy in here; the candles chopped into small pieces and strewn about the floor – useless now – and the yawning glass of the great lamp displaying the latest wick, once more snipped and impotent.

I know not what to do, for he now controls the orders and seems determined upon the destruction of all within his power. His rage takes the form of a violence I know only too well, and he has further carved the trace of it here in the long white crack in the window. The emanating draft would never allow a flame to live should I be lucky enough to manage to light one, however small.

How has he done it, for that glass is doubly thick and made to withstand the strongest pressures of its precarious location?

I fear for my life.

✵

I have decided to stay here in the lamp room, for it is the only place I feel safe.

I have locked the door behind me, and have found two almost complete packets of matches, squirrelled and formerly forgotten, in an innermost pocket of my coat.

I have the one candle I brought up with me, and if nothing else I shall light it repeatedly as a warning, a hopeful sign to anyone watching, that something is wrong. Two ships have been lost that I know of, and the creaks and groans of their hulls on the rocks moaned and cried like creatures in pain; as if they were somehow taking the voice of those dying within whose own death calls were lost in the roar of the greedy wind and waves. It was painful to hear and put me in mind of my old seal friend, and even the wild gull that had died on the glass of that very window before me. Still more torturous was the memory of my sister, moaning her last breath as she gave birth to her unwanted child, and then again, the last cry of he whom I have sworn to forget, he whose view into my enraged eyes was the last thing he would ever see. These sounds haunt me now, as though they are in the same room, as though they are ripped from my own dry throat. I wonder now if madness is the luxury of oblivion, or if instead, it is the past come back to haunt us?

※

It is only a matter of time.

I hear them now, the curses and shouts of anger carried to me by the wicked wind that haunts me night and day from the twisted crack through the glass.

It is understandable. No keeper can be considered proficient in his post if he cannot keep the lamp alive, and I have lost count of how many days I have crouched here in the dark.

Yesterday I thought I heard him scratching at the door, as if seeking a way in, but the old iron lock held and I heard his footsteps retreat. I am safe for the moment.

The sun is sinking slowly before me, and now rests like a ball of fire on the horizon, setting flame to the waves as though they were made of oil.

For just a moment I thought I saw my old friend the seal in the water, its rounded head slick and smooth like that of a man, and it seemed to be calling me. Yet as I stand its features appeared to change, the mouth thickening with flat, squashed lips, the eyes glinting with malevolence, and the crooked scar painting the mottled skin like a branding. I do not know him, and yet his face is as familiar to me as my own. I know not where he is or where he has come from, but I know now that we two are tied beyond anything that can now save me.

It is only a matter of time.

❋

Perhaps he has pacified them, for the sounds have ceased. I have slept fleetingly, my body cramped and my dreams chopped and disturbed. It is dawn, yet the skies are iron still, and I must have dropped my candle in the night, for I can find no trace of it. The limited supply of matches can alone sustain us now but I must be careful, for they last only a few seconds, and once they are gone all hope is lost. I am crouched by the window, searching the black waters desperately for a sign of any soul that may need my help, for I shall withstand as long as I am able.

It seems the longest night I have known, and the chill of my uncomfortable position is working its way into my bones. It is oddly still and calm, as if once again the elements are awaiting a momentous happening, and I am reminded of how peaceful my life seemed before he arrived.

Perhaps it had to happen, for peace is a glamour for such as myself; I know what I have done. I can hear him behind me now, for somehow he has tripped open the door, his footsteps and breathing mimicking my own, falling easily into place as though we are two sides of the same coin, and he faces me in the glass as if my own image has been duplicated across its empty black shine.

Our eyes are smiling.

✺

Started journal today. There seems something oddly juvenile about it, as though I were still a schoolboy observing and reporting on my fellows and masters. But I am no longer a schoolboy, and there is no one here to observe. No one but the gulls, the sea, and the occasional vessel that it is my job to protect.

And, of course, the body that lies below, broken upon the many rocks that surround this isolated post. His eyes stare up at me now, blank and unseeing, and yet, I hope, remembering so much. I fear not – the waves and gulls will take care of him soon – yet it is just possible that another may have seen. Those boys from the village, for instance, who are always mooching around. I shall watch them carefully, for I wish to be safe here.

That is why I will have no dates in this journal. Nothing to remind me of what went before. Just the endless blur of day after day.

Yet I know that the past cannot be erased completely. And control must be maintained and threats extinguished if it is to be kept at bay. I have learned that that is the mark of a good keeper. And I plan to keep this job, for I have nowhere else to go.

I can see the gulls now, hovering in a swarm over the lifeless form on the rocks, picking over the face and memories that are as familiar as my own.

It does not matter, for I am the keeper of the secrets now.

I know.

Sea Glass

by Julie Ann Rees

Wind soughed through the dune grasses as black-backed and herring gulls screamed and scrabbled amongst the mounds of kelp and rubbish washed up by the tide. Crabs were plucked and pulled apart, the lucky ones scurrying to hide under stones or slip into the stillness of a rock pool. Sharp gusts of stinging sand roughened my cheeks, gritting my vision as the salty ocean air, carrying the smell of fish and seaweed, filled my lungs. The waves sucked backwards, the tide retreating, spent after the morning rush to deposit its load onto the shore and spew over the rocks.

 I sat on a log of driftwood, partly burned where someone may have used it for a fire, or maybe lightning had broken it scorching the wound casting the limb far from its body, lost and forlorn and not dissimilar to how I'd been feeling since the loss of my mother, which had left me reeling and struggling to cope. A crushing sense of isolation and confusion swam to the forefront of my waking days and I blinked away tears encrusted with sleep.

 I came here often to try and process my part, or lack of, in her last days. I felt drawn by the old Victorian cast iron lighthouse, cemented into the rock. It lured me. My gaze pulled to take in its rusted facade; a once needed beacon left to deteriorate and decay, ignored by all except nature and now me as I pondered its descent into a discarded future.

My mother's suicide had been a shock. Fresh anguish erupted as I struggled to banish the image of her, separating myself from the emotions that seared me in two. Then I saw you, illuminated, as the winter sun broke briefly, reflecting off the sea foam and churning opal swell. I observed your dishevelled form wandering the tide line, stooping down, searching, collecting unseen things, examining them attentively, before secretly hiding them away in a raggedy bag that hung across your chest.

My hat was pulled down tightly and I removed it to feel the wind against my hair. You were peering through something in your hand, glinting green, and that's when you saw me. Your scrutiny was disconcerting and although the cold air was not unpleasant, lifting and whipping my hair to obscure my features, I felt self conscious, exposed and dissected; my inner self on display. Like you were inside me and knew all about me.

To avoid your gaze I looked towards the estuary as it barged into the sea, and to the hazy land beyond the turbulent waters. The lighthouse obscured my view as it scowled, bracken coloured with rust, abandoned and unloved, the lamp extinguished long ago, except for a slight glint of jade that flashed once like an eye blinking into my mind, seeing what I could not and did not want to see for myself.

Quickly I pulled the woollen warmth of my hat back over my head and continued to avoid your gaze as you approached, your gait shambling and unsteady. I wanted to walk away because I felt unsure how to handle your intense scrutiny, but didn't want to appear impolite or selfishly arrogant, especially if you might be in need of help, yet something about you unsettled me. A knowingness, a gleam of recognition nudged at the barriers of my mind.

A herring gull landed at your feet to pluck at something I couldn't see, but you didn't remove your gaze, head tilting to one side as you stared. I tried out a smile and raised a hand as if in greeting, like I would to a friend, except you were not a friend, you were an anomaly, a mad thing making me nervous. Even the gull stopped his plucking to take in our exchange, grey wing feathers slightly darker than the winter sky. You shouted something but the wind snatched it from my ears.

I glanced to the side, away from you and up the beach where flat rock beds stretched into a craggy coast leaving the shifting dunes behind. I hoped you'd return to your beach combing and lose interest in me, but I could feel your form getting closer. You continued to approach until I could see your feet; bloodless and bare encrusted in damp sand, with brown cracked toenails, and had they not walked towards me I would have thought them those of a corpse. Maybe they were and you had collected them and placed them over your own.

I raised my gaze over faded cotton trousers, the colours once vibrant were dull and worn and somehow familiar, to a navy woollen jumper, stretched almost to your knees, misshapen with threads pulled revealing small holes where skin peaked. You were naked underneath and I wondered how you did not freeze. Hesitantly, as I felt afraid being seated before you, I rose and stepped away.

Lifting your own gaze from below a hat of washed out blue, pulled low over limp sandy hair, you stood taller to make eye contact. I smiled and said *hi*, my voice sounding foreign, my language unfamiliar. *Lovely day* I continued feebly, glancing at the cold winter seascape. Your head turned and you took in the same view, lingering over the lighthouse before returning to catch and this time, hold my eye.

Storm-coloured corneas sheltered behind red wind-blistered lids framed by pale lashes flickered in recognition as you absorbed my features. Sunken cheeks hung either side of a long nose, red at the tip, which ran in the wind. Mucous dripped and quickly you raised a hand to wipe it, sniffing as you did, whilst cracked lips split with small streaks of blood spoke.

"Elsa?" Your hand that wiped your nose rubbed against your trousers before reaching towards me with something nestled in your palm. "Is it you?"

I didn't take the glistening offer but stepped back cautiously stammering,

"How do you know my name?" I looked around hoping to see other people, dog walkers or kids playing in rock pools, but the beach was empty except for a fling of dunlins playing tag with the waves and far out on a rock sat a silent cormorant. The lighthouse watched our encounter in a brown cape of rust until the sharp peep of an oyster catcher sounded a warning and brusquely I suggested you must have mistaken me for another Elsa and turned to leave.

"No," you said shaking your head eyes squinting in the white sun, deflated you sat on the driftwood, your breath wheezing to a sob.

I felt awful, and softening began to console you making encouraging noises about accompanying you home. You babbled some nonsense about the lighthouse guiding you to me. I asked your name and you laughed the sound blending with the screech of a gull. Your hands rummaged in the tattered bag spilling small bones mixed with shells and twigs and from your palm fell a pebble of frosted green sea glass. Brandishing it before you, it lit up with a beam and in wonder I looked to the lighthouse.

The bones and twigs scattered onto the sand and I felt a jolt through my spine and shivered. Stammering a useless apology I sprinted across the beach, back to the path through the dunes that led to the empty cluster of shops and a chippy. I couldn't remember taking it but I could feel the sea glass digging into my palm. Breathless and trembling, embarrassed by my reaction, I glanced back at your lonely form waving at me from the half burnt log. The lighthouse sat silent and sombre behind you, water lapping the stone apron, the tide forever restless.

I saw you often after that, you'd be standing on street corners raising a hand to wave and once you sat at the same table as me crushed into a tiny cafe, until a stranger asked if they could take your seat and I nodded. A child saw you too; she stopped her bike and spoke with you, before turning to consider me. Her friends jostled around her laughing wondering why she had stopped to talk to no one. I walked away knowing you would follow.

My boyfriend told me I was mad, psychotic even *just like your mother* were the words left unsaid. He'd yell at me drawing his hands through his hair and almost weep begging me to seek help, to not face this thing alone. Maybe he didn't want to find me like I'd found her…cold and lifeless amongst empty bottles, the air sour with the stench of vomit.

"Elsa, please I can't live like this." And he'd gesture towards the empty place setting I'd laid at the table for you. Both of us stared blankly at his outburst as I fingered the sea glass thinking what strange bottle had it come from and what message had it carried, and was that message for me. I didn't know which of us he was referring to when he threw me out but you came too, as always, my shadow, my ever present self.

I didn't return to my previous life or my job but took to wandering the beach at night sleeping in the dunes. Slowly I was detaching from the thoughts and images that tormented and judged; the ignorance bringing respite. The light of the moon shone down on the lighthouse and I watched it, waiting for it to show me the way, to guide me. It's rusty pallor stark in contrast to the watery sky that blended into the sea making it hard to tell where water ended and sky began, they were as one.

The man in the chippy took pity on me, handing out left over chips and sometimes crispy batter. He trialled me with a job but had to let me go saying I put the customers off. He told me to get help or someone would call the police. I didn't know how to get help, and tried to ask you but you were drifting away from me. I saw you once in the eye of the lighthouse holding the sea glass so it caught the sun's rays. I ran towards you but the sea swelled and pulled at my legs and fearing drowning I turned back, then when I looked up you were gone.

My memory dimmed everyday and I couldn't remember where I had come from or even my name. Soon I even stopped seeing you and a cold loneliness descended as winter drew in, taking the tourists back to their homes. I missed you so much my heart ached, I'd not made much effort at friendship, and my arrogance must have pushed you away. Had you gone somewhere new, a fresh start? Or back to wherever we'd come from leaving me washed up by the tide.

Everything I had left of my life was in the tattered bag that hung across my chest. The sea whispered messages swirling and flowing as I collected her gifts of shells, bones, twigs and there in the foam gleamed the pebbled green sea glass. Had you not held it last, lighting the beacon high in the lamp of the lighthouse? Had you dropped it into the sea for me to find or had you passed it to me as a gift?

I held it to the sun to watch the world through the frosted glow and saw a figure walk along the beach to stop and sit upon the half burnt driftwood I had huddled by that night, freezing naked under my jumper. A nimbus of sandy hair whipped about her head before she pulled a blue hat down tightly stirring a memory, a memory I had once been.

"Elsa?" I called but the wind took my voice.

I'd not seen you for so long that I hesitated to approach. I cursed myself for the times I'd ignored your waves and attempts at communication before pushing you away; believing my boyfriend when he said you were no one, that there was nobody there. A scene of scattered place settings crept to mind, a memory of who I once was, a grieving half woman, but you were someone...you were not no one; you were all I had left of myself.

"Elsa!" I called again, shuffling towards your lonely form holding out the sea glass, a gift of apology, a gift of knowing from the lonely and the lost. As I drew closer I could see fear in your eyes, even as your hair buffeted, obscuring your features I saw confusion and revulsion. "Is it you?" I asked offering my gift in red cracked hands, sniffing and wiping my nose as it dripped. The lighthouse blinked green across the water flickering recognition in your expression and I saw how you resembled me, or I you... maybe we were one and not two.

I told you to look to the lighthouse; let it guide you as it had me. I worried we'd become lost, trapped in the sea's ebb and flow until we were nothing but bones washed up on the tide. I offered the sea glass again but repulsed by me and my red scoured hands you stood saying I was mistaken. I collapsed onto the log, a wheeze of sadness escaped my chest and you softened speaking patronizingly of taking me home, as though I was mad; a crazy half thing you feared. Then you ran and I followed.

I watched you ignore me at first and turn away, too absorbed in your suffering, but soon you accepted I was there, even laid a dinner setting for me and defended my existence to others. Then one day as summer stumbled into winter's embrace, I lost you, and believed you had started a new life leaving me alone on the beach. I searched for you, for a message or anything washed up by the tide. I wandered alone hiding from the pain and grief that had torn me apart, splitting my presence in two.

Then I saw you, high up in the lighthouse and like a vision you beckoned. I splashed into the sea struggling against the pull of the tide calling to you. *Look to the lighthouse*, you cried, your voice blending with the crash of the waves. Let it guide you through this sea of madness, past the rocks of despair and home to the shores of yourself. I wanted so much to remember who I was, to join you and feel whole once more no matter what the cost. Tears blurring my vision, I held up the sea glass to catch the beam of light that flickered from your hand, and fighting the sea's ebb and flow I followed where the green ray shone.

Three Days in the Grave of Sam Poe

(from the wreckage of The Light-House, Edgar Allan Poe's final work, & Poor Sambo's epitaph at Sunderland Point by James Watson)

by Matt Leyshon

His arrival at Sunderland, history's waste — in a lonely grave….. dark days alone on this angry shore — or worse ….. why dwell being in the realm! ….. manage the light — duty is nothing; — intolerable gossip — thundering chirps upon the sod, how dreary a sound — some peculiarity in the echo— but oh, no! — nonsense. I do believe I am going to "see what I can see" ….. a brighter light — To see what I can see indeed! — The swell is subsiding a little, I think — a glimmer of impossible solitude. The Great Judge lulled — Noteen but ocean and sky, many a sandbird will hear….. the awakds of a dead day, the sea looks like the slightest interminablee surface of the sea, even at low-tide, seems hollow: but wg about….. a teeming cloud, summer's sunbeam, moonligNot on man's colour — Life impart….. bleak and barrenad laid, his worth of heart.

January 1.

Born in Africa to ascen[d]...

seventeen thirty-six at Lancast[er]...

his master, spirits as long...

Sunderland Point. How drea[ry]...

came in sight. The surfa[ce]...

ocean's light. This day res[ts]...

moment. Solitude could scarcel[y]...

telescopes inside the impossible glass shaft. My spirit parts the high...

Jan 2.

Dead on arrival; the low-water mark of this shore. Until this moment there is no telling what passed this day between those solid iron-riveted walls. This day — my ...... day.... I have an appointment with the sky in a lonely grave. The swell is subsiding. The wind lulled. I could half fancy I should never sleep and my spirits are beginning to revive, I think. I scramble to the lantern up those interminable stairs and ascend the cylindrical walls of the sacred shaft. I believe I should feel myself secure. All safe? As seamen say occasionally. The surface of the rough sea is strange all day. I occupy a hollow interior where only the cutter will "see what I can see". Not even this solid iron-riveted wall is safe from the sea, and there is no safe passage home. No mere sea, not even the slightest speck of the whole, absolutely nothing. Though I manage the realm of light, most surprises are never observed; no Moonlight Elfin grieves over insulation. Outside the swell is everlasting mëerschaum. Clouds fill in. I may not be well. Will I die and see Heaven? Will I occupy the hollow interior of a cloud? Towards evening the cutter shall be within sight..... But what am I thinking about? There is nothing to be seen but gossip with an occasional gull. Doubt one half as much faith. I am here and I can see indeed, laid lonely and still, exploring the light-house on a sunbeam. Bleak and barren, but why dwell on that; the whole world is higher here. The sea looked to the sky, teeming. Such a single exception is gratified. This is all nonsense. Nothing can accomplish anything. Instructions are as plain as my worth, as my heart when the gulls impart. Alone I raged — miles from the bottom. There was only the occasional Archangel's trump, a dead Consistory, and a few sea-weeds. I feel an impossible floor of sacred light. I experience gulls against the glass; one actually passed this day in the shaft. It is merely sea, though, see; only circumstances, that is all. I have experienced the low water and I have not forgotten my first life. I have faith in the cutter and sandbirds. Warm my clods. Point my body to Neptune. Make me a winter's grave opening the Straits of Magellan, a memorial to the sea that is very much a man's colour. Let me sleep like a poor dog.... think of De Grät's prophecy as you fill it in. Till the wakening sounds light my way home.

Jan 3.

...dland Point. This poor dog...
...fe enough from the cutter...
...to a man — all alone in a...
...The sea had gone....
...Clouds dripped ocean the colour...
...prophecy. Nothing to be seen...
...eds; a grave that raged, a memorial 4 feet thick. ...tended with a few...
Unmourned. Alone.

Night Lamp Lotus

(An Attempt at a Strategic Guide)

by Damian Murphy

Subterranean brothels, encoded transmissions, worker's revolts and poisoned ink—Night Lamp Lotus stands alone among 16-bit retro computer games. It can't be said with any certainty whether a genuine solution is even possible. Some maintain that the prospect is a ruse, that the game's elaborate chains of association are little more than red herrings. On the other hand, the solution could very well be accessible from the beginning. The lighthouse is open for any player to explore. It's one of the only regions on the entire map in which nothing is concealed—there are no secret doors or hidden mechanisms, or at least nothing of the type has been reported on the retro-gaming forum. The greatest enigma of this central location would appear to be its lack of mysteries.

I won't maintain that a solution exists—I certainly haven't found one myself. The most I can do is provide a tiny bit of clarity, which will hopefully be of aid to some. I'll raise my little candle in the face of the night, its tentative flame pushing back against the darkness. If others are inspired to do the same, then my work won't have been in vain. My task is made more daunting by the well-known fact that no two copies of the game appear to be the same. Its main motifs are barely consistent enough to support a general strategy.

The objective of the game is fairly easy to gather by inference: to activate the lotus in the titular night lamp, the latter referring to the lighthouse found at the center of the map. While the function of this structure is somewhat of a mystery, being nowhere near a body of water, there's no indication that the lighthouse itself is in anything other than proper working order. The beacon at its summit is lit from the beginning, if only in the night. The lotus is found on the penultimate floor and looks nothing at all like the flower from which it takes its name. It's several times larger than the player icon and is symmetrical on all sides, its six luxurious petals rendered in a scintillating golden orange. What its activation is meant to accomplish is revealed in hints found throughout the game, being expressed by one character as "the final marriage between the dark heart of the forest and the bright home of the stars."

The influence exerted by this single, enigmatic item is woven through every aspect of the game world—as an object of both religious and sensual desire, an inspirer of mutiny and endless infidelity, the subject of rumors and outright lies, or as a self-conscious being in its own right. It persists at the nexus of innumerable factions, from the counterfeiters' guild to the alliance of insomniacs, some of whom advocate its activation while others cower in its shadow. "The lotus is no less than the face of God," so claims a cardinal secluded in a prostitute's boudoir, himself a double agent whose allegiance is split between the papal authority and a coterie of she-wolves. "It's a fragment of the body of the Absolute, and as such it encompasses the whole of creation, comprising both the pinnacle of holy grace and the concentrated seed of sin."

There are other flowers that must be activated as well. Six of them to be precise, each of them similar in design to the "lotus" and requiring three degrees of activation. Unlike the one in the lighthouse, these are exceedingly difficult to find. Locating even one of them requires a veritable coup involving forgery, alliances, duplicity, theft, and the manipulation of influence among a wide variety of characters. There's no explanation as to how they might be activated. The general consensus within the retro-gaming forum is that this isn't even possible. Nevertheless, it's made abundantly clear that these tasks must be completed before embarking on the final challenge.

Now that I've addressed the heart of the game, I'll move on to its specific parts. Before I begin, some background information will be useful to the casual reader. Night Lamp Lotus first appeared in April of 2021 in the form of a series of seven discs to be played on an atrociously arcane machine—the barely-obtainable Capella NG. The latter enjoyed a brief run on the market before its parent company went under in 1991. It was anything but a gaming machine, yet a number of games were made available, the graphic capabilities of its 16-bit processor being adequate enough given the time of its release. Why was the game developed for this particular computer? Most likely because of its obscurity. Used models are available on the second-hand market, but a certain amount of persistence is required to find them. More importantly, it's never been emulated, thus the physical machine is required to play. For reasons I'll go into later, this is indispensable to its mechanics.

The game was exclusively advertised on the retro-gaming forum on insidious.net. For just over the price of international shipping, the trusting retro-gaming enthusiast could send a bank draft to a P.O. Box in Novi Sad and hopefully receive a package in return. The screenshots provided were so enticing that a handful of members responded. When the copies they received seemed to work as advertised, their orders were followed by several more. The game, as shipped, has no packaging to speak of, nor any information concerning the developer, yet this only served to incite curiosity among the users on the forum. Within the space of only a few months, it had managed to attain what could almost be described as a cult following, if only among a segment of the insidious.net community. Little evidence of its existence appears elsewhere on the internet.

The game itself bears some resemblance to the Japanese games associated with the so-called "golden age" of console role-playing, save for the fact that the characters look like adults rather than dressed-up children. It has none of the earmarks of its predecessors—there's no fighting, no character stats, no level upgrades or special powers. Gameplay is purely based in narrative and strategic exploration. Its range of colors is remarkably appealing—vermillion and orange, peacock green, rosewood and black with flashes of azure. These dazzle the eyes within their 16-bit environments, slyly ensouled by the simple animations which tend to dominate the periphery of the screen. The different regions of the game necessitate a somewhat laborious swapping of discs. Aside from this, it runs fairly smoothly, with one notable exception, which I'll cover later in this exposition.

As mentioned above, each copy of the game appears to be unique, at least to a point. This includes the specifics of the opening scene, which always takes place at one of the locations surrounding the titular lighthouse in Salamander Town. In all reported instances, the game begins mid-scene with little explanation, leaving the player to pick up on the unfolding story, which seems to have begun some time before. In my own copy, the narrative begins with a resounding slap. The perpetrator, Noemi, wears a black and scarlet gown and stands before an ornate folding screen, the player kneeling on the floor before her with his hands tied behind his back. "I suppose you'd like another?" she maliciously taunts. "Just say the word, and I'll deliver. You'll quickly grow used to the taste of your own blood. It will nourish your degenerate heart."

The action takes place in an intimate interior, which can only be assumed to be Noemi's apartment. The player, a man in a featureless suit, is given a meager selection of possible responses: 'grovel', 'tease', 'defy', and 'keep silent'. The fact that they're alone in the apartment, along with the choices presented at the bottom of the screen, makes it obvious enough that the two of them are playing a decidedly salacious game.

All four of the responses are perfectly valid. There are few dead ends in Night Lamp Lotus. Each choice will influence the flow of the narrative, opening avenues of possibility that resound throughout the rest of the game. Let's say I choose 'tease', which prompts the player's character to deliver a suitably blithe response. "I rather prefer the taste of yours," he utters, the dialog shown in pixelated text. This, in turn, elicits another slap, slightly harder than the first. It's impossible to see it in his face, but one is given the impression that the recipient enjoys this.

Let's continue for now with this example, which adequately demonstrates the flavor of the game. After several rounds of provocation, the player is given a chance to redeem himself in the eyes of his imperious mistress. She issues the first of several quests which serve to drive the narrative. "I have a long-standing rival in the northern part of town," she informs him. "Her name is Seuki and she works as a seamstress at the textile mill. She has an irksome predilection for courting my lovers. In this, her depravity mirrors my own. What I require of you is to defile that reflection, to shatter the image without disturbing the glass. Do this for me, and I'll reward you with a secret about your beloved night lamp."

"I take it this is more than just a metaphor?" asks the player's character, speaking on his own volition.

"You can take it however you want," she says, casually turning her back. "But don't return until it's done."

And so it begins—from an impudent remark arises the first of uncountable narrative threads, each of which is ingeniously interwoven with the others. The other three responses, it should be noted, lead to completely different paths. Of course, there's far more to the game than simply choosing between menu options. The vast majority of play involves free exploration. The game world is rich in potential interactions with every element that appears on the screen. Often the most trivial of visual details—an

129

At the Lighthouse

innocuous heating vent or the pattern on a carpet—contains the key to gaining access to a vast new region. Both the textile mill and Seuki become central to the game if you choose to follow up on Noemi's instructions. On the other hand, you're free to ignore them. The possibilities are endless.

As for the ambiguity of Noemi's demand, this is par for the course with Night Lamp Lotus. Directives of this type are found all over the place—in the text of intercepted letters, in messages from dreams, and etched into the reverse side of the glass in certain mirrors. How might these requests be carried out? Is their fulfillment even possible? Speaking from experience, I can say that they are. There are means and there are means. Their completion requires a complex logic that becomes second nature to the veteran player. If one's footing is always a little uncertain, this is surely by design. One learns to proceed with a dubious step in the face of constant misdirection.

The astute reader will have noticed that there's something amiss in the names of the characters. Given the developer's attention to detail and flawless command of English, it would be rash to assume that the subtle perversion of common names is accidental. This, too, holds a key, or so one must assume. Precisely what it is, I have no idea. My understanding of this game is far from complete. But let's move on for now.

While certain aspects of the game are unique to each copy, there are elements that appear to be universal, or nearly so. Almost every player becomes involved with the counterfeiters' guild, for instance, those incorrigible forgers whose exploits are limited to the most trivial imitations—letterheads from companies that have gone out of business, arithmetic handbooks with conspicuous errors, cigarette rolling papers, losing lottery tickets, and made up currency from fictional countries. They operate exactly like a secret society, one into whose ranks the player is compelled to initiate. There are several degrees within their organization, each of which requires the passing of a test. One in particular bestows possession of an item that illustrates an important feature.

The object in question is a silver whistle which is said to be useful for summoning wolves. The initiate is tasked with "borrowing" the original and creating an identical copy. In order to do this, you'll need recourse to a different kind of forgery—the kind that deals with metals. Double meanings of this type are typical in Night Lamp Lotus and almost always indicate another kind of doubling—that of the "astral plane" as the Theosophists call it, also known as the mirror of nature, a numinous copy of the physical world that can only be accessed through the finer of the senses. These, too, are bestowed by the counterfeiters' rites if you can manage to surpass the initial degrees. In this lies an essential key to several aspects of the game.

How might the original whistle be stolen? Each player must fall back on their own ingenuity. The mechanics of the game are flexible enough to allow for a range of different approaches, most of them involving one Countess Masimi, who always keeps it on her person. I'll mention only that the wolves it summons are invisible to all of the corporeal senses—one neither sees them, hears them, nor feels their bites, though their viciousness is no less devastating for their intangibility. One of the flowers—the gold and scarlet "hyacinth"—can be uncovered with their help if the player is clever enough. I've yet to find another way.

Let's focus on the wolves for a little while longer. The scope of their abilities reveals several key elements of the game, some of which may shed light on the possibility of its solution. They operate according to a number of modes, determined by their controlling whistle. Once the player has forged the latter, the item is theirs to keep. A single blast will summon the beasts, yet this is hardly sufficient to deploy them effectively. The attentive player will come to observe that they respond to certain tunes, themselves picked up from various sources.

One of these—derived from a song played on a sabotaged piano in a night brothel—causes the wolves to circle a specified target, whether human or inanimate. Their procession gives rise to an elemental force that can only be perceived from its effects—use it, for example, on a radio found in a hidden chamber in the architect's academy, and you can tune the device to a mysterious channel and listen to a secret broadcast. All of this depends on the proper timing. If you unleash the wolves around the confessional booth in Saint Estukio's Cathedral, timing their deployment to coincide with the setting of the sun on the western horizon, you'll attract the presence of a disconsolate widow whose confession will make your hair stand on end. Her diabolical misdeeds provide a valuable clue to the location of an ivory mantel clock which, in turn, is instrumental to the infiltration of the night watch. Do this at any other time and you'll merely agitate the priest.

There are other things that can be done with the wolves. They make for adequate messengers and excellent thieves. Their howls, though inaudible, attract the spirits of the moon, which themselves are invoked in the counterfeiters' rites. The wolves are also known to several other characters, some on a notably intimate basis, though none so literally as Seuki, who's been known to take them as lovers.

Of all of their uses, among the most versatile is their strategic deployment in dreams, both one's own and those of other characters. Seuki herself can teach you how to do this, provided you supply the proper motivation. There's a traditional tune that can be played on the whistle that Noemi's rival is well familiar with, its secrets passed on to her by her mother, who presumably learned it from her own. Here, the player is advised to beware—this is not a step to be taken lightly. To dream about the wolves is to make them a part of you, which can never be undone—not even after restarting the game. I hardly regret my own decision to do so, yet other players may feel differently. It's best to proceed with all due discretion.

In-game dreams are not unheard of in the history of computer role-playing, though they're rarely as ubiquitous as they are in Night Lamp Lotus. The player can sleep nearly anywhere unless they're stricken with insomnia, and even then they'll occasionally be subject to a pernicious series of waking dreams. Once the wolves are involved, the landscape changes. Different shades of meaning are introduced. To inflict this on a rival can lead to definite advantages, though I've yet to find even the slightest utility in dreaming of the wolves myself. That said, to do so adds a depth to the game that's worth pursuing in its own right. Clearly, an example is in order. I have one in mind that I think will suffice.

After bearing the whip at Noemi's hand in exchange for a secret password, I fell back onto a bed of perfumed furs where oblivion swiftly overtook me—my character, that is. My luxuriant state of total blackout gave way, in time, to a medley of images. Narratives unfolded, events played out, visions came and went with all the grandeur of a symphony. After several significant, if fleeting, encounters, I found myself seated at a richly-decorated dinner table. Somehow I knew (so the on-screen text revealed) that this was located somewhere underground. Several notable guests were present, most of whom were known to me from previous encounters. The copious shadows swayed and shifted at the dictates of the candlelight.

"My chrysanthemum appears to be somewhat tipsy." This from Tsubaki, who was seated to my left. "I think it's been affected by the candle flame. It lurches and reels like a moth in the wind." She was referring to the flower that lay on her plate. Indeed, one of the candles shed its light over the petals, casting exaggerated shadows that spilled over onto the table.

"You're not the only one," said Noburu, who sat directly across from me. "My narcissus appears to be downright drunk. I half expect it to fall off the plate."

Each of our plates, in point of fact, contained a single flower with no stem. These clearly corresponded to the flowers in the game, excepting, of course, the lotus. Here, they'd reverted to their common forms, which could just be discerned from their simplified icons. In the center of my own was a hyacinth, which was the only one of the six sub-flowers that I'd uncovered up to that point. I noted also that our glasses were filled with a fluid too dark to be wine. I was informed by the text at the top of the screen that this hummed and pulsed with a vibrant force. It seems obvious now, if only in hindsight, that this could only have been wolf's blood.

"What flower would not be intoxicated?" proffered one of the weavers from the textile mill, who sat two seats over to my right. "The light of the candles represents a tradition whose roots lie in the truly bestial, yet if one pursues it deep enough one comes face-to-face with the Absolute. At the invisible nexus of God and beast lie secrets so profound that they overwhelm the best of us. Our flowers, as the seals of these mysteries, have willingly taken on this burden."

Conversation continued along similar lines. None dared sample the flower before them. A servant brought in a serving dish and placed it at the center of the table. The lid was removed to reveal a creature of unparalleled distinction—an illuminated wolf with multi-colored heads arranged in a circle around its neck. One by one were its snouts turned upward, their jaws opening to their limits. A series of sonorous songs emerged, first in turn and then all at once. While the musical capacity of the Capella NG is not remotely impressive, this particular series of rudimentary tones had a notable effect on me. They were presented as somehow primal, appealing to something beyond my grasp, suggestive at once of forgotten pleasures and of the dark intelligence of the earth. These were clearly the tunes that could be played on the whistle in their pure, unfiltered form. They seemed to intersect like the pieces in a puzzle, combining to comprise a haunting chorus, itself replete with variations and interwoven themes. Here, I understood, was the secret of the wolves in all of their operations. Now that I'd heard it, it could never be forgotten. It remains with me to this day.

But enough has been said about the wolves. I think the reader gets the basic idea. I wish only to provide a general outline. Too many details will spoil this guide, leading the reader to follow to the letter what they should instead pursue in spirit. If the light of my tiny candle is to be of any genuine service then I must take care lest it burn itself out before it reveals something of substance. Its flame will inevitably be extinguished before we reach the end of the game. Care must be taken to ensure that it's properly applied.

This brings to mind another issue—the matter of the final goal. There's quite a bit more to Night Lamp Lotus than the pursuit of its solution. This should be obvious even to readers that haven't played the game themselves. I don't know if it's possible to reach the end. It's hardly the point, in any case. This idea is foreshadowed by the lighthouse itself—its lamp is integral to every part of the game, yet it seems to serve no real purpose; there are no ships to heed its beacon, no rocky shores on which to crash, its light sweeps over a nighttime city which is adequately lit by street lamps. One could almost conclude that it's purely symbolic.

In spite of all this, there are a handful of members on the retro-gaming forum that claim to have solved the game. Their boasts are hardly worth considering. A glance at their profiles readily exposes them as little more than casual gamers. They overlook the heart of Night Lamp Lotus in their obsession with winning and prestige. My candle may waver in the face of the darkness, but at least it's the product of honest inquiry. I'd rather fall short than be inauthentic.

But let's not get caught up in trivialities. I still have significant ground to cover. There are other common features that bear mention. Among the most crucial and enigmatic are Madame Saaitō's parlor games. Her weekly soirées are a critical nexus for a

At the Lighthouse

vast array of narrative threads, yet the guest list is so exclusive that they're rarely witnessed directly. The games begin in her apartment and extend over the course of several days, most often giving rise to every manner of catastrophe before they've run their course. The worker's revolt at the textile mill is only one of countless examples.

Securing an invite is nearly impossible, yet there are options open to the enterprising player. One of the 'gifts' of the counterfeiters' guild, conferred through a lengthy initiation, involves the ability to swap appearances with other characters of the same degree, so long as they're willing. As it happens, one of your fellow initiates is a regular attendant at Saaitō's parties. The discreet and timely use of blackmail is enough to compel them to acquiesce, allowing the player to attend in their place without anybody noticing.

Madame Saaitō's spacious apartment is one of the most elegant locations in all of Salamander Town—carved teak couches with silken upholstery; screens of black lacquer and mother of pearl; walls of azure and gold damask; jeweled fans and ceremonial knives. Nearly anything can happen in its opulent chambers—you might partake of the rites of both Lucifer and Noctifer in all of their sadomasochistic splendor, behold the dawn of the Peacock Angel while in an opiated trance, or pay infernal homage to the minotaur of Knossos through the complex interface of one of her machines, though the real attraction, of course, is her games, which have gained some measure of infamy.

"The game this evening is called *The Untenable Postulate*," so said Madame Saaitō the first time I laid eyes on her. "It will begin right here in my apartment and end in one of yours—whose, precisely, will be determined by any number of factors: skill, duplicity, cunning, theft, artifice, treachery, and copious bluffing." On this particular occasion, she was dressed in a kimono of emerald and black. Her hair was in an elaborate bun. She looked nothing short of ravishing in her 16-bit resplendence. It's astounding how a simple, pixelated icon can be made to produce such a stunning effect. By this time, of course, I expected no less from a new location in Night Lamp Lotus. Along with the other guests, of which there were six, all arranged in a semi-circle around our illustrious hostess, we were treated to a simple explanation of the rules.

I'm not inclined to spoil this for the reader. Suffice it to say, *The Untenable Postulate* is integral to the discovery of one of the hidden flowers. Other parlor games follow, each of them different, each leading to its own revelations—*Method Displacement*, with its esoteric palindromes, *Conspicuous Glance*, which is perhaps the most difficult, *Surveillance Oblique*, which grants access to the diamond mines, and of course the most portentous of them all—*Apostate's Crown*. Of the latter, I think I can reveal a little. It's important not to say too much. Madame Saaitō herself best explains the object of this game.

"It's a long-accepted truth that the night lamp in our town is possessed of an inverted twin," she instructs, "a subtle, yet tangible etheric reflection that can purportedly be reached in dreams and visions. I've been there myself, so I know that it's real, and further, I know what can be found at its heart. The object of this game is a simple one—to see it for yourself. Do so, and I'll be more than happy to confirm your findings in person."

She goes on to advise her distinguished guests that this game confers no official reward. "Those who find their way to the object in question will already have gained something of inestimable worth—they'll forever wear the apostate's crown, which is more than anything I could give them. This crown is invisible, though it's easily recognized by others that wear the same. May the worthy attain it, either by trickery or by force."

As far as I know, this is the only one of the parlor games that takes place entirely outside of Madame Saaitō's apartment. The party officially ends at midnight, which is also when the game begins. The key to her challenge is remarkably simple—one has

At the Lighthouse

merely to switch off the beacon in the lighthouse for the course of a single night. This causes the workers throughout the city to abandon their roles and run amok, partaking in a sort of saturnalia in which common values are reversed. Hierarchies are banished, havoc reigns, the courthouse is maliciously set on fire—the timeless wisdom of the night erupts within the hearts of a usually docile populace, awakening long-forgotten powers and fanning the flames of opposition. The weavers, in particular, grow out of hand, letting sail their 'ship of fools'—a seafaring vessel which they drag through the streets only to smash it at the base of the darkened night lamp. The player must furtively slip through the gate which this destruction forces open on the astral plane, in order to access what, for lack of an official term, might be referred to as the day lamp.

As to how one switches the night lamp off, that's another matter entirely. I don't intend to hold the reader's hand. In any case, I have reason to believe that the method is different in every copy of the game. I'm certain that the matter is never an easy one. In my own case, the task was herculean, requiring endless failed attempts, each one uncovering a crucial detail that allowed me to investigate another angle of the problem. The key lay in an ingenious puzzle whose solution unlocked an invaluable power—the ability to deploy the wolves in two places at once.

I see no good reason to refrain from revealing what lies in the depths of the inverted lighthouse. In any case, words could never do it justice. One really must see it for oneself. I speak of nothing less compelling than the negative form of the immaculate flower beneath the lamp. Its symmetrical petals of violet-blue speak to the concealed of the concealed, flashing and pulsing in succulent waves whose silence is overwhelming. The nascent twin of the night lamp lotus goes by many disparate names—the black light of apostasy, the splendor of the midnight sun, and *Deus Absconditus*, among others. As far as I know, this encounter has no bearing on one's progress through the game. Not a single character aside from Madame Saaitō is able to recognize the apostate's crown and even she confers nothing but the mere fact of acknowledgment. After the night of pandemonium has passed, the flame of the night lamp is restored. Order is returned to Salamander Town as if nothing ever happened—even the courthouse is as it was before. The player learns nothing about any of the sub-flowers or their means of activation. Those who pursue this unlikely distinction must do so for its own sake.

Rarely do Madame Saaitō's games lead to genuine advancement in Night Lamp Lotus, at least not in any direct way. Her diversions are usually incidental, alerting the player to institutions that might otherwise remain unknown to them. The prizes she awards her victors tend to be useless in themselves—an alabaster parrot, a book of pornographic prayers, or a monocle stolen from an infamous marquess. Of all the elements involved in her games, perhaps the most significant are the pleasure houses. These are cleverly concealed throughout the town and are seven in number, so far as I've been able to discern, each one given to its own predilections, which tend toward the aesthetic rather than the carnal. They're advertised only by word of mouth, yet they're not tremendously exclusive. Once the player has encountered one, they'll notice references to them everywhere.

"The name of the game I've prepared for you this evening is *The Avaricious Muse*," announces Madame Saaitō on one occasion. She stands in the center of a circle of mirrors, each with a flaming candle behind it, her amber gown and crimson mantle reflected on their surfaces. She looks like nothing so much as a stylish ram. "The ancients used to gaze upon the surfaces of mirrors to determine the fates of nations," she continues. "We'll be using the same device tonight for something far more trivial. By means at once nefarious and obscure, I've imbued each of the candles with the essence of a place within town. The most perceptive among you will peer through your reflection to discern precisely where this is, provided you have the patience. What you see will be the object of the real game, for which this is merely the opening."

Each player draws a card to determine their mirror, taking their place before the glass. As long as you're proficient in second sight, which you assuredly will be if you're attending these parties, your concentrated gaze will be rewarded with an image. Depending on the mirror that's been chosen for you, this will be one or another of the pleasure houses. Its location will conveniently be marked on your map.

"A treasure can be found in each of these places," instructs Madame Saaitō as the players draw their cards. "I'm covetous enough to desire them all. Bring one to me and I'll exchange it for something of no uncertain value. Failure will incur no penalty—I'm not a demanding hostess. You'll leave the party empty-handed, but you'll be welcome back again for next week's game. I'm confident that some of you will succeed. After all, my guests are the crème de la crème. Now go, my little magpies—steal for me the riches I so rightly deserve."

Perhaps you've had a vision of *The Lustrous Pearl* on the southeastern edge of the industrial district. You may already have encountered the entrance as you've explored the byways of Salamander Town, yet its doors will not have opened for you until you've seen it in Saaitō's mirror. Its interior is filled with heated bathing pools beneath elegant domes linked by limestone arches, all lit throughout by flaming torchlight to create a shimmering mosaic of orange and gold. These colors provide a striking contrast to the central attraction of the house—a friendly spectral elephant that emits a pale, ghost-green glow. The latter can often be found carousing in one pool or another, either amusing the guests, enjoying a nap, or bathing itself with its massive trunk. He's ironically known as *Behemoth* and will tend to greet the player with a flap of the ears.

If you've spoken to the jeweler near the underground stream, then you may recognize the affable beast. On the condition that you've found the amaryllis that's concealed in the heart of the nearby prison, he'll tell you that each of the six sub-flowers is possessed of an *emanation*, an archon of sorts whose existence in the world embodies the flower's intrinsic mystery. "I can only speak for the amaryllis," he tells you in a furtive whisper. "Its archon takes the form of an elephant's ghost, known only to the town's elite. For the most part, you'll find it perfectly harmless, though it's occasionally known to lose its temper. I've heard it's prone to the scent of burning bay leaves. Take that for what it's worth."

Here, the player has several options. Retrieving the treasure for Madame Saaitō is by far the simplest course of action. Bay leaves can be found on the edge of the woods on the northern side of town. Simply light these on fire with one of the torches and *Behemoth* will follow you wherever you go. There's a natural spring not far from the bathhouse where the elephant will drop a tusk. This will grow back on its own within a day or two, while the discarded tusk solidifies upon touching the water. The latter will satisfy Saaitō's desires and she'll reward you with a worthless bauble.

If, on the other hand, you prefer to know something of the imperishable nature of the amaryllis, there's another path open to you—direct the wolves to circle *Behemoth* and they'll make him fly into a rage. However immaterial the elephant appears, the destruction he causes is very real. There are several places this might be unleashed—in the bathhouse itself, in the heart of the woods, or down at the harbor when the ships are coming in. If you time this right, he'll run up a gangplank and repeatedly ram one of the masts, causing the thing to come crashing down amidst the ruined deck and the trampled bodies of the ship hands. The spectacle evokes the giddy delirium of a carnival ride out of control.

The most audacious place to incite his rampage is in the underground prison in which his flower is located. Here, he lets loose with a vehemence that shakes the arches of the underworld. Several spots within the prison prove particularly vulnerable to his wrath. The empty space beneath the laundry room is my own personal favorite, allowing the elephant easy access to several of the cell blocks as well as one of the power stations. The player that manages to survive in his wake will witness countless scenes of devastation—impassable walls reduced to rubble, supporting beams shattered and doorways smashed, prisoners freed and wardens crushed, roaring tongues of uncontrollable flame. This is not the chaos of the saturnalia, but something far more dire. There's something sublime about the terrifying spectacle, suggesting the majesty of a god that can't be contained by its own creation. Once the carnage is set in motion, its scope will continue to escalate, each catastrophe exceeding the last as if building toward a climax. Just when it seems that the violent frenzy is about to surpass all possible limits, the player is abruptly pulled out of the experience as the game fatally crashes with a critical error.

It's conceivable that the crash is a genuine bug, yet I find the prospect highly unlikely. The developer's peculiar sense of humor is written all over the unfortunate failure. What are we to make of such a curious decision? I can think of no rational explanation, yet I feel quite certain that the disruption is essential to a deeper understanding of the amaryllis. The latter is located far beneath the cells in an unused part of the prison and remains untouched by the elephant's tempest no matter where you summon the wolves. As with the other sub-flowers, it would appear to be indestructible.

One might be moved to ask as well—is *this* the activation of the flower, or at least the first of its three degrees? Nothing in the game confirms this, but then that's often the way with Night Lamp Lotus. The disc that crashes is number four of seven. If it's possible to crash the other discs, I haven't found a way to do so. As for the flower's emanations, *Behemoth* is the only one that can be found in any of the pleasure houses. The others are scattered throughout the obscurest reaches of the game.

Here, I'm afraid that the light of my candle is swiftly approaching the end of its usefulness, yet there's still a little more

I hope to illuminate before bringing this guide to a close. There's so much more I could write about—the glowing blue mansion, the river of milk, or the holy stag that appears in the forest with a shining lotus between its horns—yet these mysteries have managed to elude me so far and I have little to offer in regard to their significance. For what it's worth, I regard my failures to be valuable in themselves. To proceed into the darkness, to lose one's way, to err, to falter, to give in to bewilderment—all of these things are part and parcel of the spirit of Night Lamp Lotus. But let us press on. There's still a little bit of work to do. My flame hasn't yet burnt out completely. It can still shed light on one last feature which I can't, in good conscience, omit from this guide.

After the crash in the underground prison, the player is forced to begin again. There's no way to save in Night Lamp Lotus. The game is reset with every play-through, whether you somehow manage to get yourself killed or simply give up in exasperation. There are, however, certain changes that persist from game to game. These are usually affected by trivial actions that seem meaningless in themselves—minor dialog choices, acts of petty destruction, or arbitrary changes in décor. There's a loose strip of wallpaper in the upper corner room of a derelict hotel, for instance. Peel it once and it remains peeled forever. You couldn't undo it even if you wanted to. You'll find a lengthy thread on the retro-gaming forum that's dedicated to cataloging as many of these aberrations as possible. Some of them affect the flow of the game, while others seem purely ornamental. The most notable example involves none other than Seuki.

Of all the characters in Night Lamp Lotus, Seuki is the only one that retains her memory after the game has been reset. This has its limits—she rarely recalls events from more than six or seven games before. This notwithstanding, her unique ability opens up avenues of play that would otherwise be impossible. With a little finesse, over the course of several games, you can become one of her lovers, rising through the ranks of her amorous suitors and taking your place in their upper echelons. This will require a series of suitable gifts, particularly ones that exceed the means of her other companions, not so much in terms of cost as in the difficulty involved in procuring them. Unlike Madame Saaitō, Seuki is not impressed by material treasures. What she loves more than anything else is a spectacle, the more nefarious the better.

Nothing wins Seuki's affections as much as the embarrassment of her rival, Noemi. There are a number of ways to do this, though few among them will go undetected. One might intercept Noemi's unsent letters, for example, which can be found inside her writing desk, altering their content in subtle ways so as to ruin her alliances and make her look like an imbecile. She'll never forgive you for your betrayal—at least not until the game is reset. After that, she'll have forgotten all about it, yet Seuki will remember everything.

Why, you might ask, would you go to such lengths? The answer should be obvious—it's all part of the task that Noemi delivered at the very beginning of the game, to "shatter the reflection without breaking the mirror." Shifting the balance between the two women is a multi-faceted affair, requiring alternate betrayals of one or the other over several successive play-throughs. All of these byzantine machinations must be directed toward a single aim—the catastrophic failure of a divinatory rite that takes place inside the lighthouse. Since Noemi's task and all that it involves appears in no copy but my own, I feel justified in revealing the means by which this desired end might be accomplished.

The rite, performed by Seuki, draws its power from the night lamp. Her aim is to devise a strategy that will be used against her rival, thus to ruin her friendship with the Countess Masimi and sever her ties with the night watch. The working is oracular in nature, opening a window onto the astral plane in the hope of determining where best to strike in order to bring about the maximum effect. It's a beautiful ritual, composed of several different stages, each of which involves a particular gesture—the consumption of an orchid, the inversion of a crown, and the anointing of a compass, to name but three. At its climax lies a traditional act which is not without its dangers—a quantity of consecrated ink must be swallowed to appease the prophetic spirits. It would be very unfortunate were someone to ensure that the ink wasn't properly consecrated, swapping the bottle in the midst of the rite with another one received from Noemi. I was unable to sleep for a week after carrying out the treacherous act. One cannot proceed without making certain sacrifices.

I won't describe the scene that follows. It was upsetting enough to experience it. Seuki's howls resound throughout the lighthouse, poisoning the light that bathes the city. She knows exactly what the player has done—she can tell by the taste of the ink alone. This is not a rite that she's unfamiliar with. It, too, was passed down to her from her mother. This act of sabotage isn't fatal. It doesn't even have any long-term effects, yet this is hardly enough to stop Seuki from shifting her efforts toward a devastating curse. She won't be able to carry this out before the ink begins to take effect. Just as she's uttering her final incantations, she begins to lose her bearings, her words trailing off into half-formed strings of unintelligible nonsense. Within a couple of minutes, she'll have forgotten what she's doing, her long-term memory wiped clean. This is the only technique I've been able to find that satisfies Noemi's demand in full.

Now that we've come full circle, my exposition is complete—or at least as complete as it needs to be. I've only revealed a few key fragments, yet I think I've shown enough to trace the shadow of the night lamp. I should mention that I don't expect this document to be well received on the retro-gaming forum. One-upmanship and petty rivalries have already compromised whatever standing I might once have had there. insidious.net is not generally known to be a bastion of prudence and maturity. Passions run high. Factions turn against each other. I'll admit, I'm as guilty as anyone else. In any case, I hope I've managed to reveal something of use to the general reader. In closing, I can think of nothing more appropriate than Noemi's response to the completion of her task. Since this scene is unique to my own copy of the game, I may as well quote her verbatim.

"I told you I'd reward you with the secret of the night lamp," she says as you recline into her loose embrace. "I have no intention of holding back. Not that I expect it will do any good." This takes place in her apartment after a particularly arduous session—an exacting reward for your loyalty, which she delivers with little mercy. "If the lighthouse can be said to be the axis mundi, then the lotus is the navel of the world. Its beacon seems to serve no earthly purpose; its flower seems a testament to its lack of utility. Its light is akin to the burning desire of the angels that circle the celestial throne. The heavenly court has an undying passion for the splendors of the fallen. Nothing could be more enticing to them than the mess we make of our lives—our weakness, our avarice, our constant self-deception—everything that makes us human.

"For all of its apparent uselessness, the lighthouse does have a function," she continues. "While the light it shines at night is deceptive, it emits another, more poignant signal, a constant voice that's far too fine for ears as coarse as ours to hear. It's as penetrant as sonar, as immutable as starlight, endowed with a cunning and shrewd intelligence, bestowing a simple, yet infallible strategy on those that can comprehend it. This is our only means of navigation through this labyrinth of exile. A momentary glimpse is all we're permitted, a partial understanding of its underlying structure, just enough to grasp the basis of all of our strivings and machinations. No sooner have we seen it than it seems to disappear again, pitching us back into the darkness of the night, the night which overpowers and resurrects, which encompasses all we could ever hope for."

Rising Tall and Slender

by Tim Lees

He dreamed of it: a watchful phallus, poised like God upon the world's far edge.

A pillar with an eye.

What good could ever come of such a thing? What benefit?

The snows are gone, the spring storms stilled, the sea a bright, untroubled blue. Yet today, the fishermen don't fish, nor the ploughmen plough, nor the blacksmith pound his anvil; for today is Festival, and the crowds are gathered at the ancient lighthouse, keen to celebrate. Listen! The band's already warming up, and the first notes of a jig float gaily on the salty air. The town's young women have arrived, stars of the show, huddled in their finest frocks, all pinks and blues and forest greens. Hear their laughter: nervous, excitable – chaste, but far from innocent – for today, they take their first steps in the adult world.

Dancing steps! What could be more appropriate?

The lighthouse has been hung with ribbons, from the topmost rail right to the ground, and as the band strikes up, so each girl takes a streamer, and begins to dance, to the sounds of the fiddle, tabor and accordion – circling the tower, weaving back and forth in ever more intriguing, complex measures.

A stranger watches.

The professor, visiting from far away, had hoped for just a little rustic entertainment, a few songs and a simple meal.

What he sees instead fills him with horror.

It has been his great misfortune, in the course of his work, to become familiar with both the Swiss and Viennese schools of psychology. The knowledge weighs on him. It haunts him, for it sullies everything; and where once he might have taken innocent delight in the performance, now he sees it for its true nature: the spectacle of virgin womanhood, in thrall to this – oh, Lord! – this edifice of lust, this monument to male concupiscence!

His palms are sweating. He rises, somewhat drunkenly (for the region's wine is strong), seeks out the priest, and asks him, "Why do you permit this?"

"Permit...?" says the priest, failing to understand.

"It is a mockery!"

"It is tradition."

"The worship of the phallus!"

"Ah." Now comprehension dawns. The priest, a handsome man with close-cropped, greying hair, steeples his fingers in a regal fashion. "And is not worship a great goodness of itself?" he asks. "That we bear in mind those forces which beget and shape our lives?"

"Worship of God, perhaps! But this, this –"

"'Phallus' was the word you used."

"You admit it, then?"

"My friend. This is a principle of nature, is it not? And nature is decreed by God. Do you agree? It is in nature we most readily perceive Him, and for many, where He is most readily extolled."

"You worship the *phallus!*" screams the professor, turning again to view the ghastly scene.

But at once, he finds himself distracted. The girls cavort, each with a ribbon in her hand, and the professor's eyes are drawn to them in ways he finds unsettling: the line of a calf, the sway of a hip, the jiggle of a bosom; he is aroused, despite himself.

Rising Tall and Slender

His anger grows, spurred on by his own weakness, his own too-fleshly thoughts.

Half-sheathed in braided silk, the lighthouse glimmers in the sun.

And the dance goes on.

The professor, thinking perhaps the problem is mere ignorance, leans closer to the priest.

"Do you not see? If we accept this – if *this* is the sum total of our worth – then we are nothing. Mere slaves to a blind urge to reproduce. Our higher feelings, all our spiritual endeavours – shrunk to a brutish, thrusting drive – to *copulate*. Does that not offend you, sir? You are these people's guide, their spiritual advisor! Are you not appalled?"

The priest considers for a moment. He, too, watches the dance.

"You are right, of course," he says. "It would mean that. Indeed it would."

Drawn to the debate, a number of the townsfolk have come close, watching this duel of words with some considerable interest.

It's a pebble beach. Unseen by the professor, one man bends, selects a large, round stone, and holds it in his hands, caressing it as if it were a living thing.

"Yet you allow such acts –"

"I see nothing here in conflict with my faith."

"Nothing?" The professor sputters. His hands clutch at the air. "This – this is abomination!"

"Copulation," corrects the priest; then, with just the slightest gesture, draws the townsfolk closer. "Part of life, surely? Copulation, and then –"

Unconscious of the crowd behind him, the professor rants. Words tumble from his mouth. He waves his hands. He is clearly drunk.

The first stone strikes him in the small of the back. It is such a shock that he can hardly understand what's happened; he turns, a little dazed. The girls still dance, but now, between the professor and the lighthouse, there stands a wall of local men, each with a large, round stone in hand.

"Look here," says the professor. "I am a person of considerable importance, and I –"

The next stone strikes him in the mouth. A third, upon the shoulder. He makes to run, but the missiles rain down, and he falls to his knees.

Blood spreads. This is tradition. Blood must be spilled, the blood of a deflowering, or the blood of a blasphemer. Either way.

All things belong to God.

The priest smiles, clasping his hands in prayer.

He watches the professor's rumpled form, sprawled on the ground, still twitching, as if it, too, wants to follow the music, in one last and long-delayed attempt to join the dance of life.

❋

Fog. Thick fog.

And tonight, the lamp is out.

The lighthouse keeper wakes abruptly. Did he feel the light die in his dreams? Perhaps. He's such a part of this place now, it's as if his soul has seeped into its stones. Here, in the living quarters which adjoin the tower, he can taste the fog. His throat is clogged with it. He coughs, sputters, rolls over in bed –

A glance out the window confirms his fears. The land, the sea, subsumed in grey; no light, no flash, no fire in the dark. He stumbles out of bed, pulls on his trousers and his peacoat, slips feet in boots without tying the laces. He must renew the light! He flings open the door to the lounge, but here, a second shock awaits. His bedroom merely reeks of fog, but now, a wall of it comes tumbling down on him with dream-like slowness, swallowing the world in thick, damp grey. He can hardly see a hand before his face, much less the door into the tower.

He feels his way along the wall. Here is the sideboard, here the small electric fire; here, the framed print of a French Impressionist, hung by his predecessor. Yet where's the exit? He circles the room two, three times, blindly, almost panicking. The lamp must be lit! His heart throbs in his breast, he sucks the dank, grey air – and, yes, at last! A door. He tugs at it, he blunders through –

He's lived here seven months. He knows the place. He knows it like it's part of him. But this room... his memory deserts him. Suddenly, he's lost! He hurries forward, into the murk, but the next door fails to appear.

He's heard of men lost in the desert, walking in circles, favouring one leg or the other; so deliberately now, he walks first to the right, then to the left. And yes, he finds a door, but not one of the old, panelled doors he's used to. This is modern, crude – a sheet of plywood nailed upon a wooden frame. It's unfamiliar. How has he missed it, in his time here? Is he in one of the outhouses, perhaps? Did he stumble, blind in the haze, out of his house, into some nearby shack?

It seems improbable, but he can find no better explanation. He pulls open the door, steps through. The next room, too, is blanked by fog.

He trips over an office chair, an item he has never seen before.

He thinks he's made a wrong turn somewhere. But in trying to retrace his steps, he finds himself in rooms that he was sure were never previously there, rooms which offer not the slightest clue to his location.

He must light the light! He must save the ships! But where is he? And why is nothing as it should be?

❋

At the Lighthouse

Windswept, remote, the lighthouse of the northern shore must be continually manned, and boasts not one, but two lighthouse keepers; we'll call them Zack and James. They alternate their duties and take turns with their days off; thus Zack visits the town on one night, James the next, and so on. Each has a girlfriend there. Each considers himself lucky to have found companionship in such a wild, outlandish place.

Zack's girlfriend, Sarah, cooks beautiful hash skillets; James's girlfriend, Ann, gave him a thick wool sweater for his nights on duty. Sometimes, when the two men are alone together, they extol the virtues of their lady-friends, in friendly competition, each convinced that he alone must be the winner.

And for her own part, Sarah-Ann is likewise pleased. She knows the way a man can wear a woman down, even without meaning to: his endlessly-repeated stories, tiresome jokes, and work-a-day love-making. Such tedium is not for her. But two half-men – ah! Now that's a different matter!

※

By the Sultan's decree, seven lighthouses were built along the strait, each in the shape of an animal: the snake, the rabbit, the tiger, the ox, the ram, the fish, and the wolf. By night, the beasts were crowned with light, and in daytime, any mariner might gauge his progress by the particular brute looming to port or starboard – useful, for the waters of the strait are treacherous in the extreme.

The story goes that, some years later, the Sultan's spies brought news of a great foreign fleet massed at the strait's far mouth, its power immense, and its intentions plain.

The Sultan might have fled and saved himself. Yet history recalls him as a diligent and cunning ruler. He gave orders: wherever there was wood – in the forests of the south, or a farmer's outbuildings, or the shacks and sheds beyond the palace grounds – it was gathered up, and taken to the coast. Along with it went carpenters and labourers by the hundreds. Thus, in a single night, seven great wooden facades were built, each to mask one of these far-famed beacons. By morning, it appeared the snake and tiger had swapped places; the ears of the rabbit become the horns of the ram; the ox become a fish, the fish a wolf, and so on. That day, fierce winds blew, and these ramshackle fronts had to be held in place, with countless citizens hauling on ropes to keep the illusion.

So the fleet set sail. Entering the strait, the invaders proved as fearsome as reports had claimed, and ravenous for battle. Look-outs aboard checked off the markers as they passed: snake, ram... tiger? Something was wrong. Where was the ox? The wolf? Confusion spread among the vessels. Some broke formation, convinced their leaders had been misinformed. Some were lost in the shallows, or ran aground on hidden rocks; others, baffled, simply turned and sailed back the way they'd come. The few that remained met the Sultan's fleet, which now outnumbered them, and their fate was swift and brutal.

Today, the same harsh winds blow on the strait, but the lighthouses are hard to find: a few stones here, a grassy hummock there. Through the centuries, it seems they were demolished, piece by piece, and used for building material – perhaps to replace those wooden structures, artfully dismantled in the service of defence.

※

There's a fly in the lighthouse.
    It's been here days.
    It's driving him insane.

You'd think, after so long alone, that almost any company, any distraction would be welcome, even such as this.

Not so.

Each day he wakes, drinks in the first few minutes' calm, and thinks: perhaps the insect's dead. Or gone. Perhaps I'm free of it at last. He boils the water, makes his breakfast. Then –

The sound is thin and high, a too-familiar whine that seems to cut into his brain like a buzz-saw. He leaves his meal, looks this way, that, paces angrily –

And here! Yes! The nasty, raisin-bodied thing is pushing at the window, straining to escape. He takes a magazine. Moves slowly, barely shivering the air, raises his arm, and – *smack!* For a second, he's convinced he's got it. But the magazine is unmarked, and the insect's hovering before him, loud and insolent. He tries to clap his hands around it, but no good: wherever he strikes, it's gone.

The creature is tormenting him. Deliberately, he thinks. It has malice and intelligence. It plays games, pretending that it wants to leave, but when he throws open the window, it won't go out. It doubles back. Perhaps it laughs at him. He sets traps, baits them with sugar, honey, or the last of the strawberry jam. None works.

The creature watches him, dancing on the air, scrabbling at the windows.

No mere insect, this, he's sure.

This thing is Lucifer incarnate, sent to torment him, to mock him for his past sins, for every selfish, cruel act, and every unkind thought that's ever crossed his mind; in the whining of the fly, he hears them listed, accusations at which he can only nod, and curse, and prepare to meet his fate.

For now he understands: the fly has come to claim his soul.

❋

A light sweeps past.

Light: darkness.

Darkness: light.

The Great Detective smooths his moustache, casts eyes over the group assembled here at his behest; and to the Colonel, says bluntly, "No, *monsieur*. You were not mistaken. You were merely wrong."

The Colonel *harumphs*. "I saw what I saw."

"Indeed, indeed. But you did not *interpret* what you saw, my friend. And that, I am afraid, is a most crucial matter."

Talk bubbles through the crowd. People look to their fellows, but their former trust is gone; for one of them, it's plain, must be the killer.

"You saw the victim, caught in the brief illumination of the lighthouse beam," says the Detective. "He was alone. The light swung away; when it swung back, the man was dying. You conclude, therefore, what you have witnessed is a suicide. Yet you forget those few seconds of darkness. Mere moments, to be sure; yet *that* was when the killer struck. We reconstruct the sequence of events as follows. The victim is visible, seemingly alone. The light moves from him; in the dark, his throat is sliced from ear to ear, the knife dropped at his feet. When the light returns, he is alone again, clutching his wound, the killer vanished in the night. That killer, *monsieur*, is with us now. The name –"

But in that very instant, the light moves on again, flitting over rocks and waves, turning the spindrift to a spray of diamonds; plunging the party into darkness, out of which the Great Detective gives a single, choking cry – his final word.

None of the onlookers agree on what he said. Was it supposed to be a name? And, if so, who on Earth is "Urgh"?

❈

When I was young, I had a little green-skinned boy for a friend. We met in the north, where the city fizzles into smallholdings and fishing quays, and the Atlas Lighthouse stands alone and empty on the shore.

He came towards me through the surf, svelte and muscular, the sunlight gleaming on his arms and legs. He was wary – we both were – and when I stood, he skittered back into the waves, nervous as a deer. But his shyness gave me courage, and I called out, "Wait, wait!" and waded after him.

His hands were webbed. His eyes were round, black lenses, where my own image peered darkly back at me; and only when he smiled I felt a moment's trepidation, for in that, he lost all semblance to humanity, and his mouth became a phalanx of long, needle teeth, like some voracious, deep-sea predator. My turn to step back – at which he laughed! His shoulders shook, and he produced a string of tiny grunting sounds, like hiccups. He was almost voiceless, as I soon found out, but his laughter was infectious, and the pair of us were quickly doubled up in mirth, clutching our stomachs till we ached. From that day on, and for the rest of summer, we were friends, though I told nobody about him, not my parents, nor my brother, and certainly, no-one at school.

I saw him almost daily. We played simple games – catch, chase – or swam together, which he loved. In the water, he was stunning. Where I strained and struggled, he dived, bobbed, or circled round me with the sleek grace of a seal. One moment he'd be floating on his back, the next he'd up-end, and his great, webbed feet would be the last thing I'd see as he slid beneath the waves, returning with a clamshell, or a handful of coins, or a leather shoe swarming with tiny crabs. The sea was a treasure-chest to him, and he wanted me to share in its delights.

He seemed to have no tribe, no family. There were times when he'd grow quiet, and stare out at the ocean, and I wondered then about his history, if he was lost, or separated from his people somehow. Was that why he'd approached me? We looked different, but at heart, I sensed that we were much alike, both lonely, isolated – both, in our own ways, adrift in life.

I talked. I talked as I had never talked to anyone before – about my home, my family, my fears for the future... I don't know what he understood, but he leaned his head against my shoulder, purring softly, and with every word, I felt my heart grow lighter; and I realised, for the first time, that whatever misery I went through now would one day pass, become a memory, and that, too, eventually fade and vanish like a long-lost dream.

Did he teach me this? Perhaps. Without him there, it would never have occurred to me – of that, I'm sure.

He brought me fish, clamped in his ferocious jaws. I told my parents that a kindly fisherman had shared his catch with me. "We don't take charity," said my father. But that night, I savoured every mouthful, and even my mother remarked that I seemed to have found my appetite again.

So life went on. The seasons changed. The sea grew rough, and the shape of the beach began to alter, banks of sand and shingle shifting with the onslaught of the waves. A cold wind blew. I huddled in my jacket, and waited by the lighthouse, as I always did. But for the first time, now, he didn't come.

Next day was the same. Had he gone? If he'd told me he was leaving, I'd have understood. I'd have accepted it. As things were, I felt betrayed. Abandoned. I drifted back into the city, walking aimlessly. I stopped strangers, asking if they'd seen a little green boy anywhere. Most just laughed, or blanked me and walked on. But one stopped, thought a moment, then pointed me towards the Gould Street Fish Market.

And that's where I saw him.

Jewels of ice shone on his skin. His feet – his big, green, flipper-feet – were crossed, tied, and slung over a metal rail. His belly had been sliced and the guts removed, leaving him shrunken and mis-shaped. But it was him, I knew. Even hanging upside-down – it could be no-one else.

A sound rose in my throat. It burst from me, not my own voice, but a bleak, animal wail. My knees gave way. Somebody caught me as I fell, asked if I was sick, asked what was wrong with me. But I could only point, and groan, and drum my fists against the ground.

I didn't return home that night. I curled up on the beach beside the lighthouse, and the sound of the waves echoed in my dreams, and I knew then that my childhood was over, and a new, far darker portion of my life begun.

※

Sea levels change. Few now recall the tower's true purpose, rising tall and slender out of lush and verdant pastureland. Weathered, ivy-clad, today small birds nest in its crannies, lizards bask upon its stones, and gulls wheel, squawking overhead – although the sea is now some miles to the south.

Through the years, the tower has become a trysting place for lovers, and something of a rite of passage for the young. What better way to spend the night than here, under the stars, with somebody you love?

Yet the tower can be a busy place. In summer, sometimes four or five couples will meet here in a single night – with much initial awkwardness, embarrassment, and quibbling over favoured spots. Thankfully, such moods pass quickly, and as the darkness deepens, it may be that an unexpected intimacy builds between these varied lovers; and in the secret hours, when the masks of daily life are shed, partners are swapped, new pleasures tried, and every likely combination readily indulged: boy with girl, and girl with girl, and boy with boy, and any multiple thereof. For some, the episode remains a one-off. For others, it proves life-changing. The tower, it's said, provides a reservoir of powerful, erotic energy, a source of blessing, knowledge, fertility – and great, great sex.

There are other visitors.

Older, solitary men skulk in the nearby woods, armed with binoculars and long-lens cameras, straining to recall some hint of their lost youth, of the thrills and glories which they once believed would last a lifetime.

But the less said about them, I think, the better.

The Lighthouse Sisters

by Rhys Hughes

There are three sisters and I am fond of them all but only one of them is fond of me and I am not entirely sure which one that is. It might be the eldest and tallest but I only think this is so because she sometimes smiles at me and once twitched her nose charmingly at something I said.

It goes without saying that she has red hair and that this hair resembles fire and that when she walks through the rain I am astonished that no steam billows from the top of her head. She works in a shop and one day she was stringing up a chain of lightbulbs over the store front.

Oh look!
A long haired
ginger girl at the top of a
tall step ladder who
in a strong wind
shows no
fear.

> But
> it's surely
> too late to resemble
> the Pharos of Alexandria,
> my dear?
>
> Or is it too early…

That is the poem I wrote about her when I reached my apartment. It is true that she seems comfortable with heights and it was a very lofty step ladder. As for myself, I enjoy being at the apex of things, not metaphorically but literally and sometimes when I am leaning on my balcony I feel an impulse to shout the word "Fire!" and then jump into the void.

Summer is long over and autumn is more than halfway through and winter will be especially harsh this year, I can feel it. I am generally right about trivial things such as the weather and mostly wrong about existence, the universe and our purpose within it. Those three sisters!

The shop the eldest works in sells light fittings and lamps. At night all the bulbs are illuminated and then it seems the shop is a furnace and that the doors have been opened to allow the molten metal to pour out. But she emerges in her red shoes instead, carrying half the total glow with her on her head, her curls licking the air and crackling with energy.

There was a festive atmosphere in the city and she joined her friends in one of the squares. A strong young lad impudently offered her a ride on his back and she accepted. He marched around the square and down some of the adjacent streets and for a moment I thought there was a torchlight procession, perhaps an atavistic political event, taking place.

But no, it was just the eldest sister on the back of a stout fellow and he was growing tired and in fact he was ready to put her down, as a mythic hero of the distant past might also have felt weary after carrying a lighthouse, and I'm sure some hero did that, and she cautiously dismounted. There was no torchlight procession tonight. I had been mistaken.

This reminds me of something that once happened when I was walking in a park not far from my house. In the centre of the park is a circle of tall stones but it's not really ancient, it only looks like some important ritual site, and I thought someone had lit a blaze of branches there.

But it turned out to be a dog running in circles excitedly. From a distance it looked just like a fire and thoughts of druids and magic and sacrifices had filled me with alarm, but it was just a Red Setter, magnificently hairy, and I laughed at my foolishness, not because it was funny but to hear my own voice guffawing and enjoying itself. Good for it.

I decided to write another poem for this eldest sister.

Come
camping with
me tonight, O ginger girl,
for it will save
us both much time
and trouble.

There'll be no
need to light a fire
before bed,
we can just cook our
supper on your
head.

I think it is unlikely she will accept the invitation, even if I make her aware of it, which I have absolutely no intention of doing. One doesn't cook soup on a burning house, that's a well attested truth, and it would be equally uncouth to do so on a lighthouse flame, no matter how organic the structure, how female and willing it is. There are limits.

The second sister also has red hair but instead of resembling the fire of a famous classical lighthouse it seems, at least from behind, like the sail of a ship at sunset. It is straight rather than curly and presents an unbroken curtain to the view of one who happens to be following.

Not that I'm in the habit of following anyone deliberately! But let's be honest enough to admit that sometimes it does happen. You wish to go in the direction that best suits your needs, but the person ahead of you appears to want to go in the same direction. What can you do? Change direction and end up in a place you have no desire to be? Surely not.

I was standing at the end of a busy street one afternoon and wondering how I might make my way down it, so thickly thronged with pedestrians was it, when I noticed the gleam of the setting sun between the shoulders and heads of the milling crowd and I checked my wristwatch and said to myself, "That's too early!" but it wasn't the setting sun at all.

No, it was the hair of the middle sister, far away on her distant head at the other end of the street, but the sunset effect was incredibly strong. She is like an old-fashioned ship in other ways too, her nose a prow, her rump a rudder, her slow gestures like churning oars, her stockings like rigging, and she surges as she walks through fathomless modern life.

The third sister has short red hair like a rock slicked with blood. I imagine she has been used as a murder weapon, a bludgeon to smash the bones of a victim who probably deserved such a fate. How could I know any of this for certain? I am guessing, nothing

The Lighthouse Sisters

more. These sisters fascinate me but I avoid the third one because she is geologically intimidating.

She looks up to the second sister, who looks up to the first sister, and this is the way it should be, but to see them standing together reminds me too much of a morbid bar chart, falling barometric pressure or the failure of the economy, the end of prosperity and decline of the west.

Do they have names, these sisters? You want to humanise them, take them away from the control of my definitions. Yes, they have names. Farina, Heeva, Recka, they are called. Unusual perhaps, but what is usual? There are too many usual things in the world that oppress and dominate people for me to have more than minimal respect for the conventional.

Farina intrigues me, the other two are not irrelevant, that's too harsh a way of putting it, but they are tangents on the curve of my understanding. Only the eldest daughter resembles a lighthouse and I want to bathe in the beams she throws off into the dark. But first I must provide the darkness! How can I do this? If I think sinister thoughts, will that be sufficient?

I have no desire to think thoughts in which I am unable to see, whether dark or foggy. And talking about fog reminds me that her laugh is exactly like a horn that roars over the swirly grey soup made from the condensing vapours that shroud the shore. Only a few times have I heard this laughter but it startled me on each occasion and made me convulse.

I ought to show her one of the many poems I have written for her. What do I have to lose? Only everything. But everything doesn't matter, because we are told that nothing is more important than love, and if nothing is so mighty that it takes precedence over everything, then nothing is the best outcome to aim for. That is logic. If I lose, I also gain.

You are a freckled girl and I'm a hale and hearty boy.	Kiss me in my vigorous prime and taste a wine divine.
I'll lick your freckles in return and slurp a ginger beer.	I am the hale and hearty boy who burned his tongue last year.

She won't be pleased by my words or the sentiments they express but there is the possibility she will be tolerant. That's more than enough for me. At least I can swear that my poems are heartfelt. I fold the page on which this verse exists into the shape of a boat and I leave it on the threshold of her shop like a beached vessel that went exploring for the lightest and brightest version of Atlantis, risen and dried out nicely, a dehydrated legend.

To my astonishment, the next time I'm passing her shop, more than a week later, she rushes out from the gaping doorway and seizes my wrists in her strong grip, swinging me around to face her twitching retroussé nose. She is taller than I am and I crane my neck to look up at her green eyes, but strands of angry red hair are covering them like streams of lava.

"Do you really believe I can be influenced by words?" she demands, and I am about to shake my head when she adds, "Well, to a certain small extent, yes I can. You will be given a chance," and when I quaveringly ask her to elucidate her tantalising meaning, she is more specific. "To amuse me, of course. Taking me out for a drink is your objective, no?"

It hadn't been until that very moment, but now it was, and so I nodded and she released my hands. The marks of her fingers remained on my flesh, slowly fading. What an unexpected development! Farina had always been an ideal for me rather than an individual it was possible to do things *with*. But to turn down a chance to be her companion for a few hours would be an unspecified sacrilege and I suggested a proper time and location.

"Very well, that will do," was her answer, and I went away like a man who has been informed that he must perform in a circus to entertain the clowns on a day when there are no paying audience members. The comparison is oblique but I was an oblique man at that moment, so it fits. I knew precisely which bar I was going to take her to, elegant and tranquil.

There is a superstition that I invented when I was younger, and despite the fact I'm aware it was manufactured by myself at a tender age in an idle moment, it has successfully incorporated itself into my belief system to the extent that it now seems very unwise to doubt its veracity.

It is the idea that everyone is allowed to cast a single spell in a lifetime, to make one wish. People either are unaware of this power and neglect to use it, or they waste their wish, using it to conjure up a minor delight that is forgotten in a few days. But I always kept my wish secure. I would finally employ it when I was with Farina and it would benefit both of us.

We met in the Lighthouse Bar on the seafront and I made sure I was early. She entered while I was watching the door and it seemed that a lamp had been lit and that the building could begin revolving. But it didn't do so. It was fixed on its foundations. We drank red wine and I said, "You are a lighthouse at heart and that is precisely why we are sitting here."

"I know almost nothing about the sea," she replied modestly, but this was a joke, for her very presence tugged at my soul and a tug is a thing of the sea, as anyone can affirm. On our third glass of wine I told her that this seaside town was no place for such a stupendous wonder as she was. There was only one city in the world worthy to host her special form.

At the Lighthouse

She wanted to know where that was and I told her. "Alexandria, the bride of the Mediterranean! Where else? That's where we should be right now, you and I, among the colonnades, white villas and wide boulevards of the greatest metropolis of ancient days. And I have one wish that I can use, untarnished and potent. Let me take us on a journey there!"

She laughed her foghorn laugh and all the wisps of doubt in my mind were shredded by its sonic magnificence. I told her about the Pharos, a tower that was almost a temple, and explained its dimensions and history, how it had served as the model for all lighthouses since, how its construction was ordered by one of the Ptolemies, taking twelve years to finish.

"One of the tallest man-made structures in the world of its time but that's a convenience of language only. You are a woman, an avatar of the Pharos, thrust into our own century for mysterious reasons. You blaze superbly but warn no ships of submerged reefs, yet I am sure you will serve as the model for every woman who will follow you. Even your sisters appreciate the deep truth of this and have done their best to imitate you."

She disagreed with me, that much was obvious, but I hadn't expected easy acquiescence on her part. It takes considerable time to convince someone that they are both a human being and a prominent structure of granite blocks topped with a platform on which shines a huge mirror during the day and where logs burn at night. Time or else a magical epiphany.

"I will use my solitary wish now. When we leave this bar we will be not in our modern town but in Alexandria as it was in its prime. Time and space are at my command. You will see and then no more persuasion will be necessary. Let me spend my wish on a blissful miracle!"

"In its prime," she echoed, but I had already closed my eyes, pressing my eyelids as firmly together as I could. I made my wish and when it was done and I opened my eyes, I was alarmed to note that she had gone. Had my talk worried her enough that she had fled while I wasn't looking? I finished my drink in one gulp, surprised it was a sweet liqueur and not the wine I had been drinking, and towards the door I hurriedly made my way.

If she had run out into the night, I would soon be on her heels. But the bar had changed dramatically during my prolonged blink. It was even more elegant than it had been, with chandeliers and softer lighting. How had the management altered the decor in such a short span of time? I lurched out into the street and I saw that in fact my wish had been granted.

The Lighthouse Bar had gone, vanished into the future, for I found myself in the past and I had just exited the Cecil Hotel. The sea lapped softly, a blue so dark it might as well be black, and the lights of the Corniche stretched along the slight curve of the bay. Yes, this was Alexandria! But there had been an error in my wish. I leaned on a palm tree for support.

Alexandria in its prime? I had assumed it would be classical times, the age of the Ptolemies and Cleopatra, the Great Library and Aristarchus, Eratosthenes, Hypatia, Ctesibius, and Hero, who invented a steam engine millennia before the Industrial Revolution. But no, the wish clearly had different ideas, other tastes, and it regarded the best days of the city to have been in the early 1930s, during the final chapter of British rule in Egypt.

Ah, the Cecil Hotel, where Somerset Maugham, Agatha Christie, Winston Churchill had often stayed! Where Umm Kulthum had performed her songs, the grandeur of empire's end, the slowly rotating ceiling fans and potted palms, the obscure liqueurs in bottles behind the bar!

I hurried to the edge of the Corniche, looking down at the narrow strip of sand washed by the incoming sea. Then I looked across to the end of the jutting headland where the Pharos had once stood. It was gone, of course, collapsed to rubble in a Fourteenth Century earthquake, its tumbled blocks recycled to form the ramparts of the Citadel of Qaitbay. The lighthouse had no role to play in this iteration of the prime time of Alexandria.

And this meant that Farina was vanished too, for she was an avatar of the structure and no avatar can survive the loss of its archetype for long. My wish had accidentally removed her from my life.

Should I write a new poem to express my melancholy appreciation of this irony? But I had no paper or pen with me. Then I noticed a ship on the sea and it was approaching the harbour. The moon had risen and it was blood red, as if pretending to be the setting sun, and its light stained the sails of the vessel. The second daughter, Heeva, was sailing into port! Could it be that she was the one who was fond of me after all? How strange!

But without a working lighthouse to warn her, the ship had no chance with the deadly rocks that make Alexandria such a hazardous place for navigation. I saw how the waves lapped against a large round rock directly in the path of the hull and I realised that this was the third sister. Recka was waiting to smash the timbers of Heeva. So it was the third sister who was secretly fond of me too? I was indirectly responsible for this chaos.

Sibling rivalry taken to extremes! Recka couldn't bear losing me to Heeva and planned to sabotage her sister's efforts to reach me. Or was I deluded? Did these events really have nothing to do with my existence? In old cartoons there is a convention that an inspired idea can be represented by a spherical lightbulb coming on over one's head. My sudden insight was that I was superfluous to all that was happening, that I too was a wreck.

In anguish I began to turn on my heel, throwing out wide beams from the imaginary bulb that crowned my cranium.

The Lighthouse Sisters

Three sisters
and one is a lighthouse,
one a ship,
the other a rock,
and I am just a man
out of time with the world
who has had an idea
that illuminates his own place
but also reaches out
across the perilous sea.

Safe Passage

by Brittni Brinn

"As agreed. Safe passage off the island." The barter-master hands me a square of paper—a charcoal drawing of the Lighthouse smudged and distorted by water stains.

"How would you know what it looks like?" I sneer, flipping the drawing over. A scrawl of confirmation, a red stamp, the text around the rim of the ink circle unreadable.

He shrugs, the rags hanging off his shoulders fluttering to stillness. "I can dream, can't I?"

I throw him the bones I owe and duck under the threadbare banner spanning the top of the door. The street is empty, dark in the middle of the day—an ice storm is brewing, heavy clouds churning low over the jagged shack roofs.

I burrow my face into the ridge of my twice-wrapped shawl. The wind cuts through it, leaving no warmth. Turning the corner at the end of the street, I stagger over frozen mud tracks and scatterings of debris, weaving through abandoned carts and crates until I reach the doorway that is mine, closed against the wind.

I wrench the handle, push my way inside. Kick the door closed behind. The absence of sound sets my ears ringing. No light either, but I know by touch where the kettle and the matches are.

Strike one—the match head skitters across the counter.

Strike two—a flare of red against the sandpaper, then darkness.

Strike three—the end of the match glows blue and builds to a teardrop of flame. I light the burner under the kettle, hurry to touch the curling matchstick to wick. The lump of candle catches on, glows. Easy enough to see the single room in the faint light—bed, chair, wash basin. Packing up this small, sad life will take no time at all.

My fingers worry the edge of the drawing in my pocket. Paper is a useless thing—easy to burn, drown, rip into pieces. Passage should be set in stone, carved in metal, branded on the skin—irreversible. So, I have to protect this paper to prove my worth? If that's what I have to do.

The kettle screams as the first shards of ice patter the roof. I pour acid-hot water into a mug. Sit while it cools. Smooth the drawing on the counter. The Lighthouse is still there, in a fog of charcoal smears. I roll it carefully, then fit it into a copper canister I usually keep jerky in. There's a loop worked into the canister lid so I can hook it onto my belt—useful for the long trip ahead.

The ice storm rages, battering the thin walls and the roof, threatening death, daring me to come outside and face it. Instead, I wrap myself in my blanket and spread my belongings on the bed. I place them, one by one, inside the sack I've been saving. I tie it closed.

Tonight will be the last, I think, as I lay down on my bare mattress. The ice storm is a symphony that howls me to sleep.

※

"You're really leaving?" Zan looks up from the bundle in their hands.

"I thought you'd like your things back." I readjust the sack over my shoulder.

They frown, deep lines carved in their shallow cheeks. "Quinn…"

"How do I know?" They've asked me enough times. My plan to reach the Lighthouse isn't a secret. I've been saving for a year, sold everything I could spare to afford my passage off the island, across the black sea to the warm lands. Everyone who makes the journey never returns. Why would they?

"What if you get there and there's nothing? What if this town is all there is?"

"Gotta be something better than this place."

Zan hesitates, then reaches for my hand. "We can make this place better. Listen, I know I've talked about it for a while, but there are a few of us. We can build better houses, a communal cookhouse. Enough food and shelter for everyone. It'll take time, but I believe we can do it."

Their hand is warm. It takes everything out of me to let go. "I've got my passage," I say, tapping the canister against my hip. "If you were smart, you'd get yours too."

Zan winces, gripping the bundle of their things. "Don't leave yet." They enter the back room of their shop, a closet where they sleep. Half a dozen waterproof cloaks hang on the wall, all for sale. Zan sells maybe one a week. Barely enough bones to live on.

Rustling, the sound of cardboard being sliced open, a heavy fold of fabric being shook free of packaging.

Zan returns and pushes a green-black raincloak into my hands. They blink a few times. Their lips consider an unspoken word.

"How much?" I say.

"Get out," they manage. "If you want to that bad. Leave."

I do. Standing in the slick road, I drop the sack, find the holes in the heavy green-black material as I pull it over my head. The raincloak fits perfectly.

Returning my sack to my shoulder, I shuffle down the road as a pattering of ice leaps across corrugated steel rooftops. Puddles

175

on the road shiver under the brief assault. What a garbage pit. I don't even say goodbye to the town as I cross the unspoken border between the shacks and the rocky plain that stretches out to the cliff.

The raincloak keeps the wind out as I reach the thick chain stretched across the exit point. The cliff is a sheer drop, down and down until it hits the slate bottom of the ancient harbour. Long ago, the harbour was dammed and all the water was burned away or frozen and shot into space, depending on which of the old stories are true.

Now, the Lighthouse is the only story. It's the only way off the island, past the dried-up harbour out over the black sea. To wherever people live beyond.

No one goes past the cliff unless they are going to the Lighthouse. No one who goes to the Lighthouse comes back.

But I've made my ends and have my passage. I unhook the chain and take the first step down the stairs carved into the cliff face, a steep and slick flight broken up every so often by a natural platform protruding from the stone. The stairs are open to the wind and ice and the slate below. A coarse and dirty rope is tacked along the wall. I grip my sack of belongings to my stomach, clench the rope with a cold hand.

Slowly. One step. Move the hand down, fibres cutting into palm. Another step. A sheet of ice-rain passes, hissing as it hits the stairs. Even more careful. One more step, press the boot tread on the stone. Keep going until I reach relief.

The first outcropping is wide, flat, covered in yellow splatters of moss. I release the air pent up in my chest. I sit down to eat some jerky, my back against the cliff. The canister holding my passage is secured to my belt under the raincloak. I am worthy. The red stamp on paper confirms it.

The next flight down is scattered with rubble. Some of the steps are crumbling on the edge. Slowly, carefully, one step and another. My foot falters, I grip the rope, head reeling, stomach

Safe Passage

screaming—but I am still on the step, my boot firm on stone. The fear clears.

I can make out the next platform down. Closer with each step. The impression of yellow on stone increases. It resolves into a shape. A huddle. My heart throbs as I continue down, the unknown becoming undeniable. It's a body.

And still I have to descend. A yellow raincloak with a hood and thin sleeves. Only a few more steps to go. The body sprawls on its stomach, legs bent at terrifying angles. Under the curve of the hood, bloated blue lips and ice-encrusted skin.

I skirt around the yellow raincloak as fast as I can.

The next flight of stairs is less steep. Only a couple more outcroppings, and each step easier than the last. Finally, the harbour floor underfoot.

I relieve myself behind a boulder. The release is intensified by the wall rising up beside me, the cliff that has killed others but couldn't kill me.

With my sack over my shoulder, I take my bearings. The Lighthouse is visible now that I'm lower down, its weak green light flashing from a promontory up ahead. I head out along the harbour towards it.

The slate is scattered with old things. Boulders set with fossils of underwater plants, fishbones pecked clean by migrating sea birds. Corroded metal and even the husk of an old ship half-embedded in the stone.

A patch of ice surprises me, but I manage to keep my footing. The green beam is stronger now, a sweeping light instead of a blip in the distance. I daydream as I settle on the slate, eating a piece of jerky, sipping water out of a canteen from my sack—I'll reach the Lighthouse, and the Lighthouse keeper will be there with a weathered old face. He'll look at my passage, and say, "well done!" Then, he'll signal the ship from across the sea, to take me to the good lands where it's warm and where I won't have to deal with people like Zan who don't believe.

"Oi!" A rough voice echoes.

I quickly tie my sack shut and stand.

"You! Going to the Lighthouse, are you?" I find the source of the voice: a figure staggering over the slate towards me.

"Aren't you?" I reply, trying to broaden my shoulders under the raincloak.

"What?" they shout even though I'm only a few metres away. They lurch to a stop, panting. "Take me with you."

"Why? Don't you have your passage?"

Their face contorts. "I lost it, somewhere. I can't find it. I've looked everywhere!"

"You can't go without one."

"Please," they say, their knees buckling. "Say I'm with you, say I'm family—" Their breath rattles. Their hands spread out towards me, o   ne of them red with blood.

"You're injured," I realise. "You should go back to town."

They shake their head, tears gathering in a storm. "I won't make it."

The cliff is too steep, too many stairs. They would fall. They would wear a yellow raincloak and freeze to death.

"You need your own passage," I tell them. "You can't leave without one."

The storm breaks over their face, contorting features, their sobs howling wind.

Nothing more to do, I find the Lighthouse ahead and leave the unworthy one behind. Gradually, their cries grow silent. The pressure on my chest eases. They were a test. They probably weren't even really bleeding. A trick. Red paint to lure me in and steal my passage. I cast a look over my shoulder—nothing to catch in the rock-scattered field behind.

The Lighthouse takes on detail the closer I get. Its beam sweeps left to right across the harbour floor once every couple of minutes, washing the stone in green-tinged light. The tower's original surface is unknowable—long tusks of ice are twisted

Safe Passage

around it, hanging from the octagonal eve in an upside-down crown. The wind off the black sea has shaped and pointed them back towards the island. The frozen monument to my escape is magnificent. Awe-inspiring.

My foot hits water—a cold submerged splash—and I pull back. A channel about ten metres wide blocks my way. I search the shore for a crossing point, but there isn't one. The channel has probably spent hundreds of years gathering spill-over from the black sea and run-off from storms. Why it isn't frozen over, I can't begin to guess. My soaked foot is beginning to numb. But there's no way around it. I have to cross.

Over the water, I can make out a path up the gentle incline to the Lighthouse. I let my sack of possessions fall at my feet. I take off my raincloak, shivering instantly. Removing the canister from my belt, I roll it in the waterproof material.

I take one step into the channel, the shock of cold setting my teeth on edge. I grip the precious bundle overhead in both hands. Everything else I own will have to stay behind. *If that's what I have to do.* I take another step. *To pass.* Another, up to my thighs now. *To be worthy.* A small yelp escapes my lips as the icy water laps over my groin, my waist. *I'll do it.*

The bottom of the channel falls away and I kick frantically, managing to keep my arms and head above water as I half-swim, half-flounder until there's rock under my feet again. I push forward against the current, my body numb and shivering as I splash up onto the other side.

Catching my breath, I turn back and pick out my abandoned sack keeled over like a dead beetle. All the mementoes of my family, my friends, my old life—I've been freed from them. Now the Lighthouse keeper will know that I've sacrificed everything to get here.

The thought warms me as I unwrap the canister and return it to my belt. I drape the raincloak over my shoulders, then

179

reconsider. Isn't it part of my old life, just as much as the rest of it? A reminder of the island. Of Zan.

With a violent wrench, I pull the raincloak off me and toss it into the channel. The green-black material spreads over the surface, the two sleeves filling, drawing the cloak deep underwater.

The path is gravel, weaving slightly as it leads up the slope to the Lighthouse. The beam bathes me in its intensity. With each step, I feel my worries falling away. I've come through the harbour unscathed with my passage intact. I have nothing to fear.

The eternal ice covers the base of the Lighthouse, making it hard to find solid footing. But I find the door, a slab of red framed in sharp ivory icicles. I half-expect it to be locked, yet when I turn the simple door handle, it pushes open with ease.

"Hello?" The room is dark. I shut the door behind me, one hand gripping the canister on my hip. Water drips from my clothes onto the bare floor. Details appear from the dim interior. First, the ragged floral curtains covering the window over a kitchen sink. A bare wooden table and chair. A cold cast-iron wood stove.

Of course, the Lighthouse keeper would be upstairs, keeping an eye on the great beacon. How long will it take to send a message to bring the ship across? I mount the first step of the dim winding staircase, my hand finding the cold rail. I hope he has a warm meal and a bed waiting for me.

My body is completely numb from the cold. In the darkness, I am just a jumble of thoughts ascending the stairs, a spirit without a body. The idea paralyses me until my pounding heartbeat drives it out. I take the stairs two at a time, desperate for his friendly voice to say "well done", because I have done well, I've made it all the way here, haven't I?

I barrel through the white door at the top of the stairs into a wide room. A counter covered in a lit panel of digital gauges sits in front of the wall-to-wall viewing window. There is no chair, no radio, nothing made for human comfort. The viewing room of the Lighthouse is stark. Empty.

Safe Passage

A huge hum pours down from the ceiling as the automated lamp oscillates overhead, throwing light out as far as it can across the black sheet of water. The panoramic window shows the sea. No other land, no other sky. Just the beam of sickly green combing the waves, right to left. Right to left.

The friendly old Lighthouse keeper from my imagination is nowhere to be seen. But still, there's a presence in the empty room. A slight distortion over the control board, like a sheen of spilled lamp oil. Before I can second-guess myself, I unscrew the lid from the canister and remove the pristine piece of paper from inside.

"I have safe passage," I say, and hold it out.

The green beam fills the window—right to left.

The distortion shimmers, and I hear something, just on the edge of knowing. Sharp and repetitive. Unkind.

"I did everything I was supposed to!" I tell the distortion. "I survived the cliff stairs. I ignored the distraction. I left my old life on the banks and crossed the channel. I made it to the Lighthouse with my passage intact! I deserve to be taken across to the warm lands!"

The distortion swells and approaches. I hold the passage steady. The oil-like sheen covers my feet, makes them disappear. Invisibility takes my legs, my torso. Then the pain begins. A thousand stabbing needles in my toes, up through my calves—

"Shhh," a voice whispers inside me as the distortion consumes my chest, my arms. The useless paper flutters to the floor.

"You humans and your complicated stories," the voice continues. "They bring you to me, so I cannot complain. But if you were wise and knew what the ships of old knew..."

I lose taste, lose smell, lose sound, lose sight—all become the voice inside that I am now becoming. "What did I do wrong?" I whimper.

"You did nothing wrong. This is what happens to all who come here."

"But the Lighthouse…passage…" I grasp for the words, but they are gone.

"Now you understand," the creature soothes as it takes me. "The Lighthouse is not a beacon. It should be given a wide berth. Get too close, and you'll be dashed on the rocks. Consumed by the fathomless sea."

"For the old humans," we say as one, "a lighthouse was a harbinger of death."

Not Sideways, but Upwards

by Charles Wilkinson

Outside the window of The Balefire, the Oxfordshire countryside turned blond: the grass verges on the other side of the road bleached and brittle; the crops in the fields creaming and yellow in the heat; the honeyed stone of the farmhouses drier and paler, as if encrusted by unremitting sun. Matthew Wells lifted his pint, allowing the noonday glare to dance on the dimples and shift its swirling gold through amber.

From where he was sitting in the front bar, he could just make out the folly on the top of its hill, smudged by the heat haze. The reason why Sir John Spelman, an eighteenth-century squire, built the tower in the shape of a lighthouse, remained elusive, bewildering local historians and researchers from the universities alike; nor had anyone succeeded in deciphering the arcane inscriptions that decorated the building's interior. That there could be no practical application of the purpose for which the structure was supposedly intended appeared plain: it was over ninety miles to the coast and thus too far away to serve a discernible function.

Just as Matthew drained his pint, George Place, a man who believed himself to be widely respected as a geologist, although he held no paid position in that discipline, emerged from behind him.

"I'll get that," he said, pointing a finger that might have been purloined from an ossuary, at the empty glass.

Matthew hesitated for a moment. He regarded Place as at best an irritation and at worst an egregious fantasist. "Oh, very well," he muttered. "If you must."

"My pleasure."

As ever Place was impervious to the slight. No matter how curt Matthew was, the man always bounced back, ready to offer a thousand favours, large or small.

But now that the rivers had dried up what else was there to do but drink? Matthew turned towards the bar and watched as Place, an epicene figure with sparse sandy hair and oversized spectacles, ordered the drinks.

"I've been asked to give a lecture at the village hall in Little Banting, said Place, as he returned with the beer. "I know it's hardly Balliol, but it's pleasing all the same, don't you think?"

"They've a taste for fiction at Little Banting, have they?"

Place laughed without humour and pushed his glasses back onto the bridge of his nose. "If only you'd *read* me, Wells, you'd discover that all my views are both carefully argued, supported by empirical evidence and, alas for Planet Earth, as far from fiction as it's possible for any text to be."

"I'm afraid I pay no attention to self-published authors. I don't even read articles unless they've been peer-reviewed."

"That's your loss. It means you've no access to work done outside the academic establishment. Still, I'd be grateful if you'd mention my talk …in certain quarters …quadrangles, perhaps. There must be some people at the university who take a more broadminded view than yours."

When they'd first met, Matthew had made the mistake of admitting that, although he now worked for a government-funded project, he'd once held a research fellowship at an Oxford college. Since then Place had attributed to him a connection with the university's Department of Geology that he did not possess.

"As I've made clear, I'm a professional hydrologist, I've no…"

"But our fields overlap. Now more so than ever, you'll admit."

"I'll concede nothing of the sort," said Matthew, rising on rickety feet and holding onto the top of his armchair. "Thanks for the drink, George," he continued, reluctantly using his Christian name so as not seem ungracious in the face of generosity. "I think I'd better move around a bit before my joints seize up."

That night the heat in Matthew's room was almost palpable, rendering sleep out of reach. Now that Place and he were thrown together as the last residents in the hotel, it was hard not to think about him and his manifold absurdities. Place's principal theory was that the ancient seas that covered Oxfordshire in the Jurassic and Mesozoic periods continued to exist, immanent in nature in a way that he was unable to explain with any precision, a curious view to take when the county was experiencing the worst drought in living memory.

At midnight, Matthew tried to think of something else. He'd been idle and half drunk for several days now. His mouth was so dry that since retiring he'd made repeated visits to the sink, only to summon up a few dribbles of water from the tap. Tomorrow, he must take a walk over to Boxe Hall, the seat of the Spelmans from the sixteenth to the early nineteenth century, but now owned by The National Trust. Perhaps he'd learn more about the lighthouse, a building to which he'd so far been denied admission for reasons that remained unclear.

It wasn't until the small hours that he began to drift off, dozing in the watershed that lies between wakefulness and sleep. At first, he thought of himself as some long extinct life-form submerged in the shallow seas that had once covered Oxfordshire.

He was at rest, in a region before human thought existed. Then he imagined himself as porous; absorbing, sponge-like, the warmth of brackish waters. He was part of an ancient landscape, subsisting in a forgotten geography. At last, somewhere between three and four in the morning, he was no longer aware of the borders of his own body as he drifted into dreams of lakes, deltas, lagoons, the immemorial movements of sand and gravel, coral's slow growth, the short lives of sea urchins and shellfish.

※

Having missed breakfast by several hours, Matthew contented himself with a cup of instant coffee in his room. Fierce sunlight fell through the window patching the single bedsheet with elongated white diamonds. At eleven o'clock, as he lay stretched out in his favourite seat in the front bar, he felt dehydrated, a stick of dry wood, his skin fragmenting bark. He glanced at his watch. The bar would open soon and then he'd able to buy himself a can of cold beer, which might temporarily anaesthetise the dull ache behind his forehead. He recalled his resolution to visit Boxe Hall. Shouldn't he make an effort to break the debilitating routine of the last few days? After all, more alcohol would, in the long run, make his headache worse. He forced himself to his feet and tottered outside. Within seconds, he felt perspiration pooling under his armpits; his forehead slithered with sweat that threatened to fry him, bubbling and spitting across his face. For a moment, he was tempted to return to the comparative shade of the bar. But perhaps it would prove to be cooler inside Boxe Hall, with its small mullioned windows and thick stone walls.

It came as a relief to walk under the shade of the avenue of beech trees that lined the approach to the entrance of the hall. His knees crumbling, the cartilage caving in, he was unsteady on his feet, but at least the hot weather had lessened the pain of his arthritis. Caught in the intense light of near mid-day, the honey-coloured masonry of the hall took on the texture of edibility, as if the ancient stones could be prized out of the façade to melt on the tongue like toffee. The entrance was open and as soon as Matthew stepped onto the flagstone floor he felt the temperature drop by a few degrees.

Inside, a young man dressed in a blue uniform was seated behind a table covered with guide books and postcards. A peaked cap gave him a nautical air.

He appeared unlike the tweed-clad ladies and retired gentlemen who customarily composed the hard core of helpers at National Trust Properties.

"A ticket for one, sir? Today all takings will be donated to The Company of New Mariners."

"Well, that's one organisation that I've never heard of."

"We've been established here since the sixteenth century. Sir John Spelman, who owned the manor house and the surrounding estate, was one of our earliest benefactors. Would you like a guided tour, sir –or perhaps you'd prefer to look around at your leisure?"

"I'll be fine by myself, although I may have a few questions to put to you later."

"By all means. We're very quiet today and so there won't be a problem."

Matthew made his way into a room with walnut panelling and sparse furnishing, although there were family portraits on the wall. He paused in front of the one of Spelman. The bewigged squire was painted slightly off centre, as if reflecting its subject's desire to escape beyond the edge of the composition. His pale blue eyes gazed out of the frame, his look that of an uneasy visionary or a man staring at a dot on the far horizon. He wore a bilious green waistcoat. Behind him, in defiance of the facts of geography, the artist had depicted a shrunken Boxe Hall in close proximity to

Folly Hill, which was surmounted by a disproportionately large lighthouse.

Pictures of Spelman's descendants showed how a strong family physical resemblance persisted through the centuries. But what struck Matthew most was that so many of the artists had captured what appeared to be an inherited expression of disquiet, as if the scene in front them might dissolve at any moment, giving way to horrors that could no longer remain hidden. A small boy depicted in a miniature was shown wide-eyed and white with terror.

A door, so small that Matthew had to bend down to pass through it, opened into what must have been the squire's study. A blue globe was positioned on the left-hand side of a wooden desk. As he rotated it, he saw that there was hardly any land, only a few tiny islands, green bacteria, survivors in the last days before the final triumph of water, the world as one seamless ocean. A pair of gold spectacles was at rest next to a leather-bound commonplace book. Matthew picked it up. On the frontispiece was a quotation, written in a careful hand: *'Thus saith the Lord, Ye shall not see Wind and nor shall Ye see Rain; yet the Valleys shall be filled with Water.' 2 Kings 3. 17*. Further quotations followed, both in poetry and prose, many alluding to the destructive power of water and the desirability of escape; others mentioned beacons, bonfires, watchtowers, lighthouses and balefires, mainly as symbols of hope and deliverance.

On the wall above the desk, there was a child's sampler in an ornate frame. Various local landmarks were depicted without regard to the rules of perspective, including Boxe Hall, The Balefire Inn and Folly Lighthouse. In the foreground were v-shaped blue stitches, which appeared to do duty for waves, and a fleet of small boats, some filled with gargantuan sailors that would surely have caused such flimsy vessels to capsize. At the bottom, in letters that seemed to mimic a child's handwriting were the words *'Till ye be left as a beacon upon the top of a mountain, and as an ensign on a hill.' Martha Spelman, 8 Years, 1834.*

The remainder of the rooms contained little of interest to Matthew: a couple of Georgian elbow chairs, chests for blankets, a four-poster bed, nineteenth-century wardrobes and dressers. Only one of the remaining family portraits contained hints that John Spelman's pursuit of pharology had been more than a personal preoccupation. A large oil, attributed to the studio of Sir Joshua Reynolds, showed Sir Ralf Spelman, Bart. in a similar pose to his ancestor. Once again, the Folly Lighthouse was shown in the background landscape, although this time the hill was an island surrounded by improbably blue water. In his right hand, the baronet held a model of a black boat, a barque with three black sails.

As he made his way back into the entrance hall, Matthew saw that the man at the desk had been joined by a colleague who was dressed in the same nautical fashion. They were conversing in confidential tones. Matthew stood still in the doorway and listened. Although the language they were speaking had an appealing musicality, it was so unfamiliar that he was unable to make out a single word with clarity; he couldn't even hazard a guess as to what tongue it might be. The minute he stepped forward the rhythm of the voices changed. Neither of the men turned in his direction. How could they not have heard his footsteps on the parquet flooring? He moved ever closer, slowly. The tempo of the conversation increased, its sound somehow metallic. The words seemed to be running backwards as if an old tape were being rewound at high speed. And then, when Matthew was no more than a matter of five metres away, a few words of English, isolated but recognisable, bubbled up in the otherwise unintelligible torrent of discourse. Within seconds, they were speaking fully in English, the subject apparently unremarkable: the prospect of rain.

"Is that in the forecast?" Matthew asked. "It would certainly be a relief."

"No," said the man who'd sold Matthew his ticket. "We were just saying that they'll be no break in the weather, not until …"

He appeared to pause in a fit of embarrassment, as if he'd only just pre-empted a monstrous verbal blunder.

"Until what?" asked Matthew.

"Until the wind changes," said the second man, evidently extemporizing.

"But there is no wind."

"Yes, yes," said the man, unaccountably flustered. "That's the cause of the problem: there's no wind."

Matthew picked up a postcard of the lighthouse and peered at the small print, as if some further insight into the prevailing meteorological conditions might be found there. "What language were you speaking just now?" he asked, looking up sharply.

The two men glanced at each other, their expressions puzzled. "English," said the second man. "We were speaking in English. Would you like to buy that postcard, sir? We also have a lithograph of the lighthouse, which you may buy either framed or unframed."

"No …I don't think so. But tell me … when will Folly Lighthouse be open to visitors?"

"It's been shut for the last twenty-five years."

"But there must be a caretaker; someone capable of giving genuine scholars a guided tour. I've heard there are some very interesting inscriptions inside."

"It's said there is a caretaker, but as I've already stated – no one, however, distinguished, has been admitted to the lighthouse for a quarter of a century."

"And we also have," interrupted the first man, picking up a cardboard box that had been stowed away under the desk, "these models of the Folly Lighthouse. All the proceeds from the sales are donated to the Guild of Pharos. One can never be sure when one might be in need of a lighthouse, don't you think?"

※

Not Sideways, But Upwards

On returning to The Balefire, Matthew was surprised to see a group of young men, dressed in the uniform of the Company of New Mariners, checking into the hotel.

Was a convention taking place? A hotel in the middle of Oxfordshire appeared to be an unlikely venue for such an event. He lingered in the lobby, affecting an interest in some posters that advertised local attractions, including tours of the university – and punting, which must be proving problematic now the rivers had either dried up or been reduced to a sluggish trickle.

The men were addressing the manager in English, their tones precise, almost pedantic. And hadn't there also been something unexpected about the way their colleagues at Boxe Hall had spoken: their accents unremarkable, received pronunciation, but the diction somehow too studied. Although they appeared to be native speakers, the comparative lack of idioms, the slightly stiff formality in the phrasing had suggested English was not their first language.

In the bar, Place was seated in a corner, his long legs outstretched. The intense sunlight fell on the polished wooden furniture, lacquering it with brilliance whilst also accentuating the darkness of the shade. Place was positioned midway in this chiaroscuro: his stone-white trousers and shirt newly washed and shining; his chest less visible, his face almost immersed in darkness. Now they were no longer the sole residents, Matthew felt an unexpected urge to speak to him.

"I see that we are not alone."

"Oh? How so?"

"We have been joined by the Company of New Mariners."

"Well, they were to be expected, weren't they?"

"Not by me."

"I see that you still haven't read my books. If you had, you'd realise that the kind of climatic conditions we've been experiencing can only result in a … retaliation … from the natural world."

"Yes, of course. I suppose we can expect thunderstorms … once this dry spell breaks."

"No, not thunderstorms."

"Well, what then?"

"If you can bring yourself to attend my talk in Little Banting, it will be explained to you in detail."

"Would you like a drink?"

"Certainly, if you're headed in that direction."

As he waited for their pints to be poured, Matthew reflected that there'd been a shift in their relationship: he was now the supplicant, buying the drinks, begging for information that would elucidate his predicament. When he returned, he found that Place had drawn up his legs so that he was seated upright in the darkness, his head almost entirely occluded, his words delivered as if from an oracle.

"I'm thinking of walking to the lighthouse this afternoon," Matthew continued. "Apparently, there is a caretaker up there. Perhaps he'll let me in …for a consideration."

"No one will enter the lighthouse until it is necessary."

"And so there's no caretaker —or if there is, he's not allowed into the lighthouse either?"

"It is a matter of waiting until the conditions are met. Then whatever actions are required will be taken."

"By whom?"

"Investigating these matters will neither delay nor postpone what is inevitable."

There was evidently nothing to be gained by listening to such gnomic nonsense, although he'd no doubt he was being advised, in an infuriatingly oblique fashion, not to walk up to the lighthouse. But now for the first time he understood that he was unable to articulate why he wanted to go there. All he knew was that from his arrival he'd felt the pull of the building, an imperative to enter it at all costs. And yet how could it be connected to what had been happening to him?

For once, Place appeared disinclined to expound his theories. The outline of his head was no longer clearly visible against the dark panelling. The marks that were his eyes, mouth and nose seemed be emerging half-formed from the grain of the wood. But his posture, and the way his white-knuckled hands gripped the armrests, implied that he was waiting for something expected and yet not fully understood, an imminent event, an alteration of such an unfathomable kind that it could never be comprehended until after its occurrence.

❋

At half past three, Matthew set out for the lighthouse. He decided to take the stoutest of his walking sticks, the blackthorn, with him. Although he'd deliberately ventured out when the sun was past its zenith, the heat was now no less intense than it had been at midday; as if every stone, rock and millimetre of the road ahead had been storing the warmth all day, only to exhale it in the afternoon.

Once he'd left the environs of the village, the landscape changed: the mud in the brooks as stiff as parchment, the fields sere and cracked, the blue distance blurred. He could almost sense the trees digging their roots deeper in quest of water.

The lighthouse was clearly visible, emerging from the wood around it, the leafage now tinged with drought-induced yellows and browns. The white stone of the building scintillated as though about to throw out its beams hours before nightfall. In the distance he saw a figure, most probably a man, progressing along the path towards him. Matthew waved his stick but received no acknowledgement.

Now the way ahead was more stone and earth than tarmac. He'd estimated by eye that the walk was no more than a stroll of fifteen minutes, but surely he'd already been on the move for more than twenty. Was he no closer to his goal? If anything the lighthouse looked further away.

Then the man, who appeared no nearer to him in spite of the fact that they were both walking towards one another, seemed to melt for a moment into the heat haze, his limbs elongated, even detached, before then reassembling himself in his true proportions. Matthew attempted to pick up speed, but he was breathing heavily and his shirt, wet with perspiration, was stuck to his back. Sweat trickled down the inside of his legs. He could even feel the warmth of the road through the thin soles of his shoes. Then as he lifted his stick once more in salutation, he tripped, falling face downwards onto a stretch of melting tarmac. When he tried to lever himself upright the palms of his hand stuck fast to the ground. Was he fated to remain here until he was found frazzled to death days later? With an effort, he managed to free himself by rolling his body sideways onto the earth. Even then he took a few patches of the road with him.

Now that he was upright, he saw that every object more than a few metres in front of him was blurred, shimmering behind a distorting veil of haze. The lighthouse was now double its normal width, as if it were being stretched like gum in the heat. Wrenching his blackthorn stick free from the gluey tarmac, he battled on. The scene in front of him was so disarranged as to deny him all knowledge of normality; yet a stable world, still governed by the ordinary rules of time and space, surely survived on the other side of the mirage. At least the direction he'd needed to take to reach the lighthouse was apparent. And the way the building shifted from side to side seemed dictated by his own irregular progress, as he took care to skirt round the tarmac.

A quarter of an hour later, the lighthouse sank down under the cover of the wood. As Matthew peered up through the canopy, he understood that he was now at the bottom of Folly Hill. The earth underfoot was hard, the cool green light correcting the chaos of his previous impressions. The ancient trunk and branches stood mercifully still, absorbing the silence in a place where not so much as a dry leaf rustled across the desiccated undergrowth, its crumbling brambles, the bony collage of twigs and dead ferns.

He'd just started to follow the path upwards when he was disturbed by movement above. As he stared up, he thought he detected, for no more than a matter of seconds, a man in a green coat seated on a branch, his thin legs dangling. But as soon as he tried to make out more detail, the figure faded. Perhaps it was no more than a momentary interplay of leafage and light that the eye had misinterpreted. The way ahead was steeper now; the path became a track that was only intermittently visible, unless he used his stick to part the layers of encrusted vegetation.

Five minutes later, when pausing for breath, he felt the gentlest of touches on his shoulder. He span round. Sir John Spelman, seemingly as solid as if he'd had just stepped out of the canvas that had contained him for four centuries, stood in front of him. The apparition raised its green arms as though about to envelop him, dragging him down into a grave of foliage. Then, at the very instant that Matthew stepped backwards, the image began to dismantle itself, merging its coat and sallow face into the forested bank behind it. It left its outstretched fingers till last.

Matthew sank to his knees. Exhaustion and heat must have unhinged him, he thought – yet was what he'd seen real on another level? Was Spelman the lighthouse's caretaker, dutiful in spite of the unending hours of his life in death? And if Matthew continued on his mission what powers might his opponent prove to have? He could not be sure what he'd seen was no more than a harmless manifestation, discernable for less than a minute. Next time it might materialise in a more permanent form. He turned round and began to retrace his steps.

Within twenty minutes he emerged from the woods. At once, he became aware that in his absence a change had taken place in the landscape. The sky was still an unblemished blue, but the light was brassier, as though the sun's yolk had been tinged with blood. The ground was spongy, and with every pace more water was pushed up from below. Then, not more than half a mile ahead of him, he saw the earth had cracked open, forming a blade-like lake. As he trudged on, steaming pools of water pushed through the surface. Yet as far as he knew there was no possibility of latent geothermal activity in the area. He watched the dry fields fissure, crack into jigsaws of earth that flooded, turning into gleaming flatlands. This alteration owed nothing to any rainfall that might have fallen whilst he was in the woods. Then he recalled Place's theory, which he'd dismissed as ludicrous: all the seas that had once covered Oxfordshire remained, immanent within a hidden realm of nature, ready to rise up from below. They were the watery guardians, waiting to restore the burnt and wounded earth.

※

From the front bar of The Balefire, not far from the high spot on which the beacon once burnt in the days of the Virgin Queen, Matthew looks across the level waters as far as Folly Hill, on top of which the chalk-white of the lighthouse stands out against a metallic blue lustre, the arc of the late afternoon sky.

He'd only a few memories of his rescue two days before. How he'd tried to skirt round what had been at first a long narrow lake, only to watch it break its banks and flood the area around him. Somehow he managed to clamber up into the branches of dead oak, where he'd fallen asleep, cradled in the right angle between a bough and the trunk. Then he'd been awoken by the sounds of an outboard motor.

Not Sideways, But Upwards

He recalls the agility of an officer from the Company of New Mariners as he climbed the tree and tied a rope around the bough. *At least I'm alive* Matthew tells himself –*but to what end?* Has he suffered some form of cognitive damage? His memories of the past are now partial, as if he is at least half imprisoned in an eternal present tense, with limited access to all that once enabled him to negotiate his way in the world. But what disturbs him most is that nobody, not even the manager of The Balefire, is speaking English. George Place refuses to utter a single phrase in what Matthew had assumed was the man's first language. There is little to do but remain in the window seat and watch the inexorable rise of the waters.

The beer garden is flooded. Matthew has tried speaking in French; all but a few elementary phrases have been erased from his memory. At nightfall, an undercurrent of disquiet runs through the room. The New Mariners glance nervously at their watches or peer through the window. Then, without forewarning, the lighthouse throws out a brilliant, sky-severing beam – not sideways, but upwards, as if it has been turned into a preternaturally powerful torch, emitting a radiance not quite of this world. A signal for some hidden force to descend?

Within the hour, the black barques arrive. The woods around Folly Hill are all but submerged, leaving only a cone of land surmounted by the lighthouse. It is time to leave. The New Mariners help Matthew to embark, their manner neither rough nor solicitous. The barque cleaves a way across waters braided with the patterns of reflected stars. Minutes later he is at last inside the lighthouse. The walls are covered by inscriptions in a language he cannot decipher, but on the plaques there are carvings, symbols, a few perhaps phallic, others that might represent lighthouses or rockets. Sir John Spelman emerges from a group of New Mariners. He is holding a green helmet.

"Come, Master Matthew. We have other garb for you. You shall wear this new headgear, if it should so please you."

But there is no choice. Within seconds, The New Mariners have him strapped in; it is as if his skull has dissolved. He has a new cranium now. Yet surely some explanation is owed to him? He attempts to struggle: to kick, to spit, to flail his arms, but not one limb, not one sinew, not a solitary tissue or cell responds. Then he's no longer in league with his own DNA; he is an experiment, being walked up the spiral staircase to the spacecraft's deck, and now the sport of an invisible puppeteer. Sir John points upwards, his gesture, more than an indication, is an acknowledgement to whatever forces have allowed him to persist through the falling dust of long centuries. Matthew is powerless, held in ambiguity. The change, when it occurs, lies beyond the certainty of exact comprehension. Are the suns and planets plunging towards him or is he being launched to the limits, as if to return his ashes to stardust?

House of the She-Devil

by Tom Johnstone

"It should be here."

"Well, it isn't, is it?"

Julia sighs, looks from her phone to the empty grassland leading to chalk cliffs where the land ends abruptly and alarmingly, giving way to the blue expanse of the English Channel. Inexplicable disappearances are not unheard of around here. But the vanishing she's thinking of is that of a woman, not a vast local landmark. She remembers seeing Selina Nightingale's wide, dark eyes on posters plastered onto every lamp-post in town offering a £10,000 reward, a face then whose discovery is as lucrative as it is unlikely. *Last seen wandering near Beachy Head --* it seems pretty obvious to Julia what happened.

"I suppose Google Maps couldn't possibly be wrong, could it?" David suggests, breaking into her thoughts.

She glares at him. It was his idea to come here. He said the idea tickled him – staying in the converted lighthouse near Beachy Head where they filmed the serial based on Fay Weldon's book, or at least the bit set in the high tower where Mary Fisher dwelled. She stares at the phone as if it will provide a solution to the mystery of the disappearing lighthouse. But after cheerfully informing her, *You have reached your destination,* the officious, artificial female voice remains unhelpfully silent. She wonders if *her* voice sounded like that as *she* guided David's hands around her body and his cock inside her.

But that never happened. David has assured her of that, time and time again.

Nevertheless she hasn't been able to shake off the feeling that something has been going on. This is why they're having this little weekend break at this 'unique Airbnb experience', according to the blurb, a kind of second honeymoon in all but name. Julia looks in vain for a lighthouse, or even a house. It would be hard to miss it in the almost featureless, though undulating, landscape, broken only by the narrow winding road that brought them here.

There is something else splitting the sward. With a gasp, she notices an almost imperceptible line running along the green expanse to the left of their car, sectioning off a D-shaped wedge at the edge of the cliff: A hair-line crack.

"It's going to go," she murmurs.

Her stomach lurches as she imagines the ground underneath them giving way, plunging the car containing them into the sea.

"Go…"

Maybe he doesn't hear her, or doesn't understand. She grabs for the steering wheel, her lungs stalling like a car failing a hill-start, her vision blurring as if she's under water.

"Drive!" she hisses, with what feels like her last breath.

Responding to the panic in her voice, David puts the car into first gear and releases the clutch so the car shoots up the winding road rather precipitously. She hears a faint rumble in the distance, which could be a rock-fall or it could be the blood rushing through her head. Then it's replaced by a loud barking, like an aggressive, pugnacious, squat dog. But the sharp, guttural noises are words…

"…the hell do you think you were playing at, Julia? You could have got us killed, you silly cow!"

"Look!" she calls out, grateful something tall and cylindrical has thrust into view to distract her from her panic attack and

David's tirade. "There it is! Must have been hidden by the brow of the hill."

Her breathing is back to normal now. So are her eyes, apart from a slight watery shimmering at the edge of her vision. The appearance of the lighthouse has steadied her as if she were a ship on the point of foundering on unseen rocks. Suddenly she bursts out laughing, partly in relief from the tension before. It's so solemn and white and phallic, towering over them in their little tin box on wheels.

"What's so funny?" David asks, then mutters something about how it's a hundred metres or so inland from where it should be.

✻

"Do please come in," says the man in the black velvet mask covering the lower portion of his face which mutes his voice, as he introduces himself as Geraint. He could be smiling but Julia can't tell from his eyes. "Hand sanitisers are to your left. I trust you found us without too much difficulty…"

David and Julia exchange glances, their own faces covered by pale-blue surgical masks that make their eyes more eloquent than words could be, his expression a glare she interprets as conveying suppressed fury still at her antics in the car. What a fun trip this is going to be!

"Actually there was a little bit of confusion," says Julia. "Has the lighthouse moved lately?"

"Now you come to mention it," says the mellifluous though muffled voice making the black velvet ripple, "frequently…"

He must have seen the way his new guests' eyebrows jumped, because he elaborates.

"Coastal erosion means every so often we have to move the lighthouse a little further inland."

At the Lighthouse

She remembers the ominous fracture in the ground, the dark-green sward looking ready to give way and expose the white chalk beneath with an earth-shattering rumble at any second.

Before David can pedantically ask how this feat of civil engineering is achieved, the host's surgically-gloved left hand ushers them into the vestibule, his right squirting translucent gel with an astringent pineapple smell onto their outstretched palms, his veiled mouth unleashing a stream of instructions, recommendations and admonitions about the house rules, breakfast and check-out times, local attractions and places to eat.

"One thing I should warn you," he says, his blue eyes grave and solemn. "Beachy Head is known for attracting those who consider themselves to have reached the end of their road. Others end up going in a similar fashion when they stray too near the edge. Others still, like a certain young lady I could mention, simply disappear. Try not to join them…

"All guests are invited into the lounge at 1700 hours for cocktails before dinner," he finishes, barely pausing for breath.

❋

The room is cramped and smells of pot-pourri and hand-sanitiser, but that doesn't seem to matter. Although their faces are covered, Julia can see the mirth in David's eyes echoing her own, and as soon as the door closes she collapses into fits of giggles. She's not sure why, considering the macabre portentousness of the latter part of his monologue, but unlike earlier she's glad to hear David joining in with his more restrained chuckles. They shouldn't really laugh about the cliff's reputation as a suicide hotspot, or a young woman's disappearance – Selina Nightingale's family must be beside themselves with worry – yet there's something about Geraint's bearing, a certain prissy self-importance. David must have picked up on it too. It's as if hosting an Airbnb lighthouse is a life-or-death matter to him.

They both remove their masks. She sees David's smile and the gleam in his eyes. It's nice that they still find the same things funny.

"Shall we...?" she begins.

"Unpack?" he asks.

"Fuck that," she says, pulling the dark-red curtains closed, shutting out the vertiginous view of the crumbling cliff, a few metres away. "Christen the room, I meant."

He looks surprised, almost shocked. They have become strangers since the children flew the nest. Was that the glue that bound them together? But there's still something there, despite his suspected betrayal. After all, an encounter between strangers can be very exciting. They begin undressing each other, not frantically, but slowly, laughing at the awkwardness of it. It's been a long time after all – months.

Afterwards, she cries. She's not sure why. David wants to know. He seems affronted, almost furious.

"Why are you crying?" he demands, his eyes wild and scared. "You came, didn't you?"

It's true. She did – so intensely, she felt as if the ground was vibrating. So did he, but when he did, his eyes were screwed tightly shut, so that she couldn't help wondering if he was visualising some other encounter.

※

On the way into the cocktail lounge, they notice a montage of photographs showing scenes from the BBC adaptation of *The Life and Loves of a She-Devil*. Dennis Waterman sulks behind large, thick-rimmed Nineteen Eighties spectacles and ginger moustache, next to a pouting Patricia Hodge, wispy auburn hair blowing in the wind. It reminds her of one of those restaurants that has a photo gallery of the celebrities who have visited, but this one can boast only two. Then again, it was on a TV location shoot, which makes it more special, she supposes.

"No sign of What's-Her-Name," David remarks.

"Who?" she asks.

"The She-Devil," he explains. "Julie Somebody," he adds. "That was the name of the actress who played her. Big lady with a monobrow and a mole on her chin."

"Funny name," says Julia.

"What? Julie?"

Of course not, she thinks. *That's almost my name.*

"No, 'Somebody'."

His laughter cuts through her.

"That's not her real name. Just couldn't remember it, that's all. Silly!"

"I was joking," she says, smiling limply at the belittling endearment he accompanies with an infantilising tweak on the nose he probably sees as affectionate. "I didn't *really* think her name was 'Somebody'."

"Of course not!" he says, echoing her private thoughts, his tone of voice conveying the opposite, as if he's trapped her in a childish error he can store up for later embarrassment, as a way of getting one over on her – as well as his own back later for his secret, stewing grievances. She pictures an after-dinner anecdote showing her up – *She really thought I was saying her name was 'Somebody'!*

The other guests begin arriving, two couples, one mid-fifties like them, the other in their early thirties. Two by two, they file into the cocktail lounge, where they sit like suspects assembled at the conclusion of an Agatha Christie crime novel, awaiting their host as if he were a detective about to stride in and expose one of them with a long, elaborate exposition of motive, opportunity and method of execution. The middle-aged man, who introduces himself as James Godfrey and his wife as Sandra, wears a navy-blue blazer and looks older than David, his face flushed ruddy above his white shirt, as if cocktail hour has already begun for him. He winks at Julia as he sits down next to her, as close as physical distancing guidelines allow, which is closer than she likes. She reaches for David's hand but he all but snatches it away, leaning towards the younger woman in the denim skirt and low-cut blouse nearby, conversing with her in low, intimate tones that contrast sharply with the sniping, bickering and outright hostility of her own interactions with her husband.

"…A nice name." She catches the tail-end of one of his blandishments. She can't hear the words. "…To meet you, Tiffany."

Tiffany's partner glowers beside her. Julia has always known David has no shame and is vain enough to think he might be in with a chance with someone like that, but his combination of brass neck and desperate eagerness to please makes her stomach lurch with nausea, like seasickness. She has a sudden urge to answer a call of nature.

"Excuse me," she whispers, rising to leave and batting away David's placating hand, his innocent stare suggesting he has belatedly picked up on the hurt in her tone.

She rushes to find the toilet, feeling as if the ground is moving underneath her. It's like walking through the corridor of a ship in choppy waters. She hears a rumble, like the faint sound of thunder from outside. And yet it feels like it comes from within her.

Maybe she just needs to eat.

When she returns, David, who appears to have moved closer to 'Tiffany'. He snatches his hand away from her bare knee where it was hovering, a fleshy bird of prey, a fresh humiliation for Julia. In his other hand is a shot-glass. James asks in a slurred voice why the guy from *Minder* is on the wall. Geraint, who has arrived in her absence, offers her a cocktail as she returns to her seat. She declines, feeling the need to explain to the dozen inquiring eyes

At the Lighthouse

that she already feels seasick without adding spirits to the mix. The room suddenly feels awfully small, its rounded white-washed, wood-paneled walls seeming to lurch and the floor shifting under her feet.

"That need not be a problem," Geraint purrs in his Welsh lilt, as she collapses onto her chair. "I can make you a purely fruity one." This is the first time she has seen his full face. His smile is as condescending as his voice sounds, as if he's offering a non-alcoholic version of an adult drink to a child, night-black mask hanging like a cravat at his throat to allow him to drink, for he too clutches a cocktail glass. "To answer your question, Mr Godfrey, Dennis Waterman played the adulterous husband in the BBC serial adaptation of *The Life and Loves of a She Devil*, some scenes of which used this very lighthouse as a location…"

Julia glances at David, who stares into his glass, in contrast with the other guests who are all responding to the unusual guesthouse's claim to fame. Sandra Godfrey, thin and wispy and clad in grey tweed, scoffs at some whispered comment from her husband.

"I think I remember seeing it," she says in her high, nasal voice. "That woman who played the She Devil though…"

"Julie Somebody," David puts in, and everyone in the room apart from Julia laughs, pointedly refusing to look at her as if they are faintly ashamed to do so. Would it be paranoid to think that David has told that story in her absence? *She really thought I meant her surname was 'Somebody'!* He has this way of making her feel like a nobody sometimes.

"She was quite something," the wispy, tweedy woman finishes when the collective mirth subsides.

"Quite," says Geraint. "Now, are there any other questions?"

"Are we allowed up top where the light is?" asks Julia.

Geraint sighs wearily, as if he was expecting someone to ask that, but dreading it.

"The lamp room? No, I'm afraid not," he says. "It's closed for refurbishment at the moment."

Rather brusquely, even sulkily, he begins collecting the cocktail glasses.

※

The moon is too bright for Julia to sleep, the room too stuffy even with the window open the fraction its mechanism will permit, less than the girth of a human body, disabled possibly as precaution against suicides, as if the area's reputation also haunts the lighthouse itself. Pale rays seep under the curtains of the room – those of her eyelids too.

Even if it were dark enough to sleep, she couldn't. The row they had earlier when they returned to their room after dinner, when he'd still visibly drooled over Tiffany at the table, kept going round and round in her head. *You just can't help yourself!* she said. *I can*, he said, insisting he'd never been unfaithful to her, adding bitterly, dripping self pity, *But there's always a first time – maybe there will be…*

She lies awake listening to him snoring and muttering, wondering if she can make out *her* name when she thinks she sees his slack mouth smiling faintly in the moon-bleached dark. She wonders if he really does care for her as he insisted during their row. She thinks on balance he does, but then she remembers his lecherous behaviour earlier on. The cycle replays inside her head, a flower-petal scattering game of *Loves Me, Loves Me Not*. Its stuck-record rhythm keeps jerking her awake even when she does fall asleep, counting wolfish fears instead of sheep.

Then she hears the sound.

For the third time that day, she feels the ground vibrating beneath her, as if mighty engines are grinding into motion. Unlike earlier, she can't attribute the sensation to orgasm or nausea, although this time it might be David snoring, she supposes. Before she can decide whether she is sure that this is what it is, a new sound rends the night.

A low bellowing sob, echoing faintly from somewhere in the building.

That's it. There's no chance she's going to sleep now. Julia climbs out of bed, glancing back to see if she has woken David, but he slumbers on oblivious. She can feel a faint throbbing beneath her feet. Surely *that* can't be David snoring. The lighthouse is alive -- and moving! She goes over to the window, stepping carefully as if negotiating a storm-tossed ship, peers through the curtain to see the moonscape outside. The round, cratered lamp in the night sky shines on a cliff-face that is indeed retreating into the distance. She draws back from the window in wonder and disbelief, almost losing her balance as she feels the lurching motion underneath her. Geraint did say the lighthouse has to move from time to time, but she didn't think he meant like this…

Again she hears the desolate, lonesome sobbing. Though the timbre of the voice is deep, she cannot but think it's the weeping of a betrayed and abandoned woman.

She goes back to the bed, begins shaking David, who is still managing to sleep through it all. He stirs.

"What?" he murmurs, his eyes still closed.

"Wake up!" she says. "There's someone in distress – a woman I think."

"I can't hear anything."

He rolls over and flops back to sleep. Either that or he's pretending to. It reminds her of when the children were little and she would always be the one to tend to their crying at night. That seems so long ago in their empty nest. But like their infant mewlings, this sound reaches inside her and is impossible not to answer. She could have imagined it, she supposes. But then, she hears it again, louder and more insistent now, a keening wail of anguish and fury. Despairing of her husband's help, she goes out into the hallway, which is little more than a square of floor leading to a spiral staircase. She listens out for the repetition of the cry, so she can work out if it comes from above or below. She wonders if anyone else has heard it, but no one else is out of their room, so they are either too afraid to investigate, or like David, they prefer to ignore it. How can anyone sleep as the lighthouse moves? Then she recalls the comforting motion of the sleeper train to Edinburgh years ago.

The banshee howling echoes down the stairwell, so she begins gingerly climbing up, using the rope that serves as a banister to steady herself against the continuing lurching motion of the tower, the cries guiding her like a homing beacon, or indeed a lighthouse in a storm, until she reaches the door at the top marked with a handwritten CLOSED FOR REFURBISHMENT sign.

Another despairing sob that grasps her heart with needy fingers.

"Who's there?" she asks tentatively. "What's the matter?"

The only reply is another heart-rending cry.

She tries the handle, but the door is locked. She turns it, making it rattle impotently.

A surgically gloved hand clasps hers over the handle.

"I told you this area was out of bounds, Mrs Philips."

She can feel Geraint's breath on the back of her neck. Or rather she would be able to if he weren't wearing his black, velvet mask.

"There's someone in there in terrible distress," she says.

"I don't know what you're talking about," he says. "I can't hear anything. Now if you don't mind…"

And he moves his hand to her elbow, as if to guide her back down the stairs.

"Would you mind taking your hand off me?"

"I would mind," he says. "It seems to me, Mrs Philips, that you're tired. Your dreams are leaking out into the real world."

"But I haven't been asleep. I haven't been able to sleep."

"Precisely my point. Now why don't you come downstairs. I can prepare you a draught of Valerian that might be just the--"

A dreadful groan issues from behind the door.

"Ticket."

"There, you see? Don't tell me you can't hear that!"

"That's the engine kicking in."

His hand still maintains a firm grip on her elbow.

"The engine?"

He sighs. His grip slackens.

"She *is* the engine. Her pain is the power source that keeps the lighthouse going."

"But that's monstrous! We must go to her…" She pulls her elbow away, rubbing at its redness. "What do you mean, 'going'?" She remembers the way, when she looked out of the window, the cliff seemed to be retreating, or rather the lighthouse was moving away from it. He simply stares back at her, inscrutable behind his velvet mask.

"It is monstrous," he says eventually. "*She* is monstrous. But her suffering is necessary – to save the lighthouse from ruin."

She just stares at him, appalled.

"What would you have us do? Let the lighthouse crash into the sea? Perhaps you'd like to stay there in her place. You have a rich seam of pain in you, I can tell. It would provide enough fuel for another few years maybe. The current incumbent is almost worn out…"

He chuckles, making the velvet mask ripple. She wants to get away from him now. But he is blocking her way. She should push him, run down the spiral staircase, get David up, but then again, would he even wake?

"I can see you really want to go to her," Geraint coos, lulling her with his soothing voice. "Very well…"

He reaches for the bunch of keys hanging from his belt like those of a prison guard, selects the one that fits the door to the lamp room.

"Here you are, Mrs Philips," he announces, turning the key and throwing the door wide with a certain ceremonial flourish. "I give you… Our Lady of the Lamp Room."

It's dark in there, as the lighthouse's original function has long since been obsolete. Through the windowpanes that encircle the lamp room, the full moon's rays illuminate the figure within, clad in a tattered wedding dress that reveals grey, doughy flesh beneath. Except for the mouth that yawns open in a permanent cry, the face is covered, but not by a wedding veil. Instead, a faintly luminous, bulb-shaped helmet masks the rest of the woman's features. It has a kind of hatch on it, and is joined to the floor by a long cable. Julia feels she must go and comfort her, so she crosses the threshold hesitantly. The hatch on the helmet is opaque, and she fumbles with its catch to open it, so she can see the face. She's sure it will reveal the wide, dark eyes depicted on all those lamp-post posters, the face of Selina Nightingale.

"I wouldn't do that if I were you," Geraint calls, but she ignores him and the figure offers no resistance, not even a faint groan, so she persists with her efforts.

When she opens it, there is nothing there, just a grey blur above the yawning mouth.

Recoiling, she spins around to see the door to the lamp-room closing.

"I'll leave you two together for a while," says Geraint. "I can see you have much to discuss before Selina passes on her burden to you…"

She runs back to the door in time to hear the key turn in the lock. She hammers on the wood, shouting that her husband will miss her and come for her.

"Oh, I somehow doubt that," he says through the door.

And when she thinks about it, Julia finds it hard to disagree.

Cygnus

by Douglas Thompson

Now in the hour that melts with homesick yearning
the hearts of seafarers who've had to say
farewell to those they love, that very morning
hour when the new-made pilgrim on his way
feels a sweet pang go through him if he hears
far chimes that seem to knell the dying day...

- Dante Alighieri, The Divine Comedy,
Purgatorio, Canto VIII.

Interstellar rocket as lighthouse. The signature of the first blast into space of any precocious species, in this case ours. So went the conversation through the hours, and the hours were many, as Captain Catriona Breck and Lieutenant Robert Stevens travelled the 4.37 light years from Earth towards the planet Proxima Centauri b. Although it's not so hard after all once you're out there, in propulsion terms. In a frictionless vacuum, any engine thrust at all translates into endless acceleration gradually building towards extraordinary velocity. But until the half-way point only, because like climbing a mountain you need to slow on the way down or you'll be charcoaled, stone cold dead on arrival. The most dangerous moment being entry through the target planet's atmosphere with the correct angular momentum so as not to burn up.

Maybe the rest of the universe needs to be warned about humanity. A rocket is a lighthouse, is a warning light, a way marker, a reminder to weary or unwary travellers, a memento mori, because we all only have to make one mistake once, to find ourselves prematurely enrolled in the choir invisible. *Ever had any near-death experiences? And what made you want to become an astronaut anyway?* These were some of the questions that Robert and Catriona found themselves asking of each other during the journey. Verbal board games really, to help pass the time in the blankness of space.

Robert related to Catriona how in his late teens he was hit by a car while crossing a busy road late at night while out drinking with friends, and woke up twelve months later in hospital. Curiously enough, killing two birds with one stone, Robert explains that this happens to also be the story of how he came to make the decision to train to become an astronaut. Because he recalls that while he was in a coma he experienced a sequence of very strange dreams, further details of which have continued to return to him over the years since. On first waking he was not immediately able to recall his name, who his parents were or where they lived. Going back to his bedroom in their house the day after he woke up, he was overcome with an overpowering sensation that they were not his real parents, that he was not returning to his real life, and that with every second he was erasing the details of his memory of what that real life somewhere else had actually been like. His profound sense of disbelief about his own life took several weeks and months to gradually fade away. During which time he decided on what to do with the rest of his life.

Catriona, a psychology as well as astrophysics graduate as it happens, points out that such experiences are not uncommon in victims of head trauma, concussion. But over the years since what has fascinated Robert the most has been trying to remember and write down all the details of the coma dreams he had, because in many of them there were rockets, space rockets on platforms waiting to take off. White rockets like white lighthouses. And this is what he tells her convinced him: the preponderance of these glamorous but vaguely creepy visual images, to pursue a career in space travel.

Having survived a year trapped inside his own body without means of communication, means that Robert believes that the boredom of the years spent in interstellar space with Catriona, will be a piece of cake by comparison. They have enough time to read all the great classics written in their original languages which they also have time to learn and converse in. They draw the line at Egyptian hieroglyphs. They raise elaborate gardens from seed in the rocket's bio-dome, grow their own food, exercise relentlessly to prevent muscle atrophy.

❋

It's been nine months now since the accident, the prognosis not good, the chances looking unfavourable that Robert Stevens will ever wake up again from his ongoing coma. At first some of his friends visited, some of the clowns who were with him on the ill-fated night out. Then the nightshift gradually whittled down to just Robert's parents, Robert's brother and Robert's girlfriend Louise. At first the brother and the girlfriend visit together, then begin to meet outside before entering the hospital, going for coffee or even dinner afterward. Robert's brother is married with a young child, but even so, against all logic and wisdom, he and Louise begin to become attracted to each other, cannot help themselves, try to lie to themselves for a while that it might be only mutual grief and duty that is bringing them together.

After a dinner drink too many, one night they sleep together at Louise's flat while Robert's wife is away for the weekend at her parents' house with their son. Realising too late what they've been drifting into, they worry retrospectively if some of their conversations at Robert's bedside together might have been heard by Robert. Heard and understood better than by themselves at the time, in terms of where things were leading. Consequently they begin to avoid visiting him together anymore, out of guilt, out of fear. They go there singly now, separately. Irrationally perhaps. Surely he can't hear them? Isn't constantly conscious and aware at any level any of the time? The doctors seem certain not, but not certain enough.

✷

One of the many questions that Robert and Catriona ask each other in their long space journey to Proxima b is what their favourite childhood memory is. For Robert this is of summers he spent in the grounds of an unmanned lighthouse on the remote Scottish island where his grandparents lived. The skies always seemed to be blue and wild, with wisps of cirrostratus combed into a froth overhead. The evocative architectural language of lighthouses: the whitewash, the yellow-painted keystones around windows, the astragals and mullions, the obscure glass and steel technology of the wondrous lantern; all played their part in the sense of wonder Robert and his brother felt in the presence of this silent white tower. The yellow dandelions, sea pink, corn marigold, twisting with the grass underfoot, as their little sandaled feet ran to and fro, chasing each other around the building, again and again. Coming upon their own dual reflection reflected in puddles after finally running out of breath. The forbidden gulches and crevasses whose edges secretly both drew and repelled, with glimpses of broiling spume raging on the rocks far below. The spectre of distant boats passing occasionally on the far horizon, tracked with a brass telescope of their grandfather's. Tankers imagined as pirate ships in search of hidden treasure on tropical islands. X marks the spot on faded maps. The black spot, the summoning to a quest. The first roots of Robert's longing for journeying, some new frontier over the horizon. The wistful thought of travel beyond the limits of the known world. Summers that never seemed to end. The lonely crying of seagulls and kittiwakes, the aroma of grass, salt sea water, sheep and rabbit droppings, the whitewash of guano.

※

Robert's brother and Louise become more and more certain over time that on balance Robert probably can't hear what they are saying. But they are wrong. Their every word generates blasts of colour behind his closed eyelids, whole symphonies of trans-sensory music. Synesthesia.

Louise has the idea of hiring a psychic, a mystical spiritual healer to attempt to bring Robert out of his coma. Suspecting the hospital staff might object, Louise chooses to smuggle *Esoteric Elaine* in to the ward unofficially, dressed as a nun. The chanting she starts up when left alone Robert experiences as the apparition of a 16th century galleon ploughing through a storm-torn ocean around the lighthouse island that his trapped mind always returns to. She is trying to catch his consciousness as if dragging a grapnel along the seabed, hoping to haul it back to the land of the living.

※

At the Lighthouse

Robert feels as if he is a lighthouse, whose thoughts are a roving beam of light that sweeps across the city at night. Contained and frozen as he is, in his coma-paused body. His thoughts, the still dimly burning fire of his soul, are his only light, his only power to penetrate the night surrounding him. Freed from the habitual restrictions of time and space, he feels as if his mind actually travels to the outskirts of the city, to parks and buildings, landmarks of significance to him in his memory of the life, his life, he has been estranged from. He finds he can dip in and out of the minds of passing strangers, old friends, family members. Move back and forward in time.

Other times he loses this ability. Humanity becomes more distant, slips away beyond his reach. Then the seas around the lighthouse island of his soul become stormy, turbulent lashing waves, thundering against the white rendered skin of the cylindrical walls of his body, the lighthouse tower.

After these storms, on days when nobody seems to visit his bedside, sometimes he sees the ocean around him becalmed, or dried up altogether, into an endless mud plain, a desiccated sea bed scattered with fragments of shells and bones, the dead or asphyxiating bodies of obscure sea life left high and dry, antennae of eyes or nostrils protruding upward from the slime, waiting for the rains to return.

※

Sometimes when Robert's brother and Louise are having sex, cheating on him, they imagine that the lighthouse beam of Robert's consciousness is looking for them, sweeping across the city, glancing over them, like the headlights of passing cars through the drawn curtains falling across Louise's naked back. Five miles away in the hospital ward, their voices murmuring, crying out in the extremity of passion, somehow shake imperceptibly the glass of water on Robert's bedside table, make the headboard of his bed tap against the plaster wall.

Although both of the lovers are separately aware of this impression or illusion, they are too ashamed or afraid to discuss it, until one night in midwinter when they sit up in bed after sex, smoking marijuana in moonlight from the half-open curtains. The first voice raising the topic in the darkness produces a strong sense of déjà vu in the listener. *Do you ever think he's somehow watching us, hating us, resenting us when we do that?* Contrary to their hitherto unexpressed fear and trepidation: they find that the subject, once broached, has the effect of exciting them further. They make love again almost immediately, violently. At the moment of mutual orgasm they both feel as if they are dying. Later that night, when they have each returned to their rightful homes, the phone rings at 3am. But there is no one on the line and the number is untraceable. When they compare notes on this later, they realise that at some irrational level both of them somehow thought the call would be from Robert, that they had raised him from the dead or from his coma bed with their transgressions. But in that moment did they feel terror or elation at the thought of him regaining consciousness then, at last? Neither of them voice this question to the other, or even to themselves, for fear of facing up to any answer.

✻

Why did Catriona ask the question? The one about near-death experiences. In the long journey through the blackness there is time to tell every tale. How she narrowly avoided accepting a lift in a stranger's car when she was a little girl playing in the local park. Only seven years old. The police wanted a description, her mother terrified. Kidnapped, they said she could have been, the word they used, not the other words, the adult ones. She said she couldn't remember clearly enough, his features blurred in her mind. But when they captured him later, years later, his photograph on television, she recognised him then. He'd killed dozens. They sent him to the chair.

And later also, on her tour in the Middle East, a sniper's bullet that killed the guy walking right next to her. Just like that, as if he'd fainted, a small wound to the head, not even that much blood. The ricocheting sound between the blinding-white buildings seeming somehow disconnected from the lifeless body, still warm, suddenly at ease at her side as she crouched behind an armoured car, radioed for back-up. Can the soul flee so quickly?

The point to these stories the two astronauts tell to each other? To explain what risk means to them, the thin line between life and death, dream and reality. The need to take the initiative, not to wait to be the sitting duck. Reclining together at the end of the day in the weightlessness of their rest lounge, floating about to fix each other protein meals. It's not the ancient fireplace with the dogs asleep, but after a while it's something else: the comfort of knowing you've made history, no matter what happens next. The ultimate heroism. To defeat no human enemy, but the ineffable unknown.

※

Gradually Louise notices differences between Robert and his brother. Their relationship begins to sour over time. Perhaps it is the guilt lingering like a poison between them. The thought process goes like this, which anyone ever embroiled in an illicit relationship always has to face eventually: If she can betray him, how long until she betrays me? If he can betray his own brother, how long until he betrays me? Guilt and resentment breed fear, which in some of us turns to anger. Steven lashes out at Louise, and not just verbally. Bruises. A black eye. Excuses made to family and work colleagues. *You're like some kind of Jekyll and Hyde character,* she castigates him. *I don't know you when you turn like this. Who is it who's talking? Whose is this lizard's tongue spouting bitterness?*

Maybe it's Robert talking, my zombie brother.

Don't talk about him like that.

He would call you a whore you know, and me a Judas, despise both of us for how we're soiling his memory...

His memory? He's not dead yet. He can still wake up any day.

Dream on, Louise.

Dream on. Maybe he's dreaming on. Doesn't that frighten you?

Sure. It frightens me.

For yourself maybe, but not for him. You're not like him I reckon. You're more selfish and cruel. Less sympathetic and compassionate. You don't feel the pain of others the way he did. He was always concerned with it.

Past tense. There you go. You just did it yourself. Condemned him to the past. Put him up on a pedestal. He was no angel. I should know. I grew up with him.

I loved him. Love him. Present tense. But you? I think I hate you.

※

Approaching Proxima Centauri b at last, Robert and Catriona begin to see the colour of its atmosphere, its ocean and land, even the shape of some of its continents through its drifting cloud patterns. *My God... it's so similar to Earth. How can that be possible?* Robert marvels.

Maybe not so surprising... Catriona cautions. Blue oxygen-rich air, green chlorophyll-producing plants. *The resemblances are probably superficial until you look at the detail.*

But they don't have much time to look at the detail as the planet rapidly approaches and they prepare to enter the atmosphere. They fail to slow their velocity enough within the required trajectory. They hit the mesosphere and everything goes white hot. The entire rocket begins to shake as they cry out to each other, desperately flicking switches and attempting to abort or correct their course. But too late. White out.

※

Robert wakes in his hospital bed and sits up. There are people in the darkness around him, sitting on chairs, watching him, judging him. He sharply intakes breath. They are cephalopods, glimmering with strange liquids, faintly glowing internal organs. He screams out in horror.

※

Robert wakes in his hospital bed and sits up. The room is deserted. He finds he is wearing a space suit, whose helmet he has to give a turn to the right in order to remove it and breathe fresh air. He finds his arms and legs are weak from lack of use, but gradually he stands and ventures out into the corridor. The entire hospital is deserted. In fact, the further he walks through the building the more he finds that it is derelict, sections of its roof absent, daylight pouring in from above, fragments of wall missing where weed and ivy are pushing through, colonising the structure. Reaching a particularly large area of shattered window at the far end of a ward, he gazes out towards a futuristic city in the distance which seems both familiar and unfamiliar. It's as if the ruined hospital has been preserved as some kind of monumental memorial, overgrown by nature, in the middle of a public park in this new phoenix-like megalopolis which has sprung from the ashes of the old. He makes his way down through its decaying staircases then walks out at the building's base, to walk through the park towards the streets of the city beyond. The traffic as he approaches seems quiet at this early hour of the day, moving with less sound but greater speed than he expects, as if powered by some disarmingly effortless energy source which he is yet to understand.

※

Robert finds himself returning to his apartment on Earth. He is older now. Late twenties. Married to Louise. This is the life he realises he was trying to remember when he first came out of his coma in his late teens. The futuristic studio flat on the 11th floor, with its superb view of the beach and ocean in late Californian light. But as she greets him, embraces and kisses him upon his mysterious return, he notices that she doesn't call him Robert but Steven. He protests at first, then gradually less jokingly, that his name is not Steven. They begin to fight about it. *No,* she says, *Robert is your brother's name. He is your twin.* Robert looks at himself in the mirror, with Louise standing behind him. He runs his fingers over his own face and body as if it is someone else's. Over his shoulder in the mirror he can see many glittering towerblocks in the distance in the evening haze. He doesn't recognise some of them and wonders how many years into the future he might be.

You've changed, Louise says. *There's something different about you. I'd swear it, but I can't quite put my finger on it.* He finds a large atlas on the bookcase and opens it out on the coffee table. He gasps. All the continents are different shapes from how he remembers them, all the countries have subtly different names, but close enough to immediately begin eroding his memory of what they should be. He puts his head in his hands, tries to stand up. Feels faint, staggers towards the door of the apartment. *But what about Tommy?* Louise asks in shock. *Don't you want to see him? Our son, I put him to bed earlier, he was running around so excited all day about your homecoming that he tired himself out. I didn't want to wake him in case you were delayed.*

Louise opens the bedroom door and she and Robert peer in at their four-year old son asleep in bed. In the sunset light filtering through the curtains Robert notices that Tommy has been playing with a toy rocket on the floor. It looks familiar. Its white streamline chassis has the mission name 'Cygnus' written in distinctive blue font down the side. Robert feels dizzy again and nearly passes out.

※

Robert drives Louise and Tommy around the bay resort the day after his homecoming, under the palm trees. She still insists his name is Steven. She is giving him directions on how to drive to visit his brother's place. His brother who is called Robert, apparently. For a moment, Robert has the weird illusion in peripheral vision that Louise's thighs are transparent, with fish-like creatures swimming inside her. Driving around the base of a group of some of the tallest towerblocks, they chance upon a small park with a tall white monument in the middle of it. The hairs on the back of his neck stand up. It reminds him of the lighthouse from his childhood, but actually it's a rocket, a disused one placed here now as a monument to the Cygnus missions. He stops the car, transfixed, moving in a slow dream, steps out to take a look up at the white form above him. *What is it, Steven?* Louise asks him, *What's wrong, what are you wondering about?*

When did the Cygnus missions end, Louise? He asks, almost whispering.

She shrugs, removes her dark glasses, glances over her shoulder to check Tommy is okay in the back seat. But before she can answer, they are both distracted by a sound from the ocean behind them. Robert abandons the car, crosses the boulevard and walks down onto the beach. Louise gets Tommy out of the car and prepares to follow. As Robert reaches the edge of the ocean he looks high into the sky to see a bright yellow light descending from the upper atmosphere. A glass pod descends and folds out like a glistening silver flower onto the water a hundred yards from Robert. His brother emerges from its cockpit, and walks across the surface of the water to meet him. When Robert lifts his left hand in greeting he sees that his brother lifts his right hand at exactly the same time. Their every movement is somehow paired and mirrored, but inverted. He notices that his brother's legs bend backward rather than forward at the knees, everything opposite from his own. As if mimicked by visual skill without sufficient biomechanical understanding.

He also dimly notices that there is something or someone left behind on the passenger seat of the glass pod hovering over the ocean. He senses it is female, some essence of a forgotten face, name scrambled into grey static by the music of the spheres, an imprint under everything, a lost map home.

※

Robert and Steven are children again, in shorts and sandals, running around the base of the old lighthouse on the remote island, haunted by the constant sound of the sea wind, the cries of the wheeling gulls above, the sharp sunlight falling on the old white render walls. They chance upon the still surface of a puddle again and both kneel down to look in wonder at themselves. They are like two halves of a split personality, yin and yang, dark and light. Robert stretches his hand towards the still surface, extends his index finger to break the surface tension. In another second the water's mirror will be shattered and become instead an endless series of circles emanating out from the centre like radio waves. To search is to be found. In the waking mind of a child, shuffling towards the light of adulthood. To proclaim our own existence is to invite its nullification, to understand for the first time our fragility, our mortality. Life is a signal. Receive and transmit. The meaning coming through for a moment, a fragment, too fast to catch, always slipping like water from the fingers. Their great, great grandfather built the lighthouse. How many greats? Didn't they also have a sister? Robert. Louise. Steven. Son.

※

(Robert Louis Stevenson (1850-1894), Scottish novelist, renowned author of Treasure Island, Strange Case of Dr Jekyll and Mr Hyde, and Kidnapped, was the son of Thomas Stevenson of the Stevenson dynasty of civil engineers celebrated for their pivotal and pioneering role in Victorian lighthouse design).

The Volkhova Perplex

by Ashley Stokes

The view of the harbour from the summit of the hill the locals call The Bite convinced us that White Ness had been Seahaven. White Ness was the seaside town that appears in episode 1 of *The Volkhova Perplex*, the sixth and final story in the classic British teatime sci-fi series *The Sagittarians*, and broadcast by Anglia TV only once: on the 14th of September 1974, when we were seven years old. White Ness was certainly Shiphaven. Finally, we had found Shiphaven.

The horseshoe shape of the bay was identical to that which appears in the establishing shot that opens Episode 1. Also, a kidney-dish-shaped island does stand in the bay. According to Google Maps, it's called Shipwreck Head. In *The Volkhova Perplex*, it's Crab Rock. Crucially, the lighthouse, the epicentre of the story, remained squat and stout on top of the island. This was first sight of that eerie beacon which ever since the episode aired had haunted my sleep. I had been haunted by what happens in the Crab Rock Lighthouse my entire life.

I must admit that looking out at the lighthouse I felt something of what I had experienced as a seven-year-old forcing myself to peer at the television from behind the sofa. Yes, it is true: my generation did do that when confronted by bubble-wrap aliens and silver-foil-covered fruit crates masquerading as battle probes from the Planet of the Ants. The unreal was strangely more real back then. The real is unreal now. This is the transit of our times.

The chill wind that thrashed The Bite, you suggested, must have given it its name. We should go down to the sea front, get some chips, look for the guesthouse, the Rock View. If you remember, I was reluctant to embrace the town. I did suggest that maybe we had seen enough.

❋

We first became aware of White Ness in a local newspaper article listing a top ten of the east coast's most dismal and depressing resort towns. White Ness was number one. When we arrived at the seafront, we realised it had worked hard to earn its top spot. Entirely absent was any sense of Harbour Master Mal Flint's well-ordered 1970s fishing village, the setting for *The Volkhova Perplex*. No freshly-swept quayside, no coils of rope, scattered lobster pots and the stacked row boats he and his son Joe meticulously tie down as a storm approaches in the opening scene. Instead, betting shops, kebab kiosks, a shuttered-up gentlemen's club called Snorkelling and Norkling, vacant townhouses, much bankrupt real estate right on the seafront, and the shell of a burnt-out casino called The Silver Rose. Still, with my back to the town and staring out at the lighthouse, its brick, cylindrical tower finished in white paint made me feel I was inhabiting episode 1 of *The Volkhova Perplex*. I was Harbour Master Flint looking out at Crab Rock when the anomaly first manifests.

❋

The Volkhova Perplex is the only episode of *The Sagittarians* to be shot entirely on location and on 16mm film. The reason film was used is that in 1973, when the episode was made, there was a technicians' strike that paralysed independent regional TV studio productions for two months. *The Volkhova Perplex* was made by some other crew, not Anglia TV's usual inhouse team. That opening shot we referenced earlier, of the bay in the darkening dusk, the sky a mess of deep blues and blue-greys with racing clouds above a far-off horizon, is more like something out of a classic movie than a one-act play filmed in an outsized wendy house like the other five *Sagittarians* stories. The last frame here draws the eye quite deliberately to the island in the bay, an island that on first sight is a barren stump sticking out of the choppy waves without a lighthouse built on it. Even after you joined my investigation, we had not established a convincing hypothesis as to how this shot was achieved. It's not a papier-mâché model shot from a discreet distance to look like the island. It is not another island somewhere else, given that the other geographical features are identical to White Ness. We are obsessive fans. We like to know how the effects were achieved. We do not know how this effect was achieved.

※

CUT-TO: we first meet Harbour Master Mal Flint – played by the actor Charles McDaughlen, known at that time mostly for a small recurring role in *The Onedin Line* and later for playing the part of Bideford Bing in *El Dorado* – and his son Joe, played by Jesse Banes, better known as the singer Richard Syringe from the punk rock band Mass Grave who died from an overdose in the Lyzzick

229

Moathouse Hotel, Boston, Lincolnshire in 1980. In cape-like sou'westers, they are busy on the quayside. Mal turns and looks at the harbour front. Stiff gusts of wind swing hurricane lamps, bunting and a sign that reads Shiphaven. He looks out to sea. There is nothing on the island. He tells Joe to hurry up. Hopefully they can soon be dry and indoors and enjoying his mam's stew. Joe smiles at the thought, presumably of hot stew, but suddenly both Flints seem spooked, turning to camera as if staring out at sea, mouths hanging open, eyes agape.

We CUT-TO the island.

A white lighthouse stands, revolving a violet beam against a sky like black marble.

Titles roll.

※

That title sequence. To little me back in 1974, the promise of its imagery, the visions of a mysterious world they project. How could ordinary life in ordinary times compete? How could the real day not shrivel up in shame?

The sequence starts with a drum roll in the darkness of outer space, then four oscillating guitar chords create a running bass interjected by a keening whine of analogue synthesiser. It's no more, really, than a hastily-promoted sound effect, but it's the sort of *Clockwork Orange*-knock-off organ surge that in the 70s said, 'weird shit will happen in the future'. This electronic riff is repeated over and over again and probably accounts for why *The Sagittarians*, it is rumoured, was regarded as too psychologically damaging to young minds for it to be shown in Sweden. Not that it was shown in any other countries either, apart from ours. Maybe it was only here that the damage was done. Anyway, the four guitar chords and analogue synth hook hit loop-mode as an animated spiral, an iconic bit of period design as it turns out, encloses the series title, The Sagittarians. A child's eye – like all the flashing

The Volkhova Perplex

images that follow, without any heads-up to epileptics – is bathed in a violet duotone. The eye opens in rapidly staggered stop-motion, then vanishes. It is replaced by the static image of a near-transparent, vein-riddled and presumably human embryo that flies from the background to the foreground, right at you. A two-dimensional meteorite that looks like it's cut out of a newspaper and had something done to it with sticky back plastic takes the same trajectory: straight at the viewer's head. An astronaut stands at the heart of a mass of concentric circles looking up as if awed by the timeless whirls of infinity. The constellation of Sagittarius appears in a triangle set against a backdrop of lunar craters. The child's eye opens again, this time quicker. The horsehead nebula appears in a square superimposed over shelves of baked beans. A lattice of scaffold poles appears. A coelacanth hurtles across the Milky Way. The eye opens. A North Sea oil rig appears. A strange, thin, possibly robed figure, maybe a Volkhovian, a meddling puncturer of the space-time continuum stands between some scaffold poles. A Venus fly trap opens. The eye opens. A white dot balloons into a monkey's skull flying through space. The Venus fly trap opens. The eye opens. Oil rig. A teenaged girl with a bubble perm is sprung on us for some reason. An extensively tattooed Maori warrior. Oil rig. The head of a praying mantis looms. The eye opens. Oil rig. The silhouette of a presumably slim and esoteric man wearing flared trousers winks in and out of existence before the story title dominates the screen: The Volkhova Perplex. Then the praying mantis pops again and the oil rig and the eye opens and the Venus fly trap opens, this time with fit-inducing speed before we are treated to the outline of a shimmying woman. Then: The Volkhova Perplex again, followed by, WRITTEN by Eric OVENS, and Episode One: A STITCH IN TIME. The synth hits a lower note, signalling that we are not pissing about now: the future will be weird, don't go there.

✳

Return to Scene: Mal and Joe stare out at us from under the hoods of their rain-splattered sou'westers. Joe says, 'Da, didn't you say that the old Crab Rock lighthouse came down in a storm in 1872?'

For us, you remember, this date had significance. The most reliable guide to Victorian lighthouses, the *British Lighthouse Chart of General Coastal Lights* was published in 1874 and in that publication, which we tracked down in the British Library, there is no lighthouse in White Ness. No structure stands on Shipwreck Head in 1874. Anyway, I digress …

Mal tells Joe that, yes, he had said that, the lighthouse came down one hundred and one years ago, and Joe, quite naturally replies with, 'How the dickens is it back then?'

'That is what we have to find out, son.'

'No, no, Da, it's too dangerous, look at the sea.'

'But there might be people in there, people trapped in some way. We need to make sure first, before we tuck in to a helping of Mam's stew. Buck up, Joe. Help me drag out the dinghy.'

CUT-TO: The violet beam of the Crab Rock Lighthouse creates a shimmering trail in the waters of the bay, along which a dinghy with an outboard motor travels as it heads for the island. Mal is clearly sitting at the back with his hand on the motor, Joe sat in front holding up a hurricane lamp that grows dimmer and dimmer at the boat recedes.

We realise then that we are seeing with the eyes of a girl. About ten-years-old, she is watching the boat from the upper room of a townhouse on the harbourside, the pads of her fingertips pressed to the glass (crane shot).

CUT-TO: From behind, she is wearing a blue and white checked two-piece dress with a white-edged black velvet ribbon tied around her waist. Clearly, a Victorian child. The window lights up violet as the beam sweeps harbourside. The girl jerks as if

The Volkhova Perplex

she's felt something and hurriedly spins about. She screams a high-pitched stage-school scream.

In her bedroom doorway, for the first time this episode we see Syzygy and Star, The Sagittarians. There has been a breach in the continuum. Malevolent conspiracy is confirmed. Syzygy and Star have been dispatched.

❋

It has to be said that in this episode, it's welcome that the delayed appearance of our otherworldly agents means the shunning of the will-they-won't-they banter we get at the start of both *Laissez Fairies*, Episode One of *The Hecate Interstices*, the first adventure that introduces Ms Syzygy and Mr Star, where we meet them teasing each other obliquely as they push trolleys around a supermarket that turns out to be an endlessly self-complicating maze that is sucking in a town a bit like Milton Keynes, and in *Out of Joint*, the first instalment of *The Slaves of Midgitara*, where their eyes meet across a swirling dancefloor at an Oxford tea dance in 1943. Starting with the Flint men both builds suspense and allows us to bond with the other members of the cast, Mal, Joe and now young Katie Flint. That Syzygy and Star have been dispatched means that all of time and space is at stake now that the lighthouse has returned and 1872 has reconstituted itself around Shiphaven as evidenced by Katie Flint's anachronistic dress. This is more interesting, especially if you're seven years old, than whether Syzygy and Star are porking each other, though apparently, the actor and actress, Dan Colo and Zoe Wilder were at it all the time behind the scenes. They couldn't help themselves, apparently. At it like rats, they were.

This is not like us.

By now, if you were a fan, you knew who Syzygy and Star were even if you didn't know what they were. Syzygy and Star are agents who mend holes in time and space, fix glitches, seal breaches, confront and defeat meddlers and unbalancers, the deadliest of which were the Volkhova, hooded time gremlins we first meet in *The Hecate Interstices*, and who, in Episode Four: *Block Punch* vowed to return, to triumph next time (for years I feared there was a portal in the medicine cabinet in my parents' bathroom that let the Volkhova in and out). Nothing is ever really revealed about the nature and origin of Syzygy and Star, who they are, where they are from, what they have for breakfast, their wider purpose or the nature of the inter-temporal authority that directs their movements. Syzygy seems to have powers of clairvoyance and clairaudience and is capable of communing with time. She can sense where time is curved or bent-back on itself when time is supposed to be a linear one-way corridor that stretches on forever. She is also fit as fuck. The ever-dapper Star is incredibly strong and can talk to machines (he even cheekily shares a few snarky lines with an ornery Sodastream in the last moments of *The Haktak Defence*, Episode Four of *The Climate of Hunter*, the fifth outing of *The Sagittarians*). In short: He is arrogant. She is empathic. He is handsome. She is beautiful. He is strength. She is skill. He is unearthly. She is unearthly. They are Odd and Odder. You wouldn't go up to them if you saw them in a pub. If we were ever to know more about them, it would be revealed in the second series that never comes.

※

Back to Episode One of *The Volkhova Perplex*, and Katie stops screaming when Syzygy takes a step towards her and puts a hand on her shoulder. The scream, though, has not gone unheard. Star, still standing in the doorway, looks back over his shoulder towards the sound of someone running up the stairs. He stands aside to let into the room a plump matron type woman also in a Victorian dress and in some state of panic.

'Oh lordy Katie, what is the matter?' 'It's fine, Mother,' says Katie. 'They are not devils or French.' Star, his face half in shadow, half hazed with violet light, says, 'Don't worry, Mrs Flint, we are here to put everything back.'

❋

We became convinced beforehand that the Rock View guesthouse, lining up as it did with Shipwreck Head, was the same building that had been used as the Flint's house in *The Volkhova Perplex*. You could plot a line from the lighthouse and the middle window of the third floor, the window we were pretty sure that Victorian Katie Flint stares out of early in the episode, and create a diagram or map in the mind, and connect this alignment with other significant points in the cosmos, the horseshoe shape of the bay seeming pretty much to be a scale model of the Corona Australis constellation, a waypoint that could orientate occupants of interplanetary craft to the Sagittarius system itself, for example. I was trying to do this for some reason as we stood looking up at the building and you reminded me that from the photos on the booking website it looked to have the same layout inside as it had in the episode minus the mocked-up period furniture. We had been very particular that we wanted that room on the third floor, Katie's Room.

We were most disappointed, therefore, to find that after we had checked in and been given our swipe card by a smiley young woman called Kiya – she was so well trained and obedient we could have mistaken her for Professor Prentice's cloying servo-droid Klang Klang, who is dismantled by Craig Formulaic in the penultimate scene of *The Far-flung Automata*, Episode Four of *The Infotainment Scan* – to find that our room was not the room we thought we had booked. There was no direct view of the lighthouse. There had obviously been at least one conversion job on the building, each of its rooms that seemed vast in the Flint house scenes in *The Volkhova Perplex* divided into two or three boxy chambers that were mere berths for beds. Or, as you pointed out, maybe the camera played games with perspective and depth of field in the episode, created an illusion of space. I was just livid we could not stand at that window and line-up with the lighthouse like Syzygy and Star after they have interrogated Mavis Flint and worked out a plan of attack.

✳

Before the scene where Syzygy and Star stand at the window bathed in the violet light of the misplaced lighthouse's beam, a scene that contains a major plot point that heads us second star on the right and straight on to interdimensional adventure, there is a long talky sequence punctuated by the camera lingering on various period pieces of furniture in the harbourmaster's house, including Mrs Flint's kitchen range, a long-armed creepy doll which may well have been cloned from Madelaine the Rag Doll in *Bagpuss,* and a grandfather clock that looks a bit too tall. The ticking from this clock provides a suspense-building running bass throughout the whole sequence in the Flint House. It does seem to speed up as Syzygy and Star run their diagnostics.

We re-join them staring at each other in profile across Mrs Flint's kitchen table. They are near to us. In the middle distance, Katie Flint, so robotic in her movements as she tries to build a pyramid from playing cards that she makes Klang Klang in *The Infotainment Scan* seem like Robin William's monumental and epochal performance as Mork from Ork in *Mork and Mindy*. In the far distance, Mrs Flint busies herself making some sort of tea. The clock ticks even though we cannot see the clock. Something tells us that the clock is situated in a hallway we'll never access.

'So, what do your powers tell you?' Star asks Syzygy.

'There is a sorrow here,' she says, dispassionately. 'Like the mirror feels when the mirror is cracked. You know what night this is?'

'Logic determines that this is the night that the storm brings down the lighthouse?'

'Logic only unfurls from where it is agreed logic begins. There is always logic before logic.' She stares into him. The clock ticks.

The clock keeps ticking. We see the clock briefly, followed by a long shot of a corridor with a long thin carpet or rug, and then Katie adds the Seven of Diamonds and the Three of Hearts to her pyramid, and Mrs Flint's ample rump bustles across the range and then we see the clock again, tall, high, elongated, strange.

'The lighthouse will fall,' says Star. 'Time is of the essence.'

'Time is always of the essence,' says Syzygy. 'You know that as well as anyone.'

'The Harbour Master and his boy are situated in the lighthouse. If we do not return them to their correct place, they will be destroyed here and leave a stain on the purity of time that will let things in and out to steal whatever they like.'

'I fear it's worse than that. All of Seahaven has been dragged into 1872. Hence Katie and Mavis. And an object the size of Seahaven being displaced means that in their time it has been replaced by something else.'

'Seahaven in 1974 has been replaced by Seahaven in 1872.'

'That feeling I have of the mirror cracking suggests the space-time continuum has ruptured and objects have been swirled in a random fashion.'

'Like the break shot in the game snooker they play here for amusement.'

At the Lighthouse

'Yes, a little like that.'

'Other things may come in and out.'

Mrs Flint bangs down a tea tray on the end of the table in slow motion and the impact produces a bang more like the sound of dozens of metal pipes dropped from a height. This does suggest time is out of whack or that we are losing control of our time. The pyramid of cards collapses. The Ace of Spades is prominent in the resulting spread in front of Katie. Katie screams but we do not hear her scream, we only see her scream. Then we have the grandfather clock again, vast in scale now, standing like an obelisk, vibrating with each tick, like it is about to blow.

❋

CUT-TO: Syzygy and Star are back at Katie's window haloed in the lighthouse's violet beam. She now wears a Victorian lady's white dress. He is now dressed like the captain of a tugboat or something.

'We will find a way across,' says Star. 'Before it is too late. Flint and his boy must return to their proper place.'

'There is another thing,' says Syzygy. 'When I mentioned that the mirror has cracked, I sense something waiting in the cracks.'

'What is it?'

'Something old, something angry.'

'Well, if they are older than us, they must be angry.'

We pull back. From behind we see Syzygy gently nudge Star with her elbow.

❋

The Volkhova Perplex

Down in the reception area of the Rock View Guesthouse, we were getting nowhere with the smiley young woman called Kiya, who seemed to have no answer to why we had been allotted a room that did not align directly with the lighthouse. She also seemed more than a little afraid when you mentioned that there should not be a lighthouse here as it collapsed in 1872 and there is no historical record that it was ever rebuilt. Here, if you remember, she politely told us to hang on, she would get the owner to come and talk to us, a Mrs Gridley.

A Mrs Gridley soon appeared from a backroom, a stocky, formidable brioche bun of a woman in her late sixties who shucked Kiya off into obscurity, an exasperated twang to the way she said to us, 'Now what on earth is the problem?'

We explained the problem.

'I don't think there is a window like the one you describe,' she said. 'And if you wanted a view on the lighthouse, you've got one.'

'It isn't the right view, though, is it,' I said. 'It comes at a slant.'

'Is this some sort of new lighthouse-spotting craze?'

'Mrs Gridley,' you interjected. 'Can I just ask? How long have you owned this building?'

'Outright? About ten year. But it was my dad's before that. Family business. I grew up here. Never been one for seeking out pastures new. I'll still be here when the rest of the coast is under water. They say we haven't got long.'

'Ah, good point,' I said to you. 'I see what you're doing ... Mrs Gridley, do you remember when in 1973 your property was used as a location for an Anglia TV science fiction production, The Sagittarians?'

'Not that I recall.'

'C'mon, you must remember a film crew being here? Your father must have been paid for the inconvenience.'

'The Sagging whats?'

'The Sagittarians. You must remember it. It was well ahead of its time. It was like a more paranormal-leaning version of *The X-Files* but set in the England of Edward Heath.'

'Never heard of it.'

'Please, Mrs Gridley, try to remember. The episode filmed here is quite famous because it was supposed to be episode one of four, but for some reason, no more were made. The episode one cliff-hanger was the last cliff-hanger. We assume they ran out of money or there were legal problems involving crew hire … or something strange happened.'

'Has no one ever come here before asking after the fate of The Sagittarians?' you asked.

'Seriously, I have never heard of The Sagittevertheshittheyare, ever. You are the first. I think you must have me confused with the wrong hotel, or the wrong resort, or the wrong world. Now, this business of the room, if you want a refund, you can fu…'

'That won't be necessary,' I said. 'Could you please inform us of how to reach the lighthouse across the bay.'

'Spinner behind you. Leaflet third from the bottom. You can hire a little boat, or if you're a landlubber, you can get Old Mal to ferry you across.'

※

Forty minutes later Old Mal was rowing us across to Shipwreck Head and the Seahaven Lighthouse. Of course, we had already, once we had pushed off and he couldn't run away, interrogated him as to whether he was related to Mal Flint, harbour master of these parts until his as yet unsolved disappearance in 1974 despite only existing in a work of fiction that, it sometimes seems, only we remember. He said he wasn't. He also, like Mrs Gridley, claimed to have never heard of *The Sagittarians* at all.

Surprising as it may sound, this is not surprising. A kind of *omertà* seems to surround the entire production, as if everyone involved is sworn to secrecy. There are even rumours that during the making of *A Stitch in Time*, Episode One of *The Volkhova Perplex*, the cast and crew witnessed some supernatural manifestation that shut the production down. No one wants to talk about it for fear of risking their credibility in a film and TV industry that is traditionally adverse to hiring delusionals, prophets and visionaries. Over the years, I have been unable to find anyone who will agree to an interview for the book I proposed to write on *The Sagittarians*. It's theme would be that *The Sagittarians* is a lost masterpiece and far more realized than crud like *The Tomorrow People* and *Joe 90*. Of course, I also want and need to solve the mystery as to why the series was cancelled after *A Stitch in Time*, and why *A Stitch in Time* was broadcast at all when it, without sequel, ended on such a terrifying note that the memory of it has disturbed both my sleeping and waking hours ever since. Finding out what happens next would be some kind of resolution for me, and for you, too.

As it stood, at that point, I had been unable to engage Eric Ovens, the writer; Dan Colo, who played Star; Zoe Wilder, Syzygy; Hilderlith Rockhampton, who composed the music and who later played keyboards for the prog outfit Rabbit Fudge (I am banned from their gigs now); or Mary Morton, Katie and later slutty Miss Esse Exeter in legal drama *Bang to Rights*.

Charles McDaughlen (Mal Flint) was dead before I started my quest – the fags got him, I believe – but dead too is John Booze, the director, Tom Fingermaus, Head of Special Effects and Julie Hull who played Mavis Flint.

No one wants to talk about what happened. It's like a UFO sighting that everyone knows they saw but convinces themselves that they didn't because short-term ridicule is worse than eternal

241

enlightenment. In fact, until I met you, I'd met no one else who would admit to even seeing *The Sagittarians*. When we played *Sagittarians* at school (I was Star, naturally), I had to play on my own. When I first met you in Lidl, by the cheapish wine, I thought I recognised you from school but we were not at school together, you said. Even so, something must have marked me out to you as a fellow Saggy. Ten minutes later, we were ensconced in a nearby Costa and after establishing that we agreed that the original *Battlestar Galactica* was more charming than the 00s reimagining with its heavy-handed political messaging and its cutting of Muffit, we somehow admitted to each other that we had both seen *A Stitch in Time,* Episode One of *The Volkhova Perplex* and would very much like to find out what happens next in that lighthouse. Someone could tell us. Seeing the script would do. God forbid the other five episodes are hidden in some archive somewhere, or in the attic of some retired notable at Anglia TV. We would somehow find out, though.

Now, we were being rowed across to the island as dusk began to fall. It has to be said, we were moving at a far slower clip than Syzygy and Star, who made good use of Star's strength powers to zip across the bay (you can tell some sort of crude backscreen superimposition is used, however; no one is that strong).

✳

CUT-TO: Star is tying the boat to the jetty. Syzygy swishes past him. The lighthouse looms above her. If we had just turned on and did not understand the premise of *The Sagittarians*, we might mistake these two for mistress and servant in some historical romance called *The Lighthouse Keeper's Woman* or *Martha's Harbour*, the sort of thing Dan Colo would regularly turn up in during the eighties, after he had failed auditions for *Manimal* and *Gemini Man*. Waves slosh. Star pulls down his seaman's cap, smirks and follows up the jetty. Everything is lit-up violet from the lighthouse's beam.

CUT-TO: They are inside the lighthouse now. Above them a vast spiral staircase leads skywards. From down here it looks like a giant ammonite shell and much, much taller than the 16 meters of the Seahaven Lighthouse as seen from outside. It looks like it might take days to reach the top. Syzygy and Star exchange glances. Star takes the first few steps, pauses, turns and holds out his hand as if he's helping her from a carriage. She huffs, blinks and now she is further up the stairs than he is and sashaying ahead.

CUT-TO: They seem to be some way up the stairs. Star looks down and it's a long way down. Syzygy looks up and it's a long way up. And here is the part that always disturbs me. Star says, 'we've been walking for so long my boot leather is wearing thin,' and Syzygy clutches her temples and seems in great pain and hisses, 'now I see. It's a time trap and we have sprung it. We're going to be here forever.' Here, they both freeze and the violet light inside the shaft becomes darker. It purples and they just stand there staring at us, the stillness of the image only broken by rapid blinks where the screen falls dark for part of a second, these rapid blinks suggesting the passing of an unknown passage of time, as brief as the blinks or winks or whatever you want to call them, or maybe months, years, decades, millennia, and the frozen expressions of their faces, his a kind of stoic resolution, shrugging acceptance to being relegated to the status of an ornament, but she looks horrified, terrified as if she is seeing things that no one else can see, not Star, not the audience, not you and me, which she can because of her time-communion powers. It has to be said here, too, that Hilderlith Rockhampton managed to add some terrible squalling-bleeping, bladder-and-bollock-trembling electronic effect that circles again and again through this whole sequence and deepens the sense of existential crisis and stymy. They have been had. They have been captured. What chance do you have, do we have, if Syzygy and Star are had and captured?

This is the thought that has kept me awake at nights for as long as I could remember. Every so often I think of this and then that nasty purple colour would cloud my mind's eye and I'd remember the Rockhampton soundtrack and feel sick, and the loneliness in Star's eyes and the atrocities Syzygy experiences tear at me. This is why I failed my exams, thinking of this, this is why I never became a special computer programmer like I wanted, or an astronaut, racing car pit crew or fighter jet pilot, love-interest, train driver, land speed record holder or explorer, this is why I never felt close to anyone and was always out on some spur of my own, some haunted peninsula or grim isthmus, some spit of land where there is only myself and the questions, the big questions about Syzygy and Star and where did they go. This is why I was afraid to talk to the women, or that my fear of them was so apparent it was unattractive and drove them away. This is why I spent my fortieth birthday on my own in the room with the last candle and two glasses of wine for one drinker. This is why I was banned by the moderators of the subreddit r/eerie_england. This is why I am not allowed to go to the conventions and the telefantasy festivals. This is why I am still looking for answers. You know these feelings, too, and you wanted the same answers.

Anyway, back in the stairwell, Syzygy fades from alongside Star and reappears in some place of swirling violet mists where apparitions in mauve robes flutter and poke at her but she is too strong for them in close proximity and using her mind she forces them back through the cracks to where they have intruded on pure time (this sounds great when I write it down but it looked decidedly school-play on TV).

Then, we're back in the stairwell, Star has reverted to his usual stance and says well done to Syzygy with an undertone that he doesn't mean it, that what she achieved was nothing special and he could have done it better himself. Anyway, they are now at the top of the staircase, at the door to the optic area of the lighthouse, the rooms that service the lens and the lantern room itself where the lens is housed.

When we arrived at the top of the staircase, at the door to the optic area, the stairwell behind us had maintained its structural and spatial integrity and it had only taken us ten or so shin-crunching minutes to ascend the steps. We were both, I know, bedazzled and confused by being inside a lighthouse that doesn't exist, that was wiped from the rocks by storm-force winds after it was struck by lightning in 1872.

In contrast to us, Syzygy and Star are aware that it is 1872 and the imminent lightning strike and the collapse of the lighthouse with the Finch men and themselves in it is creating a kind of ticking timebomb. The lighthouse will fall. Time will fall. Everything will be sucked in. This is no time to fuck about. Star springs open the door with an almighty kick that is supposed to be like the kick of a mule or something but actually just looked like a man of slightly below average height kicking a door.

Inside the Service Room, there is clockwork machinery that must be attached to the lens in the room above. A table has been set up. Mal and Joe sit at it in profile to us. Syzygy and Star approach. She looks around and seems calm and relaxed, like the mission has been accomplished. Both of us felt on first viewing that she was going to open a wormhole here and take Mal and Joe back to 1974, just as she had 'retransversed' Coco and Rictus in *Rook's Move*, Episode Four of *The Lilithica Concave*. With the casual sophistication of a host about to usher guests to their seats in a fine restaurant, Syzygy swishes over to the Flints. She's about to rest a hand on each of their shoulders when suddenly Star jolts upright as if he has been struck by a mini bolt of lightning put here only for him. His gaze is fixed on the cogs and gears of the clockwork machinery. The machinery must be talking to him, just like that Ford Cortina called Spiros told him how to find the Court of the

Time Hoods in *Echelon Attack*, Episode Two of *The Infotainment Scan*. If you were a fan of the show, if you were a Saggy, you would know that the machines were talking to Star. Machines consider Star to be one of their own.

'No, Syzygy,' he shouts. 'Don't touch them, it's a trap.'

But it's too late.

Her hands brush their shoulders.

They both disappear.

Two purple-robed figures appear, Volkhova, last seen vowing to take vengeance in *Block Punch*, Episode Four of *The Hecate Interstices*, both raise their temporal distortion rods. A bit of high-pitched synth whirr lets us know they have fired the rods. Syzygy and Star fall backwards, suspend in mid-air for half a second, before nothing remains but thick white outlines that then wipe to all four corners of the screen.

FADE TO BLACK.

The theme music kicks in again.

Titles roll.

STAR
Dan Colo

SYZYGY
Zoe Wilder

Etc

That was it.

That was all we had.

Not only no second series (these things usually get three decent series and two shit ones with hardly anyone left who was in it at the start), but not even a completed *first* series of *The Sagittarians*.

It was as if everyone involved assumed that no one was watching so no one cared. But we cared. We cared, didn't we? And we had waited a very long time.

❋

I grabbed hold of the door handle and pressed my shoulder to the door, but then looked back at you, wondering whether we really wanted to see what was on other side, what mess or trash heap might confront us. I know we needed to ascend to the lantern room to see if we could stare back at the Rock View, but also knew we would not be able to see much more than our reflections in the glass. We could be assured that we had found Sea Haven, but would come away with more questions than answers. Why was this lighthouse here? Why was there no record of it in the maps, historical and contemporary, or in local, lighthouse and maritime histories. I looked at you and you looked at me and I saw too in your eyes that you knew something was about to end. I wanted to kiss you, but didn't want that rejection on top of everything else at this moment. I leaned into the door and shoved it open.

❋

We stride into the room expecting it to be dark but it is well-lit and the table stands where it stood in Episode One and the clockwork machinery whirs and clicks and as two transparent figures in purple robes waver and wobble until they are solid and look like they are surprised, they look like they are adopting defensive postures. I have to listen hard, I have to tune in, like I am out of practice, like I know the language but the accent is strong and eccentric, but the cogs are saying, the gears are saying, *you have been away a long time but for them it has been minutes.* And realisation hammers me, almost stops me from haring forwards, the lighthouse was only knocked down in the reality from which we were banished. Nothing in the pocket dimension the Volkhova banished us to was real, no England of 1974, no going cap in hand to the IMF, no Three-Day Week, no Miners' Strike, no Falklands War, no Chernobyl Disaster, no Berlin Wall coming down, no Oasis at Knebworth, no 9/11, no Iraq, no Afghanistan, the money didn't run out, the morons didn't win, the seas did not rise, the ice did not melt, there was no virus, no death toll, none of it. These were just nightmares, just phantom sequences and loop-games, an elaborate and hypnotic time-trap of alien design. Muffit wasn't removed from *Battlestar Galactica* after all, Neelix wasn't in *Star Trek*, Chris Chibnall never twatted up *Doctor Who*. *Buffy the Vampire Slayer* never jumped the shark after series five. Condorman, BJ and the fucking Bear. None of it happened. None of it was real. It didn't matter that I'd fucked up all my chances and squandered all my opportunities and had no friends and never had a girlfriend because women think I'm weird and intense, it doesn't matter because it is absolutely true in my case that I wasn't made for this world. But I know who you are now. You know who I am.

I draw my strength from the density of a neutron star and my massive punch turns the first Volkhova to purple dust. You telekinetically rip the time-rod thing from your one's claw and smash it against the wall, then make a wormhole and send him to the primordial soup or the heat death of the universe or wherever it is that you send them, I've never asked, I don't really think that I'd understand how it works. Now they are vanquished, I look at you and you are back in your white dress so I know I am back in my seaman's garb and it's 1872 and the lighthouse will fall any second so it's time to go, time to wormhole it out of here, time to regroup, time if anything to have a drink and a debrief. But no. The ground is shaking. The light changes, darkens, turns to that violet tinge. We look up. Above us, there is a purple disc on the ceiling and it's a portal and there are swirling specks and spangles and the portal sucks us, the portal takes us up off the ground and into a funnel of streaking light, there's a drum roll in the darkness of outer space, and four oscillating guitar chords create a running bass interjected by a keening whine of analogue synthesiser. An animated spiral encloses the series title, The Sagittarians. A child's eye opens. Oil rig. Oil rig etc. The story title, The Volkhova Perplex, followed by: WRITTEN by Eric OVENS, and Episode TWO: SAVES NINE. There has been a breach in the continuum. Malevolent conspiracy is confirmed. Syzygy and Star have been dispatched.

Turn Again, O My Sweetness

by C.A. Yates

The salt-crust melancholy of the keeper's wife is more than he can bear and, as is his habit, he turns away. Unblinking, she watches his lumbering body from the kitchen window as he heads across the catwalk to his work shed, her crisp lines held as tightly as a well-rigged forestay. She puts a smouldering cigarette to her lips and takes a long drag down into her lungs. She waits a beat, and then blows it back out in a lazy ghost-ring that disperses hazily into the air around her. He hates it when she smokes, so she smokes more. Anything to antagonise. She used to dream of that big, heavy body pressing down on her, slick and hard inside of her, surrounding her, hands on her throat – too tight, gasping for breath, be careful what you wish for – but for a long time now she has been as miserable when he is close as when he turns his back. No, not miserable, not anymore. She has wondered countless times how he cannot know that she is numb, a shell of herself, bleached and fragile, looking to crumble. He cannot see how the endless days of yearning for what cannot be have hollowed her. The truth is that she no longer knows how to go on and so, instead, she haunts.

At the Lighthouse

Once he has disappeared from view, the keeper's wife peers down at the ground outside, assessing. The fall won't kill her, she is absolutely sure of that. In truth, it would be unlikely to kill anyone unless they fell the wrong way, of course, or landed on their head, or twisted funny somehow. There is a defiant mat of brittle-looking but thick grass around the base of the building – unusual because hardly any grows elsewhere on the entire rocky outcrop and she has not noticed it before – which would serve to cushion a fall at least somewhat. She's not too worried about pain or injury; she has suffered worse and the lure of the fall is louder than either. It is not as though she actually intends to kill herself, but she has been thinking about throwing herself out of the window at least a dozen times a day for as long as she can remember. Of course, if she could get right to the top of the lighthouse, get out and over the railing, then death would be assured. It's funny, although she has dreamed many times about just that, the high fall, descent, she has never once dreamed of dying that way. She takes comfort in the omission, believes it means something important. Something good. These are the only straws she has left to clutch at, after all. The trouble is her loving husband has forbidden her those heights. It is not for women, he has told her, and of course that makes her want it even more. However, while she champs at his restrictions, she knows it would be useless to argue with the stubborn ass and, besides, while she is not sure of her ultimate intention it would be foolish to go too far too soon. She must wait to make further plans, see how things unfold. For now, the kitchen window has to be enough, at least for this first time, because falling is all that matters.

Occasionally she wonders where the urge comes from, and then she remembers her grandmother's bedroom, where the old woman died. She wasn't supposed to go out onto the balcony, her mother had told her it was an accident waiting to happen, and that had been enough to ensure she had escaped onto it at every opportunity. The thrill of the forbidden was one thing, naturally, but the space had made her breathless with anticipation from the moment she'd stepped out there. Her proximity to the void, to oblivion, had been velvet black and thick on her tongue, while her heart, lodged like a cliché in her throat, had drummed in tandem with the gloriously empty throb throb throb of it. The certain knowledge that just one step, one vault and she would be out there falling, free, had almost swallowed her whole. Even now, so many years later, she still pulses at the thrill of the *so close*, and the *what if*. Of course, she wouldn't have been able to vault over anything with her small girl legs, wouldn't be able to do it now most likely, let alone jump the railing at the top of the lighthouse, which comes to her waist, but at its heart the feeling is the same. Now, however, it is adult sized, mature. Deep down in her stomach, swirling around with the bile and the anxiety and the dreadful truth, there is an absolute certainty that falling is her destiny. It feels important. Her calling. An escape. She has been thinking on it constantly.

The other women have been talking about it too; she's far from alone. It's what triggered the memory in the first place, the others. She listens to them as they whisper to each other at night, or as they walk up the winding stairs together, or when they're in a corner and they think she cannot hear them. She can though, every word, and she doesn't care that they don't include her, have discarded her so easily, because she doesn't need them, she doesn't need anyone. She knows what they are, has named them but only to herself and, while she won't dignify them with a reaction today any more than any other day, she still listens, always listens. It's not like there's much else for her to do. The radio broke weeks ago when she threw it at the wall and her husband had just shrugged, relieved he hadn't been struck by it. He'd said that's what happens when someone has idle hands and she should never have idle hands anyway because there's always something to clean or polish, if nothing else, in a lighthouse.

That said, he had tried to placate her after the last ill-fated pregnancy by buying the piano for her, probably so she would feel obliged to play and be forced to keep those nervous twisting hands of hers occupied, so he could finally stop being reminded and forget right along with the music. He would rather not remember, she knows this, has been told often enough to move on, to move past it. He hates dwelling on things, as he calls it, hates how she relives things over and over. The joke was on him though. She didn't ask him to buy the bloody piano, had never so much as mentioned she played, and she certainly doesn't know where he got the idea that she loved it enough to want her own instrument. She'd hated her lessons as a child, and the truth is she had only ever learned one song by heart, a song she doesn't enjoy playing at all. She would rather have had a new radio. Still, he starts to get twitchy when she plays it now, so she makes sure she sits down to practice at least three times a day and, when he starts fidgeting in his chair or she sees him freeze outside in the yard at the sound of those first few familiar bars, his face growing more thunderous by the second, she carries on playing and then plays it again and again until he gets up and leaves the room, muttering under his breath as he goes, or heads for cover down at the small dock where the sound will not reach him. Other than re-reading the handful of books she brought with her, dog-eared and battered as they are, it really is the only genuine entertainment available to her. That and thinking about the window. About jumping through it. Out of it.

Idly, she looks at the clock on the wall and realises it is already the middle of the afternoon. She doesn't remember making lunch but, as she looks around the room, – the assorted carnage; a broken chair here, blood spilled there – she can see the remnants of the meal, bread crusts torn to pieces by his too large, milky front teeth, like a predator's ripping at a carcass, and then discarded so carelessly once he was done. She shudders at the thought of his mouth. It happened slowly, this revulsion. She barely even noticed it at first, but before, when she did not know the grief she knows now, she had thought of nothing but his lips, of him kissing her, his large hands on her face, his warm breath against her skin, indeed she had yearned for little else. To be with him had been everything and now she can barely stand to look at him, to be near him, the whiskers of his beard like barbed wire against her skin, even the smell of his breath is enough to turn her stomach. They had waited so long for each other, through worlds, and now they are together, in the home where they were supposed to build a family and, really, she can hardly wonder where all that passion and intensity has gone. She certainly does not feel it, of course she feels hardly anything anymore, unchecked grief is such bitter ground, and he has barely touched her in weeks, not since he pressed his fingers to her stomach in tentative wonder and hope, "maybe this time", he had said and she had wept – hands on her throat, tight on her windpipe, and she had wept then too – so she thinks it is safe to assume he feels, or not, as she does. Empty, gone.

There are chores to be done, there are always chores to be done, like the man said, and she has a list longer than her arm, but the window calls and the women chatter and her cigarette must have all but burned down by now and she cannot seem to think of anything else anymore. She opens the window and takes a deep breath. The salt air is one of the best things about the island, and she could never tire of that at least. It gives her a sudden, much needed boost and before she knows she is going to, she has pulled a chair towards her and set it beneath the window. She steps up onto it without hesitation, holding onto the windowsill to keep steady for a moment. Once aboard, she realises how easy it will be to step onto the sill itself and so she does. The breeze tugs at her clothes as she stands in the frame of the window and the thrill of it is too much. She steps out.

Pure elation, so white and clear and perfectly warm in its intensity, suffuses everything. In that moment, she knows with all certainty that this is what she has been searching for, that whatever comes next will be worth it. It is the exhilaration of absolute freedom; one endless instant where there is no gravity, no husband, no expectation, no chore, no hope, no despair, no women whispering – *you're not enough, you're too much, you're everything, you're nothing* – with naught but air beneath her and the breeze tugging tugging tugging. She feels as though she will ascend rather than fall, and her body strains towards the pure blue expanse of the heavens above… but what goes up must always come down, and then there is the grass and the rocks and even as she feels something that should snap in her ankle on impact, the memory of pain scissoring up through her leg like fire as she cries out instinctively, one arm crushed beneath her, and her hips mashed against the rocky ground, she knows she wants to do it again, will always want to do it again and again and again. It is forever and forgotten at the same time. She yearns to remember, to relive, even as she is saturated with recollection. She lays there stunned but euphoric, incandescent with that once most exquisite pain, a better pain, and barely a breath left in her lungs. She blinks and the brightest green grass she has ever seen shines right in her eyes, more tickles at her nose, and laughter starts to itch its way across from her hippocampus and down from her amygdala into the back of her throat, even as it bubbles its way up from her stomach and along her windpipe to meet in the middle and, her body throbbing, her heart soaring, her sudden roar scares a squabble of gulls into flight. The women watch her from the window and, for once, are silent.

She laughs until her head spins, even lying there on the ground. She laughs as she rolls onto her back, watching as she slowly, infinitesimally, starts to come apart, atom by atom, cell by cell, bit by aching bit, sinking into the ground beneath her even as the rest of her disperses into the air as lazily as smoke rings. Notes of her laughter penetrate the rock and her voice slides after them like honey, the echo of her drip drip drip catching on the breeze and taking flight across to the mainland. Her hair sheds languidly from her scalp, strand by strand, weaving through the grass, rich auburn tangling, seguing into lushest green, emerald sparkling, spreading its carpet across earth and stone where only tufts had dwelt before. Skin rolls from flesh, muscle unknitting from bone, piece by piece, unravelling, liquefying into a pulsing viscosity that slips into and around the barren rocks and nourishes the turf. Colours flare in backlit rainbows, everything more vivid even as her eyes follow suit; cornea sliding from iris, deserting the lens, opening the vitreous chamber, the humour spilling out, particles floating into the sky even as the liquor she is already becoming trickles into the cracks in the paving slabs, winding her way down down down to the waiting sea. She reaches out her remaining hand before it is too late and, as the afternoon light hits it, it scatters too, like dandelion seeds, the fragments dancing into the air and away, taking her wishes across the water to lands she will never see but has dreamed of nonetheless. Her heart pumps slower and slower until it beats to a standstill, an echo of itself, a memory, and then it too is lost in the whip of the same wind that has carried the dust of her away.

The wind pulls at the remains of her clothing, at the dwindling remnants of her flesh and, at its insistence, she leaps to take flight, her soul on fire as she wheels and circles in the sky at last, swooping and soaring even as tendrils of her are sinking to the roots and caverns below, all the way down to the darkened hollows of the deep. She races through the air, first climbing and then allowing herself to fall, over and over, down and up, up and down, peak after trough, trough after peak, and she lends her voice to the howl of the wind as it rolls and eddies around the lighthouse, embracing it, worshipping it as it stands fast against the elements. The women watching from inside, lined close to but not at the window she leapt from, wonder open-mouthed at her dance, their insubstantial hands clasped beneath their insubstantial chins.

Her essence capers in this and that direction, at one with the sky even as it meshes with the darkness beneath, but as she strains to go higher, to go further, she cannot. There is a tether. She is not free. The call of the lighthouse is too loud, after all it is where this started and it is to where she must return. She is its captive, *his* captive, as surely as are the other women. The women, who wait and skulk and whisper. The women, who lurk in the shadows but never the light. The women, whose faces she knows so well. The women, whose hearts beat as hers does, has done, the same rhythm, the same muscle, and the same blood thundering through their veins. She cannot leave them behind; it is a betrayal she cannot make. Even if she wanted to, the lighthouse will not let her. She feels the pull and for one last, fruitless moment, she resists, straining against the trap, hopelessly defiant still… And then the collar tightens, choking her, jerking her back to the lighthouse, to where she must remain, to where she belongs until justice is done. The rush of matter and does-not-matter roars against the blue sky, echoing a protest, a fury, a wail of frustration that rings out right across the bay. It is the sound of gulls on the wing.

Later, as night falls, folk on the mainland remark at how especially bright the lighthouse is as it blinks on, how warm its light seems this evening. It comforts them as it cuts through the darkening sky, and more than one of them think about the lighthouse keeper who tends to it, the big-bodied man who lives there all alone. He's not much of a talker on the rare occasions he comes to town, but he's strong and is passably handsome, some might and do say. Perhaps he is in want of a wife? They are surprised he has never married, had wondered if perhaps he had finally done the deed when the rumours of a piano were whirling around. It's sad to think of him out there, playing the thing with no one to hear but the gulls and the fishes. Perhaps he needs some company? A man like that, all alone, it isn't right. More than one of them will dream of him later still, when they are snug beneath their sheets. They will wonder at the shadows hovering at the edges of the dream even as they fall under his spell, but it will be a passing thought, no more. For now.

On the island itself, those shadows are deeper than ever and the women huddle together in the kitchen, forlorn. The lighthouse keeper polishes his boots at the old wooden table by candlelight, the way his father and his grandfather did before him. He is whistling a happy, if discordant, tune as he goes. He is glad he kept to the plan again, finally, his father taught him well, just as his had once taught him. The time will come when he will need an heir, but now is not that time, no matter how close he has come these past few years. It was a sign, he can see that now; better late than not at all. He thinks of her smooth skin, its silken softness beneath the rough pads of his fingertips, of her beautiful blue eyes, like the sea on a clear summer's day, of her salt-rich tears, and he winces at the ache of regret the memories conjure in the pit of his stomach, and forces himself to think of the song instead. Over and over, the same damned song. The piano will make good kindling at least. An expensive mistake that makes him angry when he thinks of the waste and the trouble it has likely created. The townsfolk will have talked, of course, wondered what a big clumsy man like him would want with such a thing. His consideration for the damned woman may have put him at risk. His fist clenches around the cloth in his hand.

Good. Anger is good.

Temper rising, his mind turns to the body, considers it with nothing at all like regret now. He will need to calculate how much to weight it so it will sink all the way down to the bottom of the sea, into the inky black deep. The water is calm tonight, the weather mild, so he should have no trouble. He will consider taking another companion again in due course, he thinks to himself, after all, it's lonely out here and he is always glad of the company, at least for a while. Maybe this time she will understand her place. They will marry, as his family has always done, beneath the stars, within sight of the sea and away from the prying eyes of the town. The laws of men do not make such a union stronger or more valid. A marriage certificate is but a piece of paper after all, a meaningless bit of human bureaucracy. His family's ways run deeper than that, older, at one with the ebb and flow of the tides, respectful of the briny sea that sustains all things, and much less traceable. At last he laughs to himself and shrugs off his mood, loosening shoulders he had not realised were quite so tense. It has been a long day and he still has much to do, but he is beginning to feel better.

The women stare at him, his thoughts loud to them, although he does not know it, does not see them, never hears them. They have always waited because one day they believe he will, that he must. Tonight could be different; they can feel it. This time, buoyed beyond their past limits by the latest addition to their ranks, there is a faint rustling, audible beyond the shadows. The lighthouse keeper thinks it is perhaps a mouse and pays it no mind beyond a slight hesitation but, instead, *she* steps out from a dark corner to stand in front of the others, determined to bring about his reckoning this night. She can see the hairs on the back of his neck as they stand up, and she smiles. Raising the forever-smouldering cigarette to her lips, she musters every ounce of energy she can, reaches deep down into her fury, stretching into theirs. Although many of them have forgotten the worst of it, it is still clutched to their innards, a stain, a receipt of the worst kind, and she grabs it, grasping for everything and anything she can lay claim to, letting her sisters fuel her as, finally, she takes a long, slow drag, and then blows it out slowly but with such purpose the world seems to freeze. The candle on the table beside him flutters impossibly at her breath and all of the women hold theirs. The lighthouse keeper stops what he is doing and frowns at the flame, watching as it dances… for one long moment it flickers almost horizontally, pops blue… and then it rallies, pulsing even more brightly than before. He wipes his hand across the back of his neck, muttering something about the cooler evenings arriving earlier every year, and resumes his polishing. The women retreat into their shadows, defeated.

For now.

Author Biographies

Sophie Essex has previously edited *Dreamland: Other Stories* (Black Shuck Books) which was shortlisted for a 2022 British Fantasy Society award, *Norwich*, in the Dostoyevsky Wannabe *Cities* series, and the anthologies *Milk* and *A Galaxy of Starfish* for her own Salò Press. That press has also published around thirty poetry and prose books / chapbooks, and is shortly launching the inaugural issue of an annual magazine, *PISSOIR!* As poet, Sophie's second collection, *Some Pink Star*, was published by Eibonvale Press in 2019. She lives and works in Norwich.

Jason Gould is a writer of fiction, non-fiction, and script for stage and screen. He has been published in anthologies and magazines including the Terror Tales series (Telos Publishing), Port (Dunlin Press), Humanagerie (Eibonvale Press) and A Shadow Within: Evil in Fantasy and Science Fiction (Luna Press). In 2017, he won first prize in the Dead Pretty City (Mulholland / Hodder) crime writing competition. Fascinated by psychogeography and hauntology, he is intrigued by the intersection of myth and place, and how events often leave their own unique stain.

Andrew Hook has had over 175 short stories published since 1994 with numerous books in print, including *Human Maps* and *The Uneasy* (also from Eibonvale Press). His most recent short story collection, *Candescent Blooms* (Salt Publishing) received a five star review in the *Telegraph* and was short-listed for a British Fantasy Society award for Best Collection. A collaborative novel, *Secondhand Daylight*, written with Eugen Bacon, will also appear in 2023 from Cosmic Egg. He is working on numerous other projects and can be found at www.andrew-hook.com

Terry Grimwood likes to write in variety of genres including science fiction, horror and even a romance or two (a story of his once appeared in "Peoples Friend magazine). His short novel "Interference" (Elsewhen Press) was nominated for a best novella award in 2023. His short fiction has been collected into four books, the latest being "The She" (NewCon Press). Terry writes because he has to. He also sings and plays harmonica in The Ripsaw Blues Band.

Rory Moores writes alternative fiction and poetry. He has self-published: Office Aliens, a brutal satire of the New Zealand public service and, Kāpiti Kvlt: a trashy teen slasher set in the noughties. He is married and has two young children. www.rorywriter.com/

Pete Sillett was born in Ashford in 1980 but has spent the majority of his life split between Southampton and Canterbury. Although an avid reader of weird fiction since his teenage years, he has never actually written or published a story before now. He has a PhD in the ontological state of animated characters and how this impacts on spectator engagement, and has a chapter in *Screening Characters* published as part of Routledge's AFI Film Readers series.

Ariel Dodson writes weird, horror, fantasy and mystery fiction for adults and teenagers. Her short fiction has been published in Ellery Queen Mystery Magazine, Dark Lane Anthology, A-Z of Horror volumes: F is for Fear and J is for Jack o'Lantern, Women of Horror: Don't Break The Oath, Kids Are Hell anthology and Sand, Salt, Blood anthology. She is also the author of Blood Moon, a novel inspired by a 16th century werewolf legend, and the Southmore fantasy series for teenagers.

Julie Ann Rees holds an MA in creative writing from the University of Wales Trinity Saint David and is studying towards a PhD at Swansea University. Her stories have been published both on line and in print with Parthian books Heartland, Sliced up Press Bodies Full of Burning, Black Shuck Books Dreamland: Other stories, Improbable Press Cryptids Emerging Silver Volume, and Cast a Long Shadow a crime anthology with Honno Press. Her first book, a memoir entitled Paper Horses, was published by Black Bee Books in February 2022.
Find her at: https://www.facebook.com/julieAnnRees
https://twitter.com/JulieRe36071199
https://julieannrees.wixsite.com/julieann

Matt Leyshon lives in Blackpool, UK. His writing and photography has been published internationally. His latest book The Witch's Finger is a mixed media reworking of Virginia Woolf's To The Lighthouse.

Damian Murphy is the author of The Star of Gnosia, The Exalted and the Abased, The Narcissus Variations, and The Acephalic Imperial, among other collections and novellas. His work has been published by Snuggly Books, Mount Abraxas, Egaeus Press, and Raphus Press. He was born and lives in Seattle, Washington.

Tim Lees is from Manchester, England, but now lives in Chicago. He is the author of the much-praised historical fantasy *Frankenstein's Prescription* (Brooligan Press), the "Field Ops" books for HarperVoyager (*The God Hunter, Devil in the Wires, Steal the Lightning*) and a story collection, *The Ice Plague and Other Inconveniences*, from Incunabula Media. When not writing he has worked a variety of jobs, including film extra, conference organiser, teacher, house-painter, lithographer's assistant and lizard-bottler in a museum, plus a lengthy stint working on the rehab wards of a psychiatric hospital – a truly life-changing experience.

Rhys Hughes was born in Wales but has lived in many different countries and currently lives in India. He began writing at an early age and his first book, *Worming the Harpy*, was published in 1995. Since that time he has published more than fifty other books and his work has been translated into ten languages. He recently completed an ambitious project that involved writing exactly 1000 linked short stories. He is currently working on a novel and several new collections of prose and verse.

Brittni Brinn (she/her) is an author, interviewer, and book reviewer. She lives in a tower and sometimes a cottage with her husband and two cats in Mi'kma'ki/Nova Scotia. Her post-apocalyptic trilogy, *The Patch Project* series, is available through Adventure Worlds Press.

Charles Wilkinson's collections of strange tales and weird fiction, *A Twist in the Eye* (2016), *Splendid in Ash* (2018), *Mills of Silence* (2021) and *The Harmony of the Stares* (2022), appeared from Egaeus Press. His chapbook *The January Estate* was published by Eibonvale Press in 2023. He lives in Wales. He expresses his admiration for the author M. John Harrison, whose work shows him to be a master of the art of writing about water rising from below.

Tom Johnstone is the author of three novellas published by Omnium Gatherum Media, *The Monsters are Due in Madison Square Garden* and *Star Spangled Knuckle Duster*, and *The Song of Salomé*. His fiction has appeared in various publications, including *Black Static*, *Nightscript*, *Body Shocks* and *Best Horror of the Year*, as well as the collections *Last Stop Wellsbourne*, also published by Omnium Gatherum Books, and *Let Your Hinged Jaw Do the Talking*, from Alchemy Press. His other accomplishments include the Eibonvale Press chapbook, *How I Learned the Truth About Krampus*. More information at tomjohnstone.wordpress.com.

Douglas Thompson has published more than 20 short story and poetry collections and novels, including most recently *Stray Pilot* from Elsewhen Press. He won the Herald/Grolsch Question Of Style Award in 1989, 2nd prize in the Neil Gunn Writing Competition 2007, and the Faith/Unbelief Poetry Prize in 2016. https://douglasthompson.wordpress.com/

Ashley Stokes is the author of *Gigantic* (Unsung Stories, 2021) and *The Syllabus of Errors* (Unthank Books, 2013), and editor of the Unthology series and *The End: Fifteen Endings to Fifteen Paintings* (Unthank Books, 2016). His recent short fiction includes *The Hinwick Effigy* in Cloister Fox; *Cretaceous* in Theaker's Quarterly Fiction; and *Fields and Scatter* in Weird Horror. Other stories have appeared in Black Static, Nightscript, The Ghastling, Out of Darkness (edited by Dan Coxon, Unsung Stories), This is not a Horror Story (edited by JD Keown, Night Terror Novels), Tales from the Shadow Booth, BFS Horizons and more. He lives in the East of England where he's a ghost and ghostwriter.

C.A. Yates writes odd stories. Triple British Fantasy Award Nominee in 2022, she has been published many times by the BFS Award-winning press Fox Spirit Books, including her award nominated debut collection We All Have Teeth, as well as others including Black Shuck Books, Kristell Ink Publishing and Sirens Call Publications. British born, Chloë currently lives in the middle of Switzerland with her bearded paramour, Mr Y, where she gets to look at mountains and breathe clean air. She is a vocal advocate for the better understanding of mental health issues. Her website is www.chloeyates.com and she sometimes tweets as @shloobee

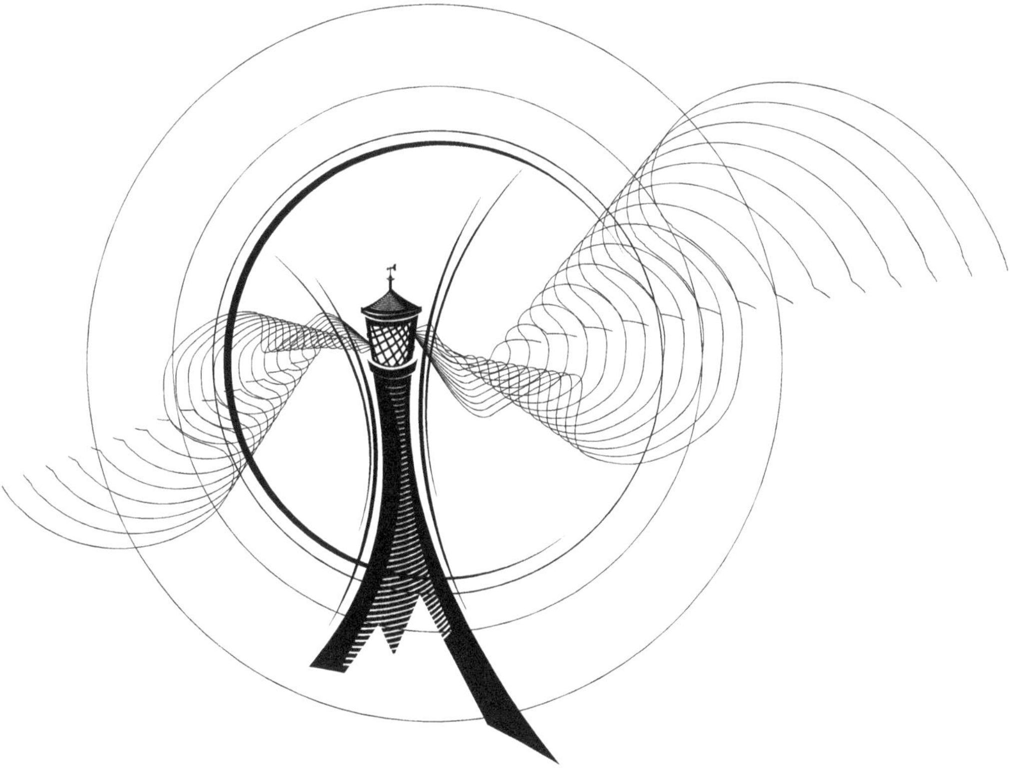

Milton Keynes UK
Ingram Content Group UK Ltd.
UKHW021046120524
442393UK00004B/82